HOT ARRANGEMENT

HOT BILLIONAIRE DADDIES BOOK 3

SUZANNE HART

© Copyright 2020 by Suzanne Hart - All rights reserved.

In no way is it legal to reproduce, duplicate, or transmit any part of this document in either electronic means or in printed format. Recording of this publication is strictly prohibited and any storage of this document is not allowed unless with written permission from the publisher. All rights reserved.

Respective authors own all copyrights not held by the publisher.

WARNING: This Book contains sexually explicit scenes and adult language. It may be considered offensive to some readers. This Book is for sale to adults ONLY.

Please ensure this Book is stored somewhere that cannot be accessed by underage readers.

CONTENTS

1. Rose	1
2. Duke	9
3. Rose	16
4. Duke	26
5. Rose	34
6. Duke	45
7. Rose	56
8. Duke	63
9. Rose	71
10. Duke	78
11. Rose	85
12. Duke	96
13. Rose	104
14. Duke	111
15. Rose	119
16. Duke	126
17. Rose	133
18. Duke	137
19. Rose	143
20. Duke	152
21. Rose	160
22. Duke	167
23. Rose	172
24. Duke	182
25. Rose	190
26. Duke	197
27. Rose	205
28. Duke	213
29. Rose	220
30. Duke	231
31. Rose	239
32. Duke	247

33. Rose	251
34. Duke	262
35. Rose	273
36. Duke	281
37. Rose	285
38. Duke	291
39. Rose	295
Epilogue	299
About Suzanne Hart	303

1

ROSE

I was happy to see my friend Karen happy. The pregnancy had been difficult for her, even though she tried to be brave and a good expectant mother. I wanted to be there for her too and I wanted her to know I would help her with the baby with whatever she needed. The way she'd helped me when I was in a bad place just a few months ago.

Of course, now when I thought about it, my problems weren't nearly as big as hers. My ex cheated on me, dumped me, and left me heartbroken and miserable. But Karen was preparing to be a single mother. A lifetime commitment and responsibility, not to mention hardships and heartbreaks too.

But it all worked out in the end. Jasper, the baby's father, the man she'd always been in love with—came back into her life and whisked her away to the sunset. It always brought a smile to my face when I thought about it. I wanted nothing but the best for Karen because she was a good person and a good friend.

I was visiting their new home today. Their baby, Jessie, was just three months old. An adorable little thing that rarely ever cried and loved being cuddled. I carried him around, swaddled like a little burrito, while Karen drank her coffee in peace. I knew she needed the break.

"Jasper is such a good daddy. He literally wakes up every time Jessie wakes up. He'll go to work sleep-deprived and bleary-eyed if he has to, but he won't miss a feeding or a diaper change. I seriously don't know how I was planning to do all this without him."

I smiled, cooing at Jessie as he blinked his eyes open.

"He's a chill guy, and so is Jessie. You're a lucky girl," I said and Karen nodded.

"I really am. Just a year ago, I was alone and living in a college dorm, trying to make some money so I could travel the world. Now I have a beautiful baby boy and a man who loves me. I can travel the world if I want to, anytime. I don't know what I did to deserve all this." Karen seemed emotional as she spoke. It had to be the hormones making her this sentimental. I sat down close to her and patted her knee while bouncing Jessie at the same time.

"You *do* deserve all this, K, don't you ever doubt that."

"You are really good with him. I didn't know you were so good with babies," she commented.

"I have three siblings. My youngest sister was born when I was twelve years old. She's only ten now. So yeah, I was old enough to look after a baby, I kinda know how they work."

Jessie tried wriggling and I stood up so I could swing him and lull him peacefully into another sleep. Karen watched me closely, sipping her coffee.

"Do you want kids?" she asked. "I don't think we've ever spoken about that before. Sorry, I've been so caught up with all the drama in my life lately."

I grinned. "Trust me, all that drama has kept me distracted from feeling sorry for myself. A year later and I would probably still be wallowing in grief over Will and our failed relationship, if you hadn't come along."

I swung my arms and Jessie was already sleeping. Karen looked at me admiringly.

"I wish I knew what to do. Most of the time I have no idea what I'm doing with him. I feel so clueless."

"You'll get there, don't worry. Both of you need time to adjust to each other. And to answer your question, yes, I've always wanted kids."

"You're a natural," Karen said. It made me blush. Kids always took well to me, especially babies. My mom used to call me the baby-whisperer because I was able to put the babies to sleep without any tears or trouble. I took it as a compliment. I liked knowing that babies felt safe with me.

"Yeah, maybe I should think about it as a profession. Like a nanny or babysitter or something."

"You're going to be a mother someday and you'll be a wonderful one," Karen said.

I was blushing again, shaking my head.

"Yeah, it takes two to clap hands, remember? Currently, I am very, very single with no prospects on the horizon."

"So what? You're just twenty-two. You have a whole life ahead of you. You'll find him. Soon. And then you'll make babies and live happily ever after."

I rolled my eyes at her and we both giggled.

"I may be good with babies, but I'm not as naïve as one of them. Happily-ever-after doesn't happen for everyone. Especially not for me," I stated. I tried to keep calm by staring at Jessie's peaceful sleeping face. I didn't want to work myself up, which I knew would happen if we continued with this conversation.

I could hear the cautionary tone in Karen's voice too, now.

"I know you're thinking these thoughts because of Will, and he did a pretty shitty thing to you. Oops, sorry, Jessie."

"Hey, I'd prefer if we didn't discuss Will. I don't want to ruin the mood. I'm happy seeing Jessie and you, and talking about you guys."

Karen cradled her hot mug of coffee, holding it close to her chest. She nodded but looked concerned.

"And you don't have to worry about me," I added. "It's not like I'm going to isolate myself or get depressed. I'm back on the dating scene. Just for fun."

"That's good. It's a good distraction."

"Yeah. I am having a lot of fun actually. There are so many interesting people out there."

Karen smiled. I held Jessie close to me, just to breathe in his sweet baby scent a bit more.

"Just be careful out there, will you, Rose?" she said.

I shrugged, not really meeting her eyes.

"I'll be fine. I've been through the worst a man can throw at me. I can pretty much handle anything now."

Karen looked at me like she wasn't really convinced. Did she think I couldn't handle it? She had no idea. I was toughened up. I wasn't going to fall for another man's manipulations again. I was never going to be foolish like that again.

"Whatever happens, I'm here for you if you need to talk or anything else. I'm usually always awake these days anyway," she said, rolling her eyes. Just then Jessie stirred and started to wake up. We couldn't help but laugh at his impeccable, comical timing.

∽

I had my own apartment now since Karen and Jasper had gotten together. It was for the best. This way we could all move on with our lives. As much as I enjoyed living with Karen, I knew I would have to face reality at some point—that I needed to make a life of my own.

And thankfully, this new job was affording me just that.

Once we graduated college, I thought I'd be so lost and wouldn't know what to do. Unlike Karen who had a strong goal in mind to travel and see the world, I didn't actually know what I wanted to do.

The only thing I was absolutely sure of was that I wanted to stop feeling the way I did. The hurt and the pain Will had caused me. I wanted that to go away, but I didn't know how. Karen helped as much as she could, but would I ever be able to trust another guy again? Everybody I met now, I looked at him with suspicion. *What was this one going to do to hurt me?*

I was so convinced Will was the one. I was sure of it. Before him, I didn't have much experience in dating. I'd been on casual dates before and had a few high school crushes, nothing serious.

Then the first year of college, I met Will and fell hard for him. Even though I wanted to focus on my coursework and on building a career, somehow, I managed to forget about all that and get tangled up in a serious relationship. Maybe I wasn't ready for a relationship. Maybe I was too young.

But Will was hot. He seemed to know what he was doing. He made me laugh and always had an arm around me. I'd spent my life not really sure of where I belonged. Coming from a family where I had to share everything with my siblings, it was easy to grow up feeling kind of lost. Like I wasn't really my own person with a unique identity.

That was precisely what Will gave me. He was able to make me feel beautiful. Like I actually stood out in a crowd. I knew the way other girls looked at him. Did they look at me and wonder what he saw in me?

Was I fat? Was I too pale? Weren't brunettes sexier than blondes?

I couldn't help but be filled with self-doubt every step of the way. But that was the thing about Will. He had the ability to push all those self-doubts out of my head. He made me feel like I was the only girl in the room. I trusted him completely.

I had wanted to build a life with him. He said he wanted it too. As soon as we were done with college, we would both get jobs so we could get an apartment together and start our new life. I invested all my energy and my trust in him.

His friends became my friends. I cleaned up around his dorm room, did his laundry, and helped him with his projects. I was neglecting my own tests and I rarely ever looked at my own reading material. I tried not to spend money on myself because I was saving up for our deposit. Everything I did was for the sake of our relationship.

I was so sure Will was doing the same.

But he wasn't.

The whole three years that we were together, Will had been sleeping with other girls. Mostly girls from the college, but sometimes random strangers he met on nights out with his buddies. I'd had no idea. All this time I had complete faith in him when I shouldn't have trusted him on a single day.

I probably wouldn't even have found out about it if it wasn't for a jealous girl he'd banged. She came up to me and outright asked if I knew Will was sleeping around. She felt hurt and humiliated. Just like I did. I burst out crying and she didn't want to console me. She felt used by him too.

I went to his friend, Stevie, first. I asked him if it was true. If Will had been sleeping around. The expression on Stevie's face was enough indication. He didn't know how to defend his friend anymore.

By the time I confronted Will, there was no way he could lie. I knew too much. I did my research. I asked as many people as were willing to speak about his adventures. Will had always been a cheater. Pretty much everyone else around us knew, except me. So I was the idiot who trusted him, who loved him despite the way he was treating me.

He made a fool of me.

Will didn't even fight it, he just accepted defeat.

"How could you do it to me, Will? How could you treat me like this?" I'd repeated those tear-stained words over and over again. For the most part, he didn't have an answer to that.

Toward the end of our last conversation, he just shrugged without meeting my eyes. I could still picture him now—lying on his bed, with his hands behind his head.

"What do you want me to say, Rosie? I did what I did because I could do it. Because it was fun. You can't tie a guy down no matter how much you try. It's just in our DNA. You shouldn't have trusted me the way you did."

I'd burst into tears when he'd said that. So it was all my fault? Will didn't shed a tear. He said he would miss me when I was gone, but that was it. It was going to be very easy for him to move on. Maybe he *wanted* to get caught so he could be free of me, finally.

I walked out of his room and went to the student council office. The only thing I could do was beg them to give me a new dorm room, far from Will. I just needed to put some distance between us. They gave me a new room. Karen was my new roommate, and if she hadn't been there for me on those miserable nights after the breakup—I would probably still be broken now.

But I wasn't broken anymore. I healed into a stronger person. I was virtually unbreakable now.

2

DUKE

I was supposed to be on vacation. My doctor had literally prescribed it to me on a prescription notepad.

"How long has it been since you last took a break, Duke?" he asked me a week ago. The only reason I even went in to see him was because I couldn't sleep at night. I hadn't slept in at least six months. I'd been surviving on a handful of hours of snatched sleep through the day. I was beginning to feel its effects on my body. Sleep deprivation was a form of torture for sure.

"A break? What do you mean?" I asked him, smirking, because I could guess what he was about to say.

"That answers my question," he mumbled while he scribbled on his pad. I saw him rip off the page and then hand it to me. "Listen to what I'm saying. You need to leave the city for a while, take a break, go somewhere quiet, away from your work."

"Is this supposed to be a joke?" I snapped, staring down at the page he'd handed me. It sure felt like one. He was a doctor. Wasn't he supposed to just prescribe some medication? Some drugs would do the trick, right?

"It's symbolic. Keep that piece of paper folded up in your wallet. Every night you have trouble sleeping or you feel overwhelmed, look at it, remember my advice. You're overworked and exhausted. That is what's wrong with you."

I stood up. This was ridiculous. Doctor Shaw had been my general physician for over a decade. I trusted him, but this was too much.

I grabbed my coat from the rack behind his door.

"Thanks for nothing, Doc," I groaned before leaving.

"You're going to thank me one of these days. Get your assistant to book you a flight somewhere."

I drowned out his voice by slamming the door behind me.

I refused to believe he knew what he was talking about. How was a vacation going to cure my insomnia? He had no idea how important my work was. How close I was to a breakthrough. If I stopped now, or took a break, I'd lose all momentum.

So I went back to work straight from the doctor's office. That visit had been a waste of my time. I put on my lab coat, washed up, and leaned into the microscope. I'd been examining a Petri dish and making notes for over a month now. The job was painstaking and slow but it would reap major rewards. I was so close to making a discovery that could help manufacture a breakthrough drug. All we needed was the approval for a drug trial.

Hours could have gone by while I remained stuck to my microscope. When I worked, I made sure nobody disturbed me. Not even Laura, my assistant who was usually constantly chasing me down with phone calls and meetings.

When I finally straightened up to take a sip of water, I

realized there was a throbbing pain at the back of my skull. I gulped the water down thirstily but the ache went nowhere. In fact, I saw black spots floating in front of my eyes. A sharp pain shot down my spine and it felt like my muscles were literally on fire.

I stood up with a jerk, so quickly that my stool fell over. My body screamed SLEEP. I tried to think back, calculate… when did I last sleep? Was it yesterday? The day before?

Now it felt like the ground was spinning underneath my feet. FUCK. Was I going to faint? Like a weak fucking princess!

"Doctor Nolan?"

It was Laura. I recognized her voice but I couldn't find the strength to turn and actually face her.

"Doctor Nolan, are you all right?" It was her voice again. Then I felt her hands on me. Laura's big sturdy hands were holding me up. I hadn't noticed how strong she was before.

"Maybe you should sit down." She helped me to a chair close by, but I shrugged her off. My ego was bruised. I sat with my legs wide apart, weaving my fingers through my hair repeatedly. I needed the headache to go away. I needed to stop feeling this out of control.

"Would you like some water?"

"I had some already."

"Okay, can I get you something to eat?"

Now I had no choice but to look up at her and meet her eyes. She looked concerned, staring at me, studying me closely. She was old enough to be my mother. If my mother was still alive.

"No, I don't need food. I need…I need you to book me a flight."

"A flight?" She was obviously confused.

"Yes."

"Okay, do you have a meeting? Where do you need to go?"

"I don't know. Pick a place. I don't have a meeting. I need to take a vacation. Surprise me."

∼

Ireland. That was where Laura booked my vacation. As it turned out, she was in full agreement with my doctor and believed some time away from Chicago and my work would do me good.

I'd never been to Ireland before. I'd probably never thought about Ireland before either, but here I was now, in a sprawling hotel room in a small village on the West coast of Ireland.

Laura insisted that I keep my phone off for the duration of my trip.

"I can call the hotel if I need you," she'd said at the airport. She'd wanted to see me off. Maybe she didn't believe I would actually get on the plane if she didn't come with me.

"Call immediately if there's an emergency," I told her and she nodded. But it had been six days and I hadn't heard from Laura at all.

I always asked the receptionist when I walked by; if there were any messages or phone calls for me. There were none. It seemed like the world didn't stop spinning even though I wasn't in my lab. It was a bitter pill to gulp down at first.

Skibbereen. How did Laura even find this place? At first, I thought it was a ridiculous place to vacation at. There were no big resorts here or thrilling nightclubs where I could meet people. The hotel I was staying at was barely four-stars, closer to three. But Laura definitely knew what she was doing.

The only thing I could do here was go on walks, have a few drinks at the local pub around the corner, and admire the architecture and the view. I couldn't remember the last time air had smelled as fresh as it did here. Had water ever tasted so sweet? It was so quiet, I could hear myself breathe.

By the second night, I was asleep. Maybe it was the exhaustion or the jet lag, or just the fact that I was bored and had nothing to do here. Or maybe it was Skibbereen. After my first night's sleep, I woke up the next day to discover I'd slept for ten hours straight.

Something I probably hadn't done since I was a teenager, unless I was blackout drunk.

I got some breakfast at the restaurant and a large cup of coffee. The only thing to do here was go for another walk. By now, I didn't even have to work hard to actively avoid thinking about work. It just slipped my mind. There were other thoughts in my head now—like why was I still living in Chicago? Why wasn't I living in Skibbereen? I could buy a house here. A mansion. I could go on these walks twice a day, for the rest of my life. I could breathe this clean fresh air all the time.

I felt free here. From everything.

And then there was the question of—who would I share it with? This life I envisioned out here in Skibbereen. Was I destined to be alone for the rest of my life? Did I want a woman to share it with? Did I want kids? A family? I hadn't had these thoughts before. Maybe it was something about hitting forty that made me revisit my priorities.

Or maybe I was just going crazy.

I blamed it on Ireland.

At the pub, I never drank alone. There were always a bunch of locals watching football and talking loudly. By my second visit there, I'd become 'one of the lads'. Nobody asked too many questions. They didn't care what I did or where I came from. They were happy sharing their drinks with me and making jokes, laughing at nothing. Suddenly, I found myself with a group of new friends who were more laidback than I could ever be.

Now, by day six of my stay here in Skibbereen, I might as well had been living here forever. I was sleeping long stretches at night and waking up with a clear head. I was eating well, drinking in moderation, and laughing more than I'd laughed in years.

This place definitely brought out the best in me. It was exactly what the doctor ordered and I made a mental note to thank him when I returned. *If* I returned. Would I return?

It was a Monday morning, not that it mattered, and I wouldn't have noticed if Laura hadn't finally left a message with the receptionist.

"She said for you to ring her back, sir," the woman behind the desk said sweetly. I was actually disappointed to hear that. By now, I was hoping I would never hear from Laura again. That I would somehow be forgotten.

When I did eventually call her, later that day, procrastinating for as long as possible, Laura had that Monday-urgency in her voice.

"Doctor Nolan, sorry, I didn't mean to bother you. I wouldn't have called you if it wasn't important."

I pressed my eyes closed. I felt that headache returning, just a hint of it.

"What's going on, Laura?"

"The ND189."

"Yeah, what about it?" I asked. It was another drug that was under clinical trial at the moment. It was a project my team had been working on for the past four years.

"It's worked," Laura said.

"Excuse me?" I thought I hadn't heard her correctly.

"Two of the test subjects returned with favorable results."

How was this possible? I was expecting it to take another year or two, if not more.

"I'm on my way," I said, banging the phone down. The receptionist looked up at me, startled a little.

This was good news. This was exactly the kind of result we'd been working toward all these years and it was finally happening. And yet, instead of feeling excited, I could feel my heart sinking a little.

I was being snapped from this gentle state of mind—back to the reality of my life. I was foolish to think I could settle here. Have a woman by my side. Maybe start a family. I didn't belong to this scene at all. I needed to be back there in the lab, doing what I'd dedicated my life to.

3

ROSE

My new job wasn't exciting, but it definitely paid well. Enough so I could afford a cool studio apartment in a good neighborhood, a gym membership (which I never utilized), and eating out several times a week. Realistically, I was now living the life I'd always envisioned for myself when I was a teenager.

I was living a life of independence. I wasn't making any big savings because I had nobody to save it for. Now when I thought about Will and the lifestyle I led when I was with him—I was ashamed. I'd forgotten myself in those three years, and now I was finally on a path of self-discovery. Will had freed me.

I'd been at this job for close to a year now. It was a clinical drugs company that focused mainly on inventing and testing new life-saving drugs. It started off small, just fifteen years ago, when its founder Duke Nolan and a small team developed a breakthrough drug for asthmatic patients. The success of that invention led them to grow the company by leaps and bounds. They'd worked on several medications since then and as far as

I knew, they worked with the highest of ethical standards.

I was wary at first when I applied for the position. Did I want to work for a big pharmaceutical corporation? But when I did my research, I quickly discovered that Nolan Pharma wasn't anything like the others. They were smaller and had no interest in expanding. It seemed like the company really and truly did want to make a difference in the medical field. They wanted to help people get better.

Besides, it wasn't like my role in the company would be significant in any way. My position was on the sales team. I was just a drop in the ocean. I hadn't even met the core team of scientists yet, in all these months of working for this company. But I liked it here.

It was a regular nine-to-five job. It left me enough time in the day to socialize and go on dates if I wanted to. I'd have enough time for the gym, if I could bring myself to go. The sales targets I was working with weren't extraordinary and I hadn't yet felt like I was under extreme pressure.

Bottom line was—I was happy with the job. My family was pleased too when I got it. My dad, who worked for the Museum of Science and Industry, was more than happy that I was working for a company that aligned with his beliefs. He'd hesitantly, over the years, accepted the fact that I wouldn't become a scientist myself. Or join one of *his* fields. But the fact that I was at least working for one of them would have to be good enough for him.

That morning when I woke up in my pull-out bed in the apartment, nothing actually felt different in any way. I'd been on another date the night before, and it had gone as well as it could have hoped for. All this guy wanted to talk about was rugby and how great he was at it. He paid for the drinks and refused to let me pay for my own food. Clearly not a guy who believed a woman was capable of taking care of herself.

It was safe to say I wasn't planning on seeing him again.

But I didn't feel regretful when I woke up the next morning. Like I was telling Karen, I was enjoying going out and meeting new people. Testing the waters. Discovering for myself how many different kinds of men existed. All of whom were being rejected one after the other.

I made my coffee and took a shower. I scrolled through my phone, looking at various news articles, while I ate my bowl of cereal on the couch. In the mirror, I closely examined myself before leaving the apartment.

A dove-grey pencil skirt accentuated my thick thighs and the curve of my narrow waist. A baby-blue silky blouse stretched over my ample breasts. I always noticed the way men's eyes were drawn to it. I was fully aware of my full figure, how men sexualized me more often than not. Most of the time, I took it as a compliment unless I was in a bad mood.

Running my fingers through my wavy, blonde hair, I rushed out of the apartment for the L train. I wanted to get to the coffee guy in time for a doughnut.

I was listening to music as I exited the station. Earplugs were deep in my ears and my hands in the pockets of my grey jacket. It was peak rush-hour now, which meant if I was going to make it for the doughnut, I would have to trample through these people who were in my way.

City-living wasn't new to me, of course. I didn't shy from using my elbows when I needed to. People came in my way and I pushed past to squeeze through the crowd. Until someone grabbed my arm, stopping me in my tracks with a jerk.

I screamed. Nobody had grabbed me like this before, not

even in the middle of a crowded street. I spun around to face this man. He released me immediately with his hands up in the air where I could see them. But I also saw the dark stain of what must've been coffee; all over the front of his white shirt. Did I do that? Had I elbowed into his coffee?

I could see his mouth moving but the music was blocking out all sound. I pulled one plug out and fumbled with the phone in my purse to shut it off. The city's loud roaring noises flooded my ears now. It came as a shock to my system.

"Can you watch where you're going?" the man was growling. I faced him again, my eyes flitting over the coffee stain once more.

"Uh…sorry, I didn't realize I did this."

His brow was furrowed, and it seemed like he was studying me closely. He had an exceptionally handsome face. Chiseled features and a strong square jaw. He was an older man, with dark hair that was greying lightly. He loomed tall over me, but I managed to keep my wits about me. I wasn't going to appear as a pushover to him.

"Again, I'm really sorry, but I've got to go. I have to get to work," I said, pointing with my thumb over my shoulder.

"What about my shirt? I was on my way to a very important meeting." Was he being serious? Was he actually looking for an answer to that question?

I gulped and looked around. There was no solution.

"Look I'm really sorry. I can give you…" I opened my purse. "I can give you some cash for dry cleaning, if that's what you're asking."

"I don't want your money," he said in a smooth voice.

People were still pushing past us.

"What do you want then?"

"A solution to my current problem," he argued.

I was feeling guilty at first, but now my face filled with frustration.

"Who carries coffee around at nine AM on this street? You were literally asking for it," I snapped.

A soft grin seemed to tug the corners of his mouth. If he wasn't *this* sexy, I would've probably walked away from him by now. But he had a kind of magnetism that was holding me back.

I knew I was late, and I knew this conversation was pointless, and yet, I couldn't make myself leave.

I was pushed forward in his direction just then, by an angry passerby who shoved me from behind. Before I knew it, I was in his arms. I'd landed right on his chest. He had his arms around me. They were strong and his chest was wide. His chin dug into the top of my head. I breathed in his strong cologne. He smelled like a pine forest. We remained like that for a moment and then I pulled away.

"So you're the kind of girl who thinks hugs solve everything," he joked with a grin. I straightened up, trying hard to get a handle on myself again. I felt flustered. I must have been blushing.

"Someone pushed me. You see, it's involuntary. These things happen in the middle of a crowded street."

I watched as he clenched his jaw tightly, and then he nodded.

"So you think I should just drop it. Let you go?"

"That would be the most reasonable thing to do, yes," I replied. I peered into his green eyes. They were bright and intelligent. What was it about him? His sturdy mouth? His grin?

"Well, you are free to leave now. Walk away if you want to. If you think that's the right thing to do."

"I don't know how I can help you. I can't fix your shirt

here. Do you want me to buy you a new shirt?"

"I told you, it's not about the money." He was speaking calmly now. I was the one who was getting worked up.

"Then what?"

"Apologize."

"Apologize?"

"Isn't that the least you can do? Tell me you're sorry for ruining my shirt on such an important day."

I looked down to the stain on his shirt. It was already pretty dry now, a lighter brown patch. How long had we been standing here talking?

When I looked up at him again, his smile had grown wider. This was a joke to him. He thought this was funny!

"Fine. I'm sorry. I'm very sorry for inadvertently spilling your coffee."

"And that you'll watch where you're going the next time."

"I promise," I said with a sigh. "I will never spill coffee on you again."

He pushed his hands into the pockets of his jacket. It had to be tailored. It looked like it had been designed for just him and fit him perfectly. So did those pants. I looked down at his well-polished brown shoes. This man sure knew how to dress.

"See, that wasn't so hard, was it?" he said.

I was snapped out of my thoughts. I met his eyes again. I felt that feeling once more. Like an electric charge running down my spine, filling my body with a shudder. I realized I wanted him. Like I'd never wanted a man before. This was totally about sex. This was about our bodies.

We were out on the streets of Chicago. A busy street where we were being pushed and shoved in each other's direction.

"Yeah, not so hard. I have to...I need to get to work," I mumbled. He was watching me still, closely, like he was studying every inch of my body. There was something else about those eyes. Not just the fact that they were magnetic. They suddenly looked familiar.

Where had I seen those eyes before?

"I'll let you off the hook this time, but only because you said sorry." He was still smiling.

I took a few steps away from him. My mind was working overtime. I knew this man. I could feel it in my bones now. I'd seen him somewhere else.

A picture of him? In a magazine? In a book? No...in a photograph. Framed. On a wall somewhere.

I continued to back away. The crowd was filling in the gap between us. He hadn't moved from his spot. He just continued to stare at me with those steely green eyes.

I whipped around and gasped as the air left my lungs. I remembered where I'd seen him.

He was Duke Nolan. The founder of my company. He was my boss.

∼

I was red-faced when I reached my desk a few minutes later. I'd forgotten about the coffee stand and my doughnut.

"You okay, Rose?" Monica asked. She was another new recruit who sat opposite me in our cubicle. Was I visibly shaking?

"Yeah, I'm fine. I was just a little rushed. Didn't think I'd make it in time." I tried not to meet her eyes as I fiddled with my bag and chair, hurriedly turning on my computer. I was afraid she'd see the truth if she looked at me.

"Okay, you just look a little jittery," Monica continued.

She swung around and around in her chair, keeping a close eye on me. I sat down, smoothing my skirt. I really needed a coffee right now, maybe something stronger.

"I...I spilled coffee on someone on the street, on my way in. I was careless. Wasn't watching where I was going."

"So? These things happen."

"Yeah, I know. It made him very mad."

"Was he like some crazy, violent person?" Monica leaned over the desk. Her curiosity was piqued now.

"No. Not violent. He was just angry at first. The coffee was all over his shirt and he said it's an important day. Something about a meeting."

"Sounds like the two of you had a chat," she said with a grin.

I glanced at her nervously. Was I sweating? I didn't know what I was supposed to do next. Confront him? Send him an email with an apology? Was this enough to cost me my job?

"Kinda. Not a chat. I guess I was rude to him. I should have apologized immediately. I don't know why I didn't."

"I don't know why you're panicking about this. It's not like you'll see this guy ever again. Forget about it, accidents happen." Monica seemed to have lost interest by now. She was already typing something on her computer.

I just sat in my chair, staring at her, trying to decide if I should disclose the truth to her or not. She looked up and caught me glaring. "What's gotten into you?"

"I think I might see him again. That's the problem," I confessed.

"How? You know this guy?"

"Not exactly. Well, I know about him, and I didn't recognize him at first, but then I realized who he was as I walked away."

"Who is he?" Monica searched my eyes.

I didn't think I'd be able to say his name out loud at first. I could've kicked myself. Why didn't I act differently with him? I had ample opportunity to make a good first impression but I didn't.

"Duke Nolan," I whispered.

"Say that again," Monica asked, leaning even further toward me.

"Duke Nolan. The one and only."

She sat back in her chair with a thump. I looked around nervously, checking to see if anyone was eavesdropping. The office buzz around us wasn't anything out of the ordinary.

"Shit," Monica mumbled.

"Yeah."

"Well, I mean, we've been working here for close to a year now. We haven't actually met him yet. There's a good chance you might never actually meet him. He might forget your face too."

I twiddled my thumbs, barely able to look at Monica anymore.

"I hope so. I really hope so. The whole thing was just extremely awkward." I left out the part about how I fell into his arms. How I felt a sexual charge between us. Maybe it was just my imagination. But there was no denying he was hunky.

"You should just relax. Keep your head down, get through the day, and hopefully this will all be forgotten soon, I mean, it was just coffee," Monica continued.

I gulped and nodded. My computer screen was staring at me. I had a few reports to write today but I knew I would be nervous and on-edge all day.

"Good morning, ladies." It was Jim, our line-manager. He'd walked over to us with a big smile on his face. "I have some good news for you both."

Monica and I straightened up. I tried to keep my chin up, not give anything away.

"I'm forming a team of my best salespeople, and I would like you both to be a part of it. It's an exciting new project."

I brightened up. This was exactly the kind of thing I needed to distract myself from the events of this morning.

"Sounds great, how do we sign up?" Monica asked.

Jim grinned.

"Well, I would like you to sit in on a meeting where we discuss a plan of action. I'm happy to say that our company is now on the brink of another major breakthrough. It's all hands on deck at the moment."

"Of course, we'd love to be a part of that," I said.

"Good. The meeting's in fifteen minutes. Conference room D. A little heads up; the big boss is going to be there."

"The big boss?" My voice turned into a whisper.

"Duke Nolan himself. He's flown in to attend this meeting, cut short his vacation, etc." Jim was backing away from us now but still smiling.

I could see he was excited, and I should have been too. But I couldn't be, not now. It felt like the world was colluding against me. I was destined for failure and embarrassment. How did it all go so wrong this suddenly?

Monica swiveled to me as soon as Jim was out of earshot.

"Okay, relax, it'll be fine. Maybe it'll be a crowded room. He might not notice you."

I faced her. The back of my neck was burning red. My palms were sweaty.

"It's fine. I'm okay. It was just a bit of coffee. This is just a job. It's not the end of the world," I said. But there was more to it than that. I was nervous about seeing him again. I was afraid of the effect he was going to have on me. The last thing I needed was to be attracted to my boss.

4

DUKE

I sat at the head of the conference table. I was early. The others were setting up the room for the meeting about to commence. Laura stood near me, reading out a list of people I was supposed to call and meet. There was a fresh cup of coffee in front of me, going cold. I hadn't touched it since Laura brought it in. I'd asked her to bring it in since my first one spilled. I had a multitude of white shirts in the cabinet in my office. I'd already changed into one. The culprit with the brown stain on the front was still in my office. I should have thrown it away. A stain like that was probably unsalvageable.

I thought about the girl who bumped into me. Maybe I was too harsh with her. She'd caught me by surprise. The coffee was hot and it stung me. I had a knee-jerk reaction and grabbed her elbow. I shouldn't have reacted that way. Did I scare her?

I was about to apologize, but then she spun around and I looked at her. At those full pink lips. Her cheeks were flushed pink too. She had the most golden hair I'd seen. Shining and framed in majestic rings around her face. They fell around her face delicately. Her eyes were blue. She could have been one of the models in a Renaissance painting.

Full-bodied, precious alabaster skin, those gorgeous eyes, and a heart-shaped face. It seemed like she didn't belong to this modern world, in that skirt and blouse she was wearing, dressed for a corporate office.

I wanted her. As soon as I saw her.

As for her, it seemed like she wanted to fight me the moment she laid eyes on me. It was just a coffee spill. Of course, it was just an accident, but I couldn't let her go. I tried to keep her, keep talking to her as long as I could, but eventually, I had no choice but to watch her walk away. But I was still thinking about her.

"Doctor Nolan?" Laura had been speaking. None of which I'd heard. I looked at her blankly now and she cleared her throat.

"Shall we begin? We can start as soon as you want. Everyone's ready."

"Yeah, bring them in." I sat up in the chair, opening the files in front of me. I hated feeling this disrupted. I needed to clear my head and focus.

Laura opened the door and spoke to people outside. I tried to read reports while the room filled with people. There was some chatter around me. When I eventually looked up, I saw Jim walking in, followed by two women. At first, when I saw her, I thought I was delusional. Losing my mind. She couldn't be here. In this office. In my board room.

She was wearing the same pencil skirt that stretched over her scrumptious curves. Her hair was the same golden color. I couldn't see her eyes because she had her face turned down. I followed her with a hard stare until she took a chair at the far end of the table, besides Jim.

There were at least fifteen other people in the room but I only had eyes for her. She was really here! She worked for me!

"Sorry for the delay, folks," I called out. They turned to me. Now she had no choice but to look too. I stared at her, catching her eyes. "I had a bit of an incident this morning on my way in. Someone spilled hot coffee all over me." I said it with a smile. The people at the table expressed their sympathy. It was all light-hearted.

But *her* face turned a bright tomato red. She looked away, embarrassed. I stood up from my chair. Laura set up a projector behind me. These people were expecting a presentation and a speech. I was usually pretty good at this. In fact, I had a lot to say today, but all I could think about right now was how much I wanted to fuck the girl sitting at the end of that table. The girl with those delicious, pink lips.

She was my employee. That would be unethical and unprofessional. I shouldn't have those thoughts whirling around in my head. I should have felt guilty but I didn't. I wanted what I wanted. I couldn't change that.

"All right, why don't we begin with Patrick? Do you want to give everyone the good news? Share the results of the tests with us?" I spoke to the head of the research team. The ones who'd been working on the drug.

Patrick stood up, beaming with pride.

"Gladly, Doctor Nolan," he said. He walked to the front of the room beside me, carrying all his files and reports. We smiled at each other. This was big news for the company. Years of hard work were paying off. Before Patrick started, I placed a hand on his shoulder and nodded.

"I just want to make it clear, for everyone here, that we will continue with our philosophy. I want you all to remember, including the sales team, that we work for the people who *need* this drug. We have made our profits in the past and we're still reaping its rewards. The goal now is to spread awareness, to make this drug accessible to the people who really need it. It's not about making money." I thumped Patrick's back.

He started speaking and I took a chair. I tried not to, but I couldn't help but glance at the girl again. She was sitting with a straight back, hands clasped on the table. Her cheeks were still flushed. I caught her looking at me, but she quickly looked away.

I was dying to know what she was doing here in this room.

∼

The obvious answer was that she was on Jim's team. She was one of the new sales recruits Laura had told me about a few months ago. But that didn't dawn on me until I'd spent a lot of time at the meeting being distracted by the way she sat with her breasts thrust forward. I'd spent too long memorizing her face in profile. A thirst was taking over. A thirst for her body.

The meeting ended on a high note. Everyone was happy and excited with the good news about the drug testing. People were enthusiastic to start working on it, as was I.

After the meeting, people stood around the table, talking. I walked up to Jim as he was speaking to a group of his salespeople. She was there too, purposely avoiding my eyes. I knew she'd sensed me walk up to them, but she refused to look at me.

"So, Jim, I haven't been introduced to most of your team here," I said.

"No, you haven't met Monica and Rose, they are our

latest recruits," he said. Monica, the other girl, was quick to extend her hand to me. I shook it.

I knew her name now. She had no choice but to meet my eyes now.

"And you must be Rose," I said. Neither of us made a move to shake hands. I was conscious of the others watching us as we all stood close together.

"It's nice to meet you, Doctor Nolan," she said. Her voice had changed from the one I remembered out on the streets. She was less confrontational now. It was more like a murmur.

"Yes, Doctor Nolan, it was extremely inspiring to hear you speak," Monica added. I glanced at her and smiled, but she wasn't the one I was interested in.

"We're going to come up with the best sales plan for this. I'm sure there will be some lobbying involved here. I need to get on the phone with Harry and talk logistics," Jim said.

I tried to focus on him, but Rose was standing too close to me. Close enough that I could smell her perfume. Or was I imagining it?

"Yeah, you do that, Jim. Just remember, we're not being aggressive with our sales yet. Sarah in marketing is going to work on a press release first and then you can start contacting the suppliers," I said.

"Yep. Got it," Jim said. Monica and the others with him were beginning to walk away. Technically, our conversation was over. But neither Rose nor I were ready to walk away yet. I could sense Jim waiting in confusion. Why were Rose and I standing together like this? Why were none of us speaking? This was awkward.

"Rose..." I began.

"Johnson."

"Right, Rose Johnson. Can I speak to you a moment please, Ms. Johnson?"

She glanced at Jim, who shrugged and then walked away, thankfully followed by the rest of his group. The board room was emptying out. Rose and I were practically alone by now.

"Doctor Nolan...I want to start by apologizing."

"You look like you've seen a ghost," I interrupted her.

She looked up at me, licked her lips, and then rubbed a hand over her forehead. I could see her freaking out. She was taking this way too seriously.

"I shouldn't have behaved the way I did this morning."

"You mean charge into me and nearly burn me alive?" I said with a laugh. Rose didn't seem to find any of this funny. Her face was a deathly pale color now. Laura was still in the room, putting the projector away. I caught Rose glance at her cautiously.

"Laura, could you give us a minute, please? Thanks."

I waited until the room was empty now. Nobody else. Just Rose and me.

"I should've been watching where I was going, and I was rude to you too."

"It was an accident," I said.

Rose clamped her mouth shut. Our eyes met. She had the sexiest mouth. Did she even realize how much I wanted her? Could she feel the electricity between us?

"Yes, it was, and I will totally understand if you want to speak to Jim about it and get me off the team."

My brow furrowed. "Over a cup of spilled coffee?"

"My attitude was all wrong. I feel ashamed, I guess. You all do such good work here and I wouldn't blame you if you don't want me on your team. If you don't trust me."

I watched her mouth move. If only she had any idea

about the thoughts going through my head now—she wouldn't think of me as the person she imagined.

"I will not be removing you from the team, you don't have to worry," I said.

Rose nodded.

"Okay, thank you, and I will work on my people skills."

"You shouldn't be the only one apologizing. I kind of kept you from leaving. I made a bigger deal of it than I should have."

She blushed again and shook her head.

"You had every right to be mad at me. I wasn't being cautious."

"All right, we're both to blame. We've apologized enough," I said. This time, when she met my eyes, she was smiling. I smiled too.

She looked even sexier now. I wanted that mouth on mine. These were not appropriate thoughts to have about an employee.

Laura knocked on the door and popped her head around.

"Mr. Enright is on the phone for you, Doctor," Laura said. I caught her glancing suspiciously at Rose.

"I'll call him back in a few minutes."

Rose had stepped away from me. There was some distance between us now. The moment had passed us. She extended her hand to me.

"I hope you have a good day, Doctor Nolan. Again, I'm very sorry about the coffee, and thank you for letting me work on this new project." We shook hands. Our skins touched and there was that pulse again. I felt it in my groin.

I had to do everything to not pull her to myself and hold her by her butt. Feel her body against mine. Rose stepped away. She glanced at me one last time before leaving the conference room.

I needed a moment to compose myself. A few more minutes alone with her and who knew what could've happened.

I wasn't used to feeling this way. This girl was dangerous.

5

ROSE

When I returned to my desk, Monica was waiting for me, full of questions.

"What did he say? Are you okay, Rose? He didn't seem angry, *was* he?"

I sat down, feeling zombie-like. I shook my head.

"No, he wasn't angry. He was okay with it. We shook hands," I answered.

"Phew! I knew he wouldn't be. It was such a small thing. Isn't he charismatic, though?"

She had no idea.

"Yeah, he's good. At talking, I mean."

Maybe Monica could see I was still flustered. She leaned over her desk even further now.

"So what are you going to do?"

"Nothing. What is there to do?"

"Did he say anything else?"

"No!" I snapped. I didn't mean to. I just needed some space to think about what just happened. About the way I was feeling right now. Was this the last time we would interact? Realistically, he had no reason to speak to me again. But

I kept looking over my shoulder, hoping he would come to speak to me again. I didn't know why. There was no reasonable explanation.

Monica sank back in her chair.

"I was just wondering. You guys seemed to be in there, talking for a while."

"I was apologizing, as I should have."

She returned to her computer, but even so, I could sense her keeping her eyes on me. I knew she was bursting to say something else.

"It's really nothing, I was worrying for no reason," I said.

"He's handsome though, isn't he? Like *really* good-looking. What age is he? Like forty?"

I wished she'd stop talking.

"Maybe, I don't know. I don't know him at all." I looked over my shoulder again.

"Do you know if he's seeing anyone? I know he's not married, but I'm sure women are throwing themselves at him all the time," she continued.

I thought about how I fell into his arms that morning. Is that what he thought happened? That I'd thrown myself at him on purpose? Could he see it in my eyes? That I wanted him.

"I don't know anything about him. I barely knew what he looked like before this morning."

Monica was thinking.

"I'm just curious, I guess," she added.

I sat silently at my desk for a while. There was only the sound of Monica tapping at her keyboard. She was thinking too. I could sense it. She was probably thinking the same thing—how hot did Duke Nolan look without his clothes on?

Inappropriate. Highly inappropriate! He was my boss. My super boss.

"So, ladies, what do you think?" It was Jim. He'd found his way to us again. Monica jumped up.

"That meeting was exhilarating," she said.

"Very exciting," I added. Forcing a smile. I could feel Jim's eyes on me now.

"So…Rose, have you guys met before? You and Doctor Nolan?" he asked. There were awkward moments between us back there. It was obvious why he was curious.

"We met this morning, happened to bump into each other on our way to work. I accidentally spilled some coffee on him, so I wanted to take the chance back there to apologize to him," I said. I wanted to come clean. There was no reason to hide it anymore.

Jim gave me a curt nod.

"Okay, well, he wants you on the core team. To be the first point of sales contact for this project. You'll have to sit in with me for a few more meetings."

I gulped. My mouth went dry. I was confused and a little afraid. I'd never done anything like this before. It was a lot of responsibility.

"Me?"

"Yes, you, Rose. I just got off the phone with him. Clearly, you've made an impression."

I didn't know what to say. What was this supposed to mean?

"I'm flattered," I said.

"You'll do it, right?"

"I don't even know where to begin."

"I'll supervise, of course. It's a huge responsibility."

"Thank you, yes, I know. I'd be lost without some guidance."

Jim tapped his knuckles on the cubicle wall.

"Good. We can discuss it this evening. You and me. I have a few meetings and then we can talk."

"Okay, thank you, Jim," I said, still fumbling with my words. None of this was making sense. Why would he ask for me specifically? How could I possibly have made a good impression on him?

Jim spoke to Monica briefly and then walked away. She flipped around to me immediately.

"Oh, my God! What is happening?" she breathed in an excited, hushed tone.

"I don't know. I don't understand it."

"Do you think...maybe. I don't know. He..."

"No!" I snapped before she could say the actual words. I knew what she was hinting at.

"Because that would be...you'd be so lucky..." Monica continued.

I stood up and walked past her briskly.

"It isn't what you think it is, Monica. Isn't it possible that he based his decision on Jim's recommendation?"

She was about to say something more but I walked away. I didn't want to hear it. The idea that Duke Nolan wanted me on his core team because he wanted to sleep with me made me angry.

Who did he think I was? What kind of a woman did he take me as? That was never going to happen.

∽

In my apartment that night, I couldn't sleep. That scene kept replaying in my head. His hand on my elbow, spinning me around, the look of annoyance in his eyes at first—then a grin. Did he decide right then that he wanted to sleep with me?

Wasn't that what I wanted too? I was immediately attracted to him when I saw him. I'd studied his features closely. I'd pictured him naked.

But *he* was taking it to a whole other level. He wanted us to start working together when we had no justifiable reason to. What was I supposed to do now? I could quit.

I was lying in bed when my phone rang. It was Karen.

"Can't sleep. Jessie kept me up all night and now I can't fall asleep," she complained when I answered.

"How are the boys?" I asked. I was happy for the distraction.

"They're good. We're good. I'm exhausted most of the time, but we're happy, you know."

"I think my boss wants to sleep with me," I blurted. I didn't mean to burden Karen with this. She had enough going on in her life with a new baby.

"What? Where did that come from? Your boss? That Jim guy?"

"No. Oh, my God!" I laughed. "Not him. Duke Nolan. The founder, Doctor Nolan."

"And this idea isn't as hilarious as Jim wanting to sleep with you?" she asked. She'd caught me. There was an obvious difference there.

"N...no, I don't know. Duke Nolan is hot."

"Hot?"

"Very, very sexy."

"So you want to sleep with him too?"

"Maybe."

"Rose?"

"Yes. Definitely. I wanted to sleep with him the moment I

met him. Bumped into him. I spilled coffee on him. He had to change his shirt."

Karen giggled. "Sounds interesting. Cute. Quite perfect actually."

"It's not though. I don't know why I feel offended by this. I mean, we both want to do it, but it feels so wrong."

"Why would it be wrong if it's consensual? Jasper and I were in the same position, remember?"

"Yeah, but I like this job. I want to *keep* this job. My manager likes me. He recommended me for this big project. I thought I was going to make a success of myself based on my merit. Not because the boss wants to have sex with me and keep me close."

Karen was silent for a bit. "I guess when you put it that crudely, it does sound a little wonky."

"And what happens after we have sex?"

"Things didn't fall apart when Jasper and I did. Well, I guess it did, for a while, but we found our way to each other eventually. Trust me, honey, it's not such a terrible thing."

"It isn't the same, K. Duke and I...We're not in love. We were two strangers this morning who were sexually attracted to each other. Now we work together, that's all. But the attraction is still there."

Karen sighed. "Well, I guess, you shouldn't allow yourself to feel used."

"No. That is exactly what I want to avoid."

"So what are you going to do?"

"I can't quit. I don't want to quit. I enjoy my job. It's pretty much the perfect job for me."

"You could be upfront with him, I guess," Karen suggested.

"What do you mean?"

"You could talk to him directly about the problem. Tell him you guys need to work at a distance to avoid any awkwardness. You can't sleep with him if you want to keep working there on neutral ground. Once you cross that line..."

"I know," I interrupted her.

"Okay, good. I just want you to do what makes you happy."

"This job makes me happy. There are so many other men out there, right?"

"Yeah, right."

"It's just sexual attraction," I added.

"Mmhmm," she mumbled.

But I didn't know how to explain it to her. Would she understand if I told her he made my body physically shudder with desire? That he had big masculine warm hands. I could still feel the pressure of his fingers on my arm where he'd grabbed me. I thought about how his heart beat so fast in his chest when I fell on him. Was I going insane?

Why did it feel like I'd never experienced this before?

"You going to be okay?" Karen asked.

"Yes, I think so. I'll speak to him the first chance I get. If I get a chance at all."

"That's good. You should put your foot down and lay the ground rules."

"Thanks."

We ended the call soon. Jessie had started crying and Karen needed to go attend to him. I lay back in bed, staring up at the ceiling in the dark. I replayed that scene again.

I could feel the texture of his jacket under my fingers. Butter smooth. That stain of coffee on his white shirt appeared to be darker in my imagination. His cologne smelt fresh in my nostrils.

If I could slip my hands under his shirt, I'd feel the rock-hardness of his abs. There was no doubt in my mind that Duke was sexy without his clothes on. I was wet thinking about him. I tossed and turned some more.

What was I going to say to him? What were the ground rules here? He was a highly successful businessman, a world-renowned scientist. He was handsome and rich and intelligent. Who was I in comparison?

Rose Johnson. Twenty-two, bright-eyed, and naïve. A girl whom her long-time boyfriend had been cheating on. A girl who was just now beginning to get the hang of her new job.

Wasn't I lucky that he even spoke to me? Was Monica right about that? I blushed when I remembered the way he looked at my body. His bright green eyes burning me up. Why did he want me? When he could have any woman he desired.

I wouldn't sleep tonight. No way. I was going to stay up all night, feeling a growing urge between my legs and dreaming about the sexy Duke Nolan and his big, strong hands.

∽

I arrived early at the office the next day. Monica was nowhere in sight, neither was Jim. I sat at my desk nervously for a few minutes and then I picked up the phone and called Laura on the top floor. I'd never spoken to her before but I knew she was Duke Nolan's assistant. As far as I knew, this man was known to live and breathe in his lab upstairs. I hoped he was in early and I'd get a chance to speak with him in private.

"Is Doctor Nolan in yet?" I asked Laura when she answered the phone. She sounded busy.

"What is this about? Rose Johnson, right?"

I remembered the suspicious looks she'd thrown me yesterday after the meeting.

"It's about the meeting. I wanted to discuss a few things with him."

"You'll have to set up an appointment, through Jim," Laura stated.

"Doctor Nolan will understand, if you just speak to him," I insisted. When she didn't say anything, I spoke again. "I'll come up and talk to you directly. It'll only take a few minutes if he can spare it."

I ended the call before she could continue. I stood up, smoothing the front of my dress. I wasn't sure where I suddenly had this much courage. I wasn't usually the type of person who was this bold. Especially not in my workplace. Maybe the chat with Karen did the trick. Like she said, I needed to set some ground rules before things got out of hand.

I took the elevator up to the top floor. There weren't many people around here either. It was too early.

Laura was at her desk when I walked toward her. She was flipping through some files. When she looked up, she fixed her big round glasses. Her lips were pursed tightly. I could see she was angry with me for my behavior.

"You can go straight through. He's waiting for you in his office," she snapped.

I quietly breathed a sigh of relief. It would've been very insulting if he refused to see me right now.

Keeping my back straight and chin up, I made my way to his office at the far end of the floor. I knocked once and opened the door. He was in the process of taking off a white coat. His lab coat. He'd been in the lab, working, just as I predicted.

"Good morning, Doctor Nolan. Thank you for seeing

me on such short notice." I entered quickly, shutting the door behind me. I just needed to get this done with. I knew I'd chicken out of saying anything if I kept it hanging too long.

"You know, Laura isn't too pleased with you," he said. He hung his lab coat on a peg on the other side of the wall. Next to a row of framed certificates of achievement and a few degrees. This man had spent the better part of his life working toward high success.

"I'm really sorry that I came on too strong, but I wanted to speak to you first thing today. I *needed* to speak to you." I was standing with my hands clasped tightly together. If I paid attention, I would've noticed my body melting. My stomach churned nervously.

The early morning sunlight filtered through the tinted glass wall behind Duke Nolan as he stood across the room. Hands deep in the pockets of his pants. His white shirt impeccably crisp and framing his chiseled muscular torso. Everything about him was so deliciously perfect, including that devilish grin he had on his face right now.

"You *needed* to speak to me?" he asked. The grin grew.

When was the last time I'd eaten? All I could do was think about this man. It needed to stop. I needed him to see how important this job and my career were to me.

"I just want to set the record straight before I begin working on this project...with you."

"With me?" he asked. His brows arched up in surprise, but he was still finding this funny.

"Jim told me yesterday that you requested for me to work on the core team. To lead the sales strategy for this drug."

Duke reached for the back of his high leather chair. I watched as he took in a deep breath and nodded.

"Yes, I did mention it to him. No decisions have been made yet."

He suddenly sounded dismissive. Did I overstep a line?

"Oh, okay, Jim made it sound like it was already decided."

He stared at me without responding. He was expecting me to continue—to get to the point.

What was the point? I was beginning to lose track here.

"I...uh...just wanted to make things clear to you."

"Make what things clear to me, Rose?" He crossed his arms over his chest now. His brow furrowed. That grin was gone from his face. I was beginning to lose my voice.

"That I don't want to work on this project if the only reason you are giving me this task is to...is to...because you think it could lead to something."

"Lead to something?" His face darkened now. I was ready for the floor to open up and swallow me whole.

"Something between us," I added. His face turned even stonier now. He was clenching his jaw tightly.

"Are you trying to accuse me of something, Rose Johnson? Because if you are, you should just come out and say it to my face. I don't believe I've behaved inappropriately with you in any way."

I had to do everything to keep looking at him.

"No, you haven't."

"Then what is this about?"

"I couldn't think of a reason why you would want me on your team. I assumed it was because of something else."

Duke glared at me for a few moments. I thought he'd end up bursting into flames.

"You should give yourself some credit. Jim recommended you and I accepted," he said.

6

DUKE

Rose was standing across the room, in the far corner. It seemed like she was too anxious to take a step in my direction. I wanted her to come closer. I *wanted* her. But now she looked embarrassed.

I wasn't lying when I told her Jim recommended her to me. He did. In fact, I was sure he had a crush on her. I couldn't blame him. Rose Johnson was probably one of the most delicious women I ever laid my eyes on.

"That's not what he said. He told me you asked for me specifically," she continued. Her voice had dropped down by several decibels. I wished I could've put her out of her misery.

"I didn't. He came to me with this suggestion and I accepted it. He spoke very highly of you," I replied. It was the truth. Although I left out the part that I was more than happy to accept his suggestion. Guess Jim wanted to work as closely with Rose as I did.

She sighed, stared down at her feet, and shook her head.

"I didn't know. I didn't realize."

"Obviously, poor Jim wasn't expecting you to come to me with this, to verify this arrangement."

"No, clearly he wasn't," she said.

"If you feel harassed by him or feel threatened in any way, I can take care of it."

She looked up at me and her blue eyes were burning up. With anger? Embarrassment? She shook her head again.

"No. No, he's never given me any reason to feel that way. And I'm hoping he made this suggestion because he truly believes in me."

"Yes, it's likely," I said.

But then why would he pretend I made the suggestion unless he had something to hide? He wanted to work more closely with her, that was obvious.

"I'm sorry for bringing this up with you. I should probably apologize to Laura too. I was way too upfront with her. I acted unprofessionally this morning."

I wanted to pull her into my arms. I wanted to kiss that mouth. If only she knew the thoughts that were going through my head. She had no idea.

"I'll deal with Laura," I said.

"Thank you."

We looked at each other now. I felt that electricity in the air again. I couldn't control the urge—to push her up against the wall, to pull up her dress, feel her body in my hands.

"So you came to see me to tell me off?" I asked with a grin. Rose wasn't smiling.

"I didn't want to be given this job for the wrong reasons."

"I hoped my reputation would speak for me," I said.

She nodded.

"It does. I mean, I should've known better. I feel silly now. I don't know why I thought there was something else."

There was. She wasn't wrong. I wanted her and maybe she wanted me too, but now it was out of the question.

"You are an employee in this office, Rose," I continued, trying to be firm.

"I know that."

I took a few steps toward her. Closing the distance between us felt powerful. I was being drawn to her like she had some sort of magnetic force.

"I shouldn't be here. If Jim finds out..."

"I won't tell him and he doesn't need to know. It's just a misunderstanding."

She nodded. "Thank you."

I could reach for her now if I wanted to. I hadn't stopped thinking about her body. How she'd felt against my chest yesterday. Soft, supple, deliciously curvy. I wanted to grab a bunch of her hair, tug her head gently back so I could look into her eyes. Kiss that incredibly pink mouth.

"You should go," I said. Maybe I spoke too gruffly because she looked up at me with a snap. There was surprise in her eyes. Like she was expecting me to say something else. I had nothing more to say to her. I wanted her to leave. Now. Before I did something stupid.

"Yes, of course, I'll go. Thank you for seeing me. Thank you for...everything," she was speaking hurriedly, backing away from me one step at a time.

I watched her back up to the door. She fumbled for the door handle and then pulled. We held each other's gazes. I was like a wild animal, waiting to pounce, and she was a poor deer fumbling to make its escape.

Without another word, she was gone. The door shut gently and I breathed heavily. What was she doing to me? No other woman had this effect on me before. It was dangerous to even just speak to her. Maybe it was because I knew I couldn't have her.

I had never been attracted to an employee before.

I was alone in my office for a few moments before the phone started buzzing. I was tempted to just let it ring. I needed a few seconds to gather myself. But it didn't stop ringing and eventually, I picked up. It was Laura.

"Everything okay, Doctor Nolan?" she asked in her usual motherly voice.

"Everything is fine, Laura. And you don't need to worry about Rose Johnson, we just had some things to discuss."

"Of course," she spoke curtly.

The last thing I needed was Laura gossiping. I trusted her, but did I really know her? She was an employee, too, after all, and she'd just seen a young new recruit walk out of my office early in the morning. What would she think? I didn't care.

I sat at my desk, swiveling in my leather chair for a few moments.

That was right, I didn't care what anyone else thought. I wanted Rose and I was going to have her.

By coming to see me this morning, she'd proved she wanted the same thing.

~

I spent the rest of the day in my lab, dreaming about Skibbereen and the pub I spent most of my vacation in. I knew I would never see my drinking buddies again. I'd left suddenly, without an explanation, and now I was yearning to return. But I couldn't go back now. I had important work to do here.

And then there was the matter of Rose. She was on my

mind. All the time. Especially since she came to see me in the morning. She knew, just as well as I did—that the sexual charge between us was palpable.

It was late in the evening when I returned to my office from the lab. Laura had left already, leaving a pile of files and notes on my desk. Apparently, I'd missed a few meetings and many phone calls. It didn't matter. I just wanted to work. I wasn't a businessman. I was lucky the company kicked off. I was just as happy being stuck at the lab.

When I was leaving the office, Jim was headed in my direction. For a moment, I thought maybe Rose had spoken to him about the mix-up. But clearly she hadn't, he was in a good mood.

"Doctor Nolan. I was just coming to see you. I have those reports you asked for. Sales figures and estimations."

I took the files from him. "Thanks for that. You headed home?"

I'd always liked Jim. He was a nice guy, not overly friendly, but friendly enough. Although now I was looking at him in a different light. I saw him as a man who wanted Rose. Just like I did? It was obvious to me.

Jim looked at his watch. "Nah, I don't think so. The rest of the team is headed to a bar. You know, to celebrate the good news and the project coming up. We are all very excited."

"You're celebrating? The whole team?"

Jim looked nervous suddenly. "Yeah, and you are welcome to join us, of course."

"Which one is it?"

"The Dutchman. Just around the corner. I wasn't sure if I'd go. I thought I'd be stuck here 'til much later."

"So you're going?" I asked.

"Yeah."

"Good, we can go together."

It was a spur-of-the-moment decision. I'd invited myself. I never socialized with my employees—as a rule. But the idea of potentially seeing Rose again, in a different environment outside the office, was too tempting.

Jim and I walked together silently to the elevator. It was evident he'd stepped on his own feet by talking about the bar. He didn't want me there amidst the team's celebrations. Who would want the company's CEO raining on that parade? But I didn't give a shit what anyone else thought.

I just wanted to see if Rose's eyes would light up or not.

And they did. Jim and I had walked into the bar together. My first action was to search her out in the dimly-lit crowd. The team was in a big group by the bar. Rose was among them, cradling a bottle of beer.

Jim waved at them and everyone turned. Their reception of us changed immediately when they saw me. Most of them looked confused and nervous, nobody was expecting me to be here. Neither was Rose.

She stood at the back, beside her friend...Monica? She watched me as the others in her team congratulated me and fell over each other trying to hold a conversation with me directly.

I was accustomed to this behavior from people who worked for me. What I wasn't used to was being ignored. Which was what Rose was doing on purpose now. She wanted to avoid me. It was obvious.

"What can I get you, Doctor Nolan?" Jim asked, rubbing his hands together. "First round is on me."

The others cheered.

"Please, everyone, call me Duke. At least when we are outside the office. Whisky. On the rocks for me, please."

Jim smiled and went away to get the drinks. The others

surrounded me again, Rose kept to herself. She was the only one I wanted to speak to. Did Monica know? She was eyeing me suspiciously too.

The problem was that I had no choice but to spend the next twenty minutes having inane conversations with people I didn't really want to talk to. Everyone was trying to make an impression. To stand out.

Rose continued to ignore me, talking privately with Monica or someone else the whole time. I couldn't blame her. This morning, I made it very clear to her that she'd let her imagination run wild. She said she felt silly coming to me with her problem. I blamed the whole thing on Jim. He wasn't completely innocent in this, no, but neither was I.

Now I wasn't sure how to break the ice with Rose again. Would she drop out of the team? Would she quit her job? The idea made me turn away abruptly from the group and walk straight up to her.

She was in the middle of a conversation with Monica.

"How are you guys getting on?" I asked, interrupting them. They turned to me, both a little pale-faced.

"Good, thank you, Doctor Nolan...umm...Duke. We're excited to work on this."

"Yeah, that's good, and you, Rose? Are you still interested in the position Jim offered you on the project?"

She had no choice but to face me now. I was expecting her to say no. To make up some excuse. But she looked squarely at my face and then nodded.

"Of course. Why wouldn't I be? This would be a great learning opportunity for me."

I could sense other eyes on us. Jim was staring too. Wasn't it obvious there was something between us? Wasn't it plain for the others to see? I'd walked straight up to her. Picked *her* to talk to especially.

"Good, because I've heard such great things about you from Jim," I said.

Rose looked past me at her manager and smiled.

"Thank you, Jim," she said and then swinging away from me, she walked to the bar, leaving me standing like a fool. Not for too long, of course, there were plenty of others to talk to. But Rose knew exactly what to do to make me want her more.

∼

I couldn't take my eyes off her, even though other people were talking to me. I mumbled mechanical responses while others spoke. From the corner of my eyes, I watched Rose.

She looked way more relaxed this evening. She laughed and talked, touched a coworker's arm lightly, ran her fingers through her curls, threw back her head as she emptied the beer from the bottle. It was like she hardly even noticed I was there.

Everyone was discussing the new drug and its future potential. Yes, it was exciting stuff but I'd spent the whole day in the lab—I was exhausted. Besides, there was only one person I wanted to talk to right now.

I had my second chance when she broke away from the group she was with. It seemed like she was about to make her way to the bar, so I walked away from the conversation I was having. The others might have been eyeing me like a hawk as I followed Rose.

She weaved through the crowd and so did I. When she got to the crowded bar, I was directly behind her. She caught sight of me over her shoulder and looked taken aback for a moment. Then she got a hold of herself and said, "Oh!"

"Let me get this drink. What are you having?"

"Just a beer, any beer," she said. I raised a hand for the bartender to take notice. I was taller than most others around us, so I was noticed fairly quickly. Beside me, Rose smiled.

"Thanks for that," she said.

"It's the least I can do."

"Why? You don't owe me any favors."

She was right. I had no response to that. I needed to change the subject.

"Are you enjoying the evening? You guys all seem to get along."

"Yeah, we work well together. Everyone sort of keeps out of each other's business, which is nice. There's very little competition."

I watched her speak. Her bright blue eyes searched the crowd as she spoke. It seemed like she didn't want to look at me directly. She was doing everything she could to avoid that.

"I'm glad you enjoy working here," I continued. Our drinks arrived, but we remained standing at the bar. I was glad she wasn't rushing away. Rose nodded as she held the bottle to her lips.

"I do. I couldn't have hoped for a better job, as my first real job, straight out of college. And Jim...he's a good manager. I am grateful to him for the opportunities he's giving me."

"Have you spoken to him? About our meeting this morning?"

"No. Whatever reasons he had for giving me the impression it was you who asked for me specifically, I'm sure they were good reasons. I don't want to put him on the spot."

I nodded. Maybe she was right, but I wanted her to be careful. Not that I had any real reason to care.

"But if he makes you uncomfortable somehow…" I started to say.

"I know, I'll go straight to HR." She was stating the obvious, that she wouldn't come to me. She had other options for help. I cleared my throat and nodded.

"Yeah, of course, go to HR."

"I don't think it will come to that. Jim is harmless."

"I'm sure he is," I replied and looked away. A few moments of silence passed between us. I was half expecting her to walk away at this point.

"But that's not what you think of him, do you?" she asked.

I faced her again. I gripped my glass of whisky tightly.

"Jim is a nice guy. I've known him for years."

"But you think he has an ulterior motive for wanting me on this project? To work closely with him?"

"I think you should be careful."

She nodded. Took another swig of her beer.

"Thank you for your concern."

"I'm not trying to tell you what to do. I'm sure you're capable of looking out for yourself."

"Okay," she replied. There was a fire in her eyes now. Her voice seemed strained too. It was almost like she was mad at me.

"Your personal life is your business, of course," I added.

"Yes, it is, as is yours. You're my boss, I am nobody. We shouldn't even be talking to each other," she said. We were staring at each other, right into each other's eyes. I couldn't keep away from her. I was being pulled toward her, despite the noise of this bar. Despite the crowd around us.

Rose licked her lips. I saw the tip of her pink tongue poke out. I could feel my cock move in my pants too. She was watching me.

"I need to use the restroom," she said. But she didn't make a move. It was like she was trying to tell me something else. "I'm going to go now," she added.

When she did begin to walk away, she threw a look over her shoulder at me. Was it an invitation to follow her? I didn't want to misread her signals. This was a crucial moment and I didn't want to get it wrong.

But then she'd walked some distance from me and turned to look again. This time it was obvious—that look in her eyes. She wanted me. I wanted her. What were we waiting for?

I emptied the remaining whisky down my throat and banged the glass down on the counter. The drink warmed the pit of my stomach. Rose had walked over to the back corridor, presumably where the toilets were. She turned to watch me again, waiting for me to follow her.

A smile crept up on my face. This felt like a miracle.

7

ROSE

The truth was I had no idea what Duke was actually going to do. What did he really want? Was he just being a supportive boss by coming to speak to me?

I didn't know if he'd follow me to the toilets. Chances were that he wouldn't. He wouldn't want to do something he was accusing Jim of, right? But it was what I wanted. I was trying to lead him on. Did he get my signals?

He denied it this morning. He embarrassed me by making me feel like I was making it all up in my head. But I knew I was right all along. There was an undeniable sexual chemistry between us. This was why he was here at the bar tonight. Why he kept watching me from the corner of his eyes the whole time.

I knew he was waiting to get me alone. He was itching to speak to me. I just wanted him to admit that he wanted me too. My body.

And now he was following me. Through the crowd of the bar. Right up to the corridor I was about to walk down. It was dimly lit. Music from the bar seeped in. I waited for him, watching his big shoulders rise and fall as he came toward me.

He'd left his drink at the bar, and so had I. He came up to me, looming tall over me so I had to tip my head back to look into his face. His jaw was clenched tightly and his green eyes burned into mine. He'd taken his jacket off at some point and his shirt sleeves were rolled up. It was like every time I looked at him, I discovered some new sexy detail about him.

I gulped.

"Do you want me to follow you in, Rose? I will not do it if you don't want me to." He spoke in a deep, guttural growl. Even his voice was dripping of sex.

"I want you to follow me," I replied. My own voice was choked. I could hardly get the words out.

I turned and walked down the short corridor until I reached the women's bathroom. Duke followed me in. Like he wasn't the least bit afraid of being seen by someone else in there. But it seemed empty.

He turned the lock on the door. We were locked in now, alone, together. There was only one purpose to this and I didn't know how to say it. I'd never experienced something like this before—acting out of pure sexual desire. Dulling out every logical thought that popped in my head. I let my body take charge.

Duke took a few steps toward me and I backed away. Not because I wanted to get away from him, but because I wanted to prolong this moment. He reached for me just as the back of my waist struck the cold, granite counter.

His hands were on my arms. He held me tightly, nearly squeezing me, then he leaned forward. I got a whiff of that cologne again. It made me dizzy, just as he took my mouth in his.

That kiss seemed to come out of nowhere even though I was expecting it. His tongue thrust into my mouth, and I welcomed him in. Our bodies relaxed. I rose up on my tiptoes so I could wrap my arms around his neck.

Duke was the guide. He was leading me through that kiss, navigating it for me with his tongue. It was an overwhelming, surreal experience. I felt like I was falling and rising at the same time. That kiss was taking over my whole body.

His hands found their way over my breasts and I pushed up against him. I could feel the strength of his body now. He was big and strong and I shuddered against him while he kissed me deeper. He squeezed my breasts and I gasped. His thumbs grazed my taut nipples through the dress.

I was out of breath by the time he pulled away from me. Panting, my shoulders heaving, I stared at him. He was peering into my eyes, maybe waiting for me to say something. I didn't know what to say. *That was amazing? Kiss me again? Touch me some more?*

"You are so fuckin' hot," he growled.

I felt like I wouldn't be able to balance on just my feet if he let me go now.

"I didn't know what you thought of me," I murmured.

"Wasn't it obvious?"

I turned my face up toward him. I wanted him to see what else I wanted. He reached for my face, cupping my chin with one hand. My lips were parted as I stared at him hungrily.

"Duke..."

"Nobody says my name like that."

"I want you to..."

"Shhh..." He covered my mouth with his again. It was a shorter, quicker kiss this time. He held me by my hips and before I knew what he was going to do, he flipped me around. I leaned over the bathroom counter.

A wide sparkling mirror was in front of me. I could see him clearly. I could see myself.

Duke stood behind me, pressed up to me. I could feel his growing cock on my butt. He was unbuckling his belt. His pants fell to the ground. I could hear everything perfectly. Then his hands were on my dress, he was pulling it up.

I felt my butt exposed to him. His hands were on my thin lace panties and he was tracing the shape of it on my butt. I could see his reflection, focused and serious. He studied my body carefully and I moaned.

I couldn't wait. I could feel the pressure building up between my legs. Wet and hot. I needed to know what his cock felt like. Inside me. I could feel it—throbbing and growing and hot.

"Is this what you want, Rose?" he asked. His eyes were focused but glazed over at the same time. He stared at me in the mirror. All I could do was nod. He pulled down my panties. This was it. There was no turning back now. I was about to have sex with my boss. My very sexy boss. A surge of electricity ran through my body as he gently parted my legs.

It was going to happen. I held my breath. And then it did.

He thrust his cock deep inside me. I cried out with pleasure. I was pushed up against the counter, but he was holding me too. His arms encircled my waist while he started pounding into me. His cock dove deep into me and then pulled out.

My whole body shook with the intensity of his power. His cock felt so good. Big and powerful. We moved together, as one entity. I knew he was going to make me come soon.

Just his cock was enough to make me feel like I was powerless.

But then he moved his hand in front of me, reaching for my wet, sensitive clit. I cried out again when he found it. So gentle with his strokes. He knew exactly how to touch me. Nothing had ever felt so good before. No man had been this amazing.

His mouth was in my hair, next to my ear, I could hear him groaning and grunting with every thrust. He lifted me off the floor a little with every thrust.

I grabbed his strong arms, clinging to him while we moved together. I was losing all control. I knew I was very close to the edge. His cock deep inside me and his hand teasing my clit. It was double trouble. And just like that, I was coming.

I huffed and moaned when I released. I couldn't look at the mirror anymore. It was too sexy. Too powerful and perfect. I had to shut my eyes as I came. All I could do was focus on the overwhelming sensation of my orgasm.

I heard Duke grunt. The pressure of his arms became more intense and I knew he was going to release too.

I felt it. His cum shot deep inside me like an explosion. We both groaned together because it was so perfect. We were still rubbing against each other. His cock was deep inside me while he filled me up.

Damn! We hadn't used any protection. The thought hit me and I grew very still all of a sudden. Duke was breathing hard into my ear but he noticed the change in my body language.

He stopped, pulling out of me quickly and with force. He took a few steps back while I hurriedly pulled my dress down. My panties were around my ankles on the floor.

I couldn't look at myself in the mirror. Nothing made

sense. How did I let this happen? I was so determined to behave professionally here and keep my job.

I brushed my hair with my hands repeatedly. Tried to fix my dress and pulled up my panties. I refused to turn and face him, but I could sense him dressing behind me too.

Eventually, he cleared his throat, trying to break the ice. One of us had to do it.

"Rose, are you okay?" he asked. He had a neutral tone of voice. It didn't sound like he actually cared.

"I'm fine, I'm great," I replied. What was I supposed to say now? Did he expect a thank you? I knew I was blushing. My body was burning up. I could still feel him against me. His cock inside me.

Should I bring up how we just had *unprotected* sex? Had the thought even occurred to him? I was usually so careful, but I wasn't thinking straight tonight. I just wanted him. It was a hungry animal desire that took over me. And now I couldn't take it back.

There was a thud on the door just then. Somebody was trying to open it. Then they knocked.

"Hello? Is this thing locked from the inside?" A woman outside was trying to pull open the door.

I looked at Duke, panic written all over my face.

"I'll handle it. I'll leave first," he said. I nodded and took a few steps back. The only thing I could hope for was that the woman on the other side wasn't somebody from our office. Being embarrassed in front of a stranger, I could handle.

Duke gently unlocked the door and swung it open. Over his shoulder, I saw Monica's stunned face.

"Doctor Nolan," she said in a low squeaky voice.

"Sorry about that. The door was stuck for some reason. All good now," he said. Monica nodded, her brow furrowed in confusion. Without giving me another look, Duke slipped past Monica and disappeared into the noise and dim lights of the bar.

I wanted to melt away. There was no escape for me. She'd stepped in and looked up to find me standing near the wash basins. A ghostly figure.

"Rose?" She was confused at first and then realization dawned on her. "You and Doctor Nolan?"

"We were just talking...umm, about the coffee thing," I tried.

She glared at me. Her hands were on her hips.

"You seriously want me to believe that?" she snapped, rolling her eyes.

My throat was dry. I wanted to cry. Everything about tonight was wrong. But it felt so right at the moment. Did I really regret it?

"It just happened. I don't know how or why," I said. I covered my mouth with my hand and stared at Monica pleadingly. Her nostrils were flared. She looked angry, like she'd been personally offended.

Then her shoulders relaxed and a smile spread on her face.

"You lucky bitch!" she declared.

8

DUKE

I left the bar soon after I escaped from the bathroom. I didn't want to hang around and face Monica and Rose. Things had taken a sudden awkward turn and I knew it was all my fault. I should've handled the matter more delicately. What were the HR implications of this situation?

The last thing I needed was a scandal, right when we were beginning a new project.

If she hadn't knocked into me on the streets. If she hadn't spilled coffee all over me—none of this would have happened.

In my apartment, I poured myself another drink. My castle of solitude. I tried to recall if anybody had ever spent the night in this apartment with me. No. Nobody. All the women I slept with here were politely asked to leave soon after I came.

That was my rule.

I sat sprawled on my couch, with whisky glass in hand and music playing loudly on the sound system. I wished I was back in Skibbereen. Would it be so bad if I left everything here and bought a house in Ireland?

Alone?

Did I want to spend the rest of my life alone?

What other option did I have? It wasn't like I was in a position to have a family. Have kids.

My phone had been ringing for some time and I finally coaxed myself to get up and answer it.

There was only one person who could be calling at this time of the night.

"Diane," I said, gruffly.

"You sound like you're drinking by yourself," my sister spoke with a laugh in her voice.

"You know me too well. But what do you want? I was just about to hit the sack."

"No, you weren't. You can't fool me. You were going to stay up late and pity yourself for all the things you don't have. Obviously, you'll forget about the things that you *do* have."

"So, you called me to discuss my shortcomings?"

"They're not your shortcomings, Duke, just some little tiny flaws. Don't worry, we all have them. It's what makes you human."

I leaned my head back, staring up at the ceiling. Diane was the only person I knew I could be completely honest with. She was the only person I trusted.

"I slept with an employee tonight. Well, it was more like a quickie in the bathroom of a bar."

A few moments of silence passed between us as the words slowly sank in. Diane might have been shocked.

"Are you serious, Duke? You banged one of your employees in a bathroom somewhere?"

"In a bar. We were there along with the rest of the sales

team, celebrating the start of a new project." There was no point explaining the nuances of the drug trial to my sister. She was a musician and never had any interest in my line of work.

"This isn't a joke?"

"Diane, I'm a hundred percent serious, okay?"

"Okay. I'm just making sure."

"Why would I joke about something like this?"

"I don't know, Duke. I just find this very hard to believe. It's quite unlike you. This isn't the sort of thing you do. Not with an employee."

I breathed out slowly and nodded.

"I know."

"So why did you do it? Were you drunk? Was she drunk?"

"Neither of us were drunk. We were both perfectly in our senses. There's been a kind of...sexual tension between us since we met. And tonight, it just exploded. Like we had no control over it."

"So, what does this mean? Is it going to happen again? Are you dating one of your employees now?"

"No!" I snapped. Probably a little too abruptly. "It's not like that. It was just a one-time thing. I mean, I'd gladly have sex with her again. She's very beautiful. But nothing more than that. She's a lot younger than me, and we should probably keep our distance from each other anyway."

I could nearly see Diane rolling her eyes at that.

"And when has that ever stopped you?"

"It didn't stop me. The sex was amazing. I'll be fantasizing about her for many, many weeks."

"Okay, so what's the problem then? Why do you sound worried?" Diane asked.

"She's an employee. How are you not seeing this?"

"You are also two consenting adults."

"She's supposed to work closely with me on this new project. I might be seeing a lot of her."

"So, you're worried she's going to fall in love with you?" Diane asked with a laugh.

"That is not what I said."

"Oh, come one, Duke. That's what you're thinking right? The last few women you've banged have all fallen in love with you, and you think that's what'll happen with this girl too."

I sighed, relaxing my shoulders a little. It was funny how Diane always knew how to surgically extract my thoughts, even if I didn't know what exactly I was feeling.

"Maybe," I replied.

"Well, you're an expert at letting women down gently. I'm sure you'll figure it out, big brother. I don't know why you're wasting any thought on this."

I took a sip of my whisky. It relaxed me a little, just like my sister did. She was right. Why was I thinking about Rose? It was over. I got what I wanted. It was time for me to move on.

"Okay, so why are *you* calling me in the middle of the night?" I asked.

"Finally! We can talk about me. I'm in Las Vegas and it looks like my band broke up."

"Broke up?"

"Yup, right in the middle of a gig. Tommy and Jack have been having it out for a while now, but tonight they really went for each other. Right up on stage too. It was horrible and hilarious at the same time."

We both laughed a little at that.

"So what are you going to do, sis?"

Diane sighed.

"Maybe hang around here for a while, see if I can score a few solo gigs. If not, I'm headed straight to you."

"You're welcome any time," I said. The idea excited me. I hadn't seen Diane in months, probably close to a year. She was always so busy with her tours and I was always busy in the lab. Maybe this was exactly what I needed. To spend some time with my sister.

∽

Jim was waiting for me outside my office when I arrived at work the next day. From the expression on his face, I could sense something was up. He hadn't simply stopped by to drop in a few files and reports.

"Morning, Jim," I said while he and Laura followed me into my office.

"Good morning, Doctor Nolan. I was hoping to speak with you privately for a moment."

Laura glanced at me and she probably saw a look of annoyance on my face.

"Jim, it might be easier if you booked an appointment with me for some time later in the day. Doctor Nolan has a few important phone calls to attend to right now."

But Jim wasn't paying attention to Laura. He seemed to be glaring at me as I sat down at my desk.

"It's okay, Laura. I can spare a few minutes. What did you want to discuss, Jim?" I asked.

Laura pursed her lips together tightly and forced herself to walk out of my office.

"Do you want to sit down?"

Jim kept standing.

"It's about Rose. Rose Johnson."

My back stiffened. I had no intention of discussing her

with Jim ever again. I had no idea what this could possibly be about. I weaved my fingers together on the desk and tried to remain stern. I just needed to remember I was still boss here.

"What about her?"

"Maybe she's not as perfect for the role we were...I was thinking about," he said. A nervousness entered his face. It made me curious.

"Why? What's changed your mind?" I asked him. Jim shifted on his feet.

"It's nothing major. It's probably not something I need to discuss with you."

"Spit it out, Jim. You're taking up too much of my time already," I snarled.

He rubbed a hand over his forehead and cleared his throat.

"I think she's sleeping with someone from this office," he said sheepishly.

I glared at him with my eyes narrowed. What the actual fuck?

"I overheard her speaking to her friend last night at the bar. Monica. They were discussing someone Rose had recently...had relations with. I could tell it was someone from the office. Possibly someone senior, like in management."

"So, you were eavesdropping?" I snapped. Jim's face paled and he shrugged.

"No, I wasn't. I was just standing near them."

"You were eavesdropping on a personal conversation between two of your subordinates." I realized my voice was becoming gruffer and harsher by the minute. Jim looked even more nervous now and that was when I realized—he was jealous.

"How does this matter to you?" I snapped. Jim stared down at his feet.

"I think it's inappropriate. I thought highly of her, but now I don't anymore."

"Because she has a sex life?"

"Because she's sleeping with someone from the office, Doctor Nolan," he continued in a pleading tone. He made me sick—his jealousy and vindictiveness made me want to punch him in the face.

"And what about the guy? The man in this office who slept with her. What do you think of him?" I had to ask. Jim chewed on his bottom lip and shrugged.

"She's a gorgeous young girl. What man would turn away a chance with her? She obviously manipulated him for favors," he replied.

"Get out of my office right now. Get out!" I thundered, jumping up from my chair. I felt an urgent need to protect Rose. To defend her. And Jim was being an arrogant, chauvinistic bastard.

He backed away to the door, looking confused.

"I just wanted to bring it to your attention."

"And what do you want me to do with this information? Someone's personal information."

"I didn't think you'd want her working in your team."

"You have a very narrow worldview, Jim, and I want you to fix it. Or you lose your job, do you get it? I am not going to allow you to treat our female employees this way."

Jim's back was to the door now and I could see he was itching to leave. Good. I didn't want to look at him again.

"Fix it!" I growled and he pulled open the door. He was gone, and I sat back down at my desk.

Covering my face with my hands, I growled repeatedly. This was going too far. This wasn't just a harmless quickie with a sexy stranger anymore. Things were getting complicated around here. The last thing I needed was for Rose to feel persecuted because we slept together.

Sure, I slept around a lot. I enjoyed sex with beautiful women, but I would never undermine her abilities or think any less of her because of our sexual history.

I needed her to know that. Whether she wanted to continue working in this office or not was up to her. Not me. And definitely not up to Jim.

I tried to ignore that voice in the back of my head that was saying I wanted to see her for other reasons, too. Because I'd been dreaming about her last night. Because I couldn't get that kiss out of my head.

"Laura, please send up Rose Johnson to see me," I spoke hurriedly into the intercom. I could sense she was about to make some comment but I ended the call before she did. I didn't need another person asking stupid questions.

I just needed to clear the air, set the record straight, and then we could move on. After all, it was just sex, right? Nothing complicated about that.

9

ROSE

Initially, I was horrified that Monica found out. She'd literally caught us red-handed last night, but as it turned out, I really needed someone to talk to.

She took it well.

She made jokes and wanted to know details until she realized I wasn't actually taking this lightly. I *liked* Duke Nolan. I really liked him. More importantly, we had unprotected sex and now I couldn't help but be worried. Monica said she understood and she'd spent the rest of the night trying to calm me down. Thankfully, Duke didn't stick around. I couldn't have faced him after everything.

I tried to get to the office on time the next morning, but I ended up being late. I was too frustrated and sleep-deprived. Monica was at her desk when I got there. She jumped up and greeted me with a hug.

"Hey, how are you feeling?" she asked. We were sitting down and speaking in hushed tones now. This was an extremely sensitive matter. Not everyone else in the office would take the news as light-heartedly as Monica did.

"I don't know. I guess I should feel nothing. It was just

sex. But I can't help but feel like something is going to go wrong," I whispered.

Monica patted my shoulder and made a pitying face.

"It'll be fine. You're both grown-ups. There was an attraction there and it happened. It's over now."

"But I don't know how I'll keep working here or on the new project. I feel like I'll be sick if I have to face him again."

"But I thought the sex was good?"

"Yeah, it was. That isn't the problem. It was too good, I guess, is what I'm trying to say."

"You mean you wish it was more than just sex?"

I sighed and sat back in my chair.

"I've been on a dating spree for the last year. Ever since my previous relationship ended. I started seeing a ton of guys and going on dates every chance I got. Just to numb myself."

Monica nodded. She still looked at me sympathetically.

"But I've not felt like this before, not in the past year, not once with all those guys I went on dates with. This strong physical connection like it's supposed to mean something, and I know it sounds insane because he's my boss."

Monica chewed on the end of a pen, staring at me as I spoke.

"That sounds amazing, actually," she said and I smiled.

"It is. I finally feel something. But for the wrong man. How am I supposed to get past this? He's my boss and clearly not interested in me in the same way."

Monica shook her head. She was out of ideas too. "I don't know what to tell you, Rose. I've never been in your position before. But my advice would be to forget about it and move on. These kinds of things don't lead to anything, especially when it's a man like..."

"Good morning, ladies." It was Jim. He was interrupting

us again. Monica and I both smiled politely at him. He nodded at her and then swung directly around to me.

Jim was usually cheerful, but today, he looked like a man on a mission.

"Rose, we need to talk," he said. I glanced at Monica, who swiveled in her chair over to her computer. Jim placed a hand on my shoulder, which was uncalled for, but I let it slide. He led me a few steps away from the cubicle. What could be so private?

"Look, Rose, before we start working on this project and before I entrust all these new responsibilities on you, I want you to know you can come to me with anything. If there is anything you want to talk about, you can bring it to me."

I stared at him for a few moments in surprise. What was he talking about? It was definitely a strange thing to say to me out of the blue. Nonetheless, I smiled and nodded.

"Of course, thanks for that, Jim," I said. He peered into my eyes, carefully studying my face. I was reminded again of that conversation with Duke. He told me to be careful with Jim. I insisted he was harmless. Was he really?

Jim took a few steps closer to me. My back was against the cubicle wall. He was too close now and I wasn't sure what to do.

"Is there something going on with you, Rose? Something secret? Did something happen with you and someone else in this office?"

My heart was beating too fast in my chest. Was it purely coincidental? But it sounded like Jim knew something. Had he seen us enter or leave the bathroom last night? Did Monica spread the gossip? I felt dizzy and wanted to push him away.

"I don't know what you're talking about," I said.

Jim's eyes were like two sharp darts piercing my skin.

I'd never perceived him like this before. He was a completely different man to me now. I was even a little bit afraid.

"I think you do, Rose, and you're keeping it from me."

"I really don't know what you're referring to."

"Rose?" It was Monica. Jim and I looked at her standing some distance from us. She'd noticed the strangeness of our situation too. She actually looked worried for me. "That was Laura on the phone. She said Doctor Nolan wants to speak to you."

"Thanks," I murmured. Jim stepped away. "I've gotta go," I said to him.

He had his jaw clenched. "Sure, yeah, do that. Come see me afterward. I have a few notes to give you."

With that, he walked away. Monica came up to me.

"What the hell was that about? He was all up in your face."

"I don't know. Seems like he knows something. Maybe he saw us last night. I don't know. I can't tell if it was a warning or genuine concern."

Monica let out a deep sigh. "Anyway, you should probably go speak to the boss. See what he has to say."

∽

Duke Nolan was sitting at his desk with a cup of coffee at his side which looked like it had been untouched for a while.

This was the man who was inside me last night. Whose cock I could still feel thrusting deep between my legs repeatedly. His fingers were on my clit, stroking me to dizzying heights of pleasure. His gruff moans were still ringing in my ear.

That handsome, chiseled face. His sharp nose and green

eyes. He had an intelligent face, along with being strong and calm. A man you could rely on.

But now, he was sitting with his fingers weaved together on the big desk. He stared at me with narrowed eyes under those sharp eyebrows.

"Thank you for coming up to see me," he said.

Just hearing his voice was enough to make me feel like I was about to melt. I stood by the door, barely able to meet his gaze. I was afraid that if he looked into my eyes, he'd see how desperately I wanted him to kiss me again.

"What did you want to discuss?" I spoke meekly.

"Jim. He came up to see me this morning with a complaint against you."

I snapped up my head to look at Duke. "A complaint?"

Slowly, he started to stand up. "Yeah, he said he overhead you and Monica talking last night. From what he could gather, he thinks you slept with someone in senior management in this office. He doesn't want you on the team."

My hands turned to fists on my sides. How dare he! My nostrils flared. I was angry.

"He eavesdropped on our conversation!"

"He shouldn't have," Duke supported.

"And even if he did hear us talking about someone I slept with. It's *my* problem. A personal issue. He had no right to bring it up with you! That is discrimination."

Duke nodded. "Yes, and I told him so."

My chest was heaving. I felt like I was out of breath.

Duke came around his desk, taking a few steps toward me.

"That's what I would have told him; regardless of whether this concerned me or not. Who you sleep with is none of his business, and it definitely doesn't affect your ability to do your job."

I stared at him, feeling my heart racing now that he came closer to me.

"No, I guess it doesn't."

Duke was standing directly in front of me now. His breath fell hot on my face. Without wasting another moment, he reached for my face. Gently, he ran a finger along my jaw. His touch was electric. I wrapped my hand around his, forcing him to keep his fingers on my face. I wanted him to keep touching me like that forever.

"I've been thinking about you, Rose," he spoke gruffly.

"I haven't stopped thinking about you," I said. I could feel the wetness between my legs again. A sharp, desperate ache. The only way it would go away was if he was inside me.

I loosened my grip and his hand traveled down...down my neck...until he covered my left breast with his big, strong palm. One soft, slow caress and that was enough to make my nipples go sharp and sensitive with desire.

"Spend the night with me, Rose," he murmured. Our faces grazed together. Our lips touched for a hot moment. I looked into his eyes. How could I say no?

I nodded.

"Come to me tonight. After work. I'll have some wine ready," he said.

I bit down on my lip. Had I ever been this excited about anything before?

The phone rang on his desk. He let it ring for a few seconds before he tore himself away from me.

"Yeah? Okay. Yeah, all right. Give me a few minutes and then make the call. I have the reports here on my desk, I can look through them." Duke put the phone down and looked at me. He sounded busy. Of course, he was. He was a busy man!

I felt like I could explode any moment now.

"Will I see you tonight?" he asked.

"Yes, I'll be there. At your place."

"Nine?" he said. I nodded and then walked to the door.

He remained at his desk but he was watching me closely. I was now overly self-conscious of my own body. The way my hips swung in that tight pencil skirt. I knew he was drawn to my breasts. The way I was drawn to his wide strong chest and those chiseled abs.

I stepped out of his office, forcing myself to not look back at him. How was I supposed to get through the rest of the day without bursting into flames?

Laura threw me a look when I walked past her desk. Maybe she saw the big sloppy grin on my face. Maybe Duke did this all the time and she was accustomed to it.

Either way, I didn't care. I just wanted to enjoy the moment. I just wanted to see him again tonight. Alone. That look in his eyes—he wanted me with a burning desire. I did too. That was enough for me. At least for tonight.

I forgot about Jim. I didn't care what he thought of me. In fact, I was glad he went to Duke with his complaint and was put in his place.

Back at my desk, Monica looked at me expectantly. She could see the flushed, excited expression on my face.

"What did he say?" she asked. I smiled, I couldn't help myself.

"We're seeing each other tonight. At his place."

She was shocked but thrilled at the same time.

I couldn't sit still. This was amazing. I still couldn't believe Duke Nolan wanted me!

"And we're having wine," I added.

10

DUKE

It seemed like a good idea at the time—inviting Rose over to my apartment. Now that I had a chance to think about it, I wasn't so sure.

I wanted her. She wanted me. Technically, nothing could go wrong, but I couldn't shake off the feeling that we were doing something bad. Because I was her boss? Because Jim knew something was up?

I prepared the wine and arranged some olives on a plate as a snack. This was probably the earliest I'd been back home in a while. I was anticipating her arrival. But there was also a part of me that hoped maybe she would change her mind and not show up. Then I wouldn't have to let her down.

But then security called me from the lounge downstairs about a guest. Rose was here. I stood at the door while she took the elevator up to my penthouse.

I was prepared to see her, or so I thought. I wasn't prepared to see her like this.

Rose stepped out of the elevator dressed in a short wine-red dress. It clung to her body deliciously. The neck scooped low to reveal her cleavage. She had big hips, wide thighs... everything about Rose was scrumptious and I had a feeling she knew it. She knew exactly the effect she had on me.

"Hi," she spoke softly when she came up to me.

"I wasn't sure if you'd actually turn up," I said.

I led her in and once again, we were alone together. This time, we were *truly* alone. Nobody could interfere.

Just seeing her was enough. I'd changed my mind about everything. This felt very, very right.

She followed me to my den.

"Wine?" I asked, walking over to the bar in the corner.

"I'm not a huge wine drinker, I have to be honest."

"So what can I get you?"

"A beer would be nice," she said.

When I brought a bottle over to her, along with the plate of olives, Rose was already sitting on my couch. Her long legs were crossed. Her dress had ridden further up her thighs. I noticed the way her curls fell softly over her shoulders. I couldn't help but picture her lying next to me in my bed. Naked under the sheets.

"Thanks. This place is really well looked after. Not like the usual guy-apartment I'm used to," she commented.

I sat on a chair across from her.

"So you visit a lot of guy-apartments, is it?"

Rose rolled her eyes.

"*That's* what you take away from the comment?"

"Just wondering. I'm not jealous or anything."

She was smiling. "I was in college last year. I hung out with guys in their apartments a lot, as all college students do."

"Of course. I was only pulling your leg, wasn't looking for an explanation."

Rose sipped her beer. I wanted her. The beer and the

olives and the conversation—these were all just a front. Could she see it in my eyes? Because she shifted in her seat and smiled at me again.

"So..."

"The last thing we should talk about right now is work," I said.

"Good, because I wouldn't want to discuss that either."

I put down my drink and so did she. I leaned closer to her and she smiled.

"In fact, the less we talk about anything, the better it will be."

Rose nodded.

"My thoughts exactly."

I studied her, examining every inch of her. She was too beautiful, too young, too sure of herself. What was I doing? What would happen in the morning?

"Do you know how beautiful you are?" I asked. The color rose in Rose's cheeks. She shied away from me.

"You definitely know how to make a girl feel like she's on top of the world."

"You are. On top of the world, Rose."

We stared at each other in silence for what seemed like one whole minute before she stood up and came closer to me. She was the one standing above me now.

"I don't want to waste any time, Duke," she said.

I reached for her, wrapping my arms around her legs. She lowered herself a little and I pulled her toward me. Within moments, she was in my lap, laughing with delight as I wrapped her up in my arms.

We were tangled together. I was close enough to taste her and that was exactly what I wanted to do now. Rose turned her face to me. Her blue eyes were shining. I took her mouth in mine and parted her lips with my tongue. Rose moaned in a really sexy way. I knew I was done for. There was no turning back now.

She was in my lap, my tongue was down her throat, and now my hand started to push up her dress so I could caress the softness of the inside of her thighs.

Rose parted her legs, moaning some more as she kissed me back ferociously. Her skin was butter-soft, smooth...I could touch her all night and I'd still want to touch her some more.

Slowly, my hand traveled up until I could feel the heat from between her thighs. That delicious pussy. My body hardened quickly at the thought of possessing her again. My cock throbbed with rage in my pants. Could she feel it?

But first, there was something else I wanted to do tonight. I pulled my mouth away from Rose. She stared at me quizzically. Her lipstick was smudged a little. She looked even more beautiful.

"I want that dress off. Every last bit of your clothing. On the floor, now."

It took her a second to register my words. I was in command here. She'd given her body to me and I was going to make her come for me. Rose stood up and started taking off her clothes. I sat in the chair and stared at her beautiful naked body being revealed to me.

It felt like I'd never wanted anything more than I wanted her right now.

∽

She wasn't self-conscious of herself and there was nothing sexier than that.

Rose stood in front of me with her arms on her side, staring at me from under her thick heavy eyelashes. Her beautiful blonde curls fell on her shoulders like a luxurious curtain. Her breasts were full and swollen, her pink nipples were taut with delight.

My eyes traveled all over her body, taking in every inch. Those gentle curves around her hips, the shape of her legs... I knew what her skin felt like under my fingers. Soft and tender.

While sitting in my chair, I undid my pants. She was watching me intently, waiting for the next step.

I needed to free my cock. It was throbbing and thrashing in my pants and now it was in my hand. Rose gasped a little when she saw it.

"I want you to touch yourself." I groaned as I started stroking my cock. I wanted to stare at her a little longer. I wanted to worship her body.

Rose's hand moved down to her pussy. I watched as she started rubbing her clit with her forefinger. Her breasts moved gently with the rest of her body.

"Your finger. Put it in," I said.

She thrusted her chin upward. Her mouth parted a little. Her middle finger was sliding into her pussy and finally she moaned. It was that sweet sound I'd been thinking about since I first fucked her. The sound of Rose's soul.

"Harder," I commanded her.

She thrust her finger in and out, her moans grew louder, and her whole body shook. I wanted her to rush to the edge of an orgasm, to teeter on that cliff, but I would rein her back.

Her moans became louder and more intense. She was still staring at me but beginning to lose control of her body.

I was stroking my cock but I stopped when I knew she was about to come. I stood up from my chair and walked over to her. Rose moved her finger out of her pussy. I grabbed her by her hips and kneeled in front of her.

Her legs were parted in front of me. I moved my face closer to her pussy. Close enough to feel the heat and wetness of it. Of her core.

She weaved her fingers in my hair, holding me in place as I moved my tongue to her pussy. I tasted her then. The sweetness of her being. She moaned even louder now.

"Duke..." she breathed my name as her hips rolled. My tongue thrust in and out of her pussy while I stroked her clit with my thumb. Every cell of my body was focused on giving Rose pleasure.

She moved against me, over me, while my tongue pushed her over the edge. She squealed with delight just as she was about to come. I flicked her clit more and licked her ferociously until she was coming in my mouth. She let go.

I could feel the reverberation of her orgasm, the way she was moaning was driving me nuts. I needed to be inside her. I released her quickly when she was done and straightened up.

Her mouth was all over me. She was kissing my chin and neck, feeling my chest, then she was unbuttoning my shirt. When she reached for my cock, I grabbed her by her waist, pressing her closer to me. Our bodies were fused together. Her hand moved up and down my cock, taking control of me. She was ready for me again.

"Wait," I grunted. My cock had a mind of its own. Before we went any further, I released her so I could go get a condom from my wallet. Rose waited for me with her bare shoulders rising and falling. She was watching me closely as I put on the condom. Then I lunged at her, pulling her to myself again.

We kissed. Our damp bodies slipping and sliding

together. I lifted her up by her waist in the next instance. Rose squealed with joy. I carried her over to the couch and laid her down.

She looked up at me now with a smile on her face. Her legs were parted wide, inviting me in. I lay down on top of her, covering her with my body. The couch squeaked from the pressure of us.

I could feel her lifting her hips up to meet me. I pinned her down to the couch with both hands until she couldn't move. Then I thrust my cock in.

We moaned together. This was exactly what I had been waiting for since the last time I was inside her. We moved roughly, maniacally, with an animal desire for each other's bodies.

She had her arms wrapped around my shoulders while I plowed my cock into her like a machine. Then it was over. We were both going to come together. There was no holding us back now.

My orgasm felt like a blackout. I emptied myself, shooting deep inside her while she wrapped her legs around my hips, keeping me in place.

We were both breathing harshly, losing control, but it didn't matter. This was the purpose of tonight—to fulfill our crazy desire for each other. And now it was done. I had my fill.

Rose's cheeks were flushed red even as her orgasm started to dim. I pulled out of her with force, groaning as I moved off the couch. She lay there for an extended moment before she quickly sat up again. Still naked. Still so bloody beautiful!

We stared at each other now. Neither of us moving or saying a word. What now? Usually, I would ask a woman to leave soon after. But I wanted Rose to stay.

11

ROSE

Did he want me to leave? Duke had a look on his face right now which I couldn't quite decipher. I had no idea what he wanted me to do next. Regardless, I needed to put on some clothes.

I broke my gaze away from him and started reaching for my clothes on the floor. He started gathering his clothes too. I was still jittery from the explosion of feelings inside my body tonight. Were my hands shaking? I couldn't quite tell anymore.

"Hey..." He was about to say something, but I wasn't quite ready to hear it yet. I could feel it. He was about to ask me to go.

"Can I use your bathroom?" I interrupted him as I zipped up the side of my dress.

"Yes, of course, it's down the hall to the left, right at the end," he said, stepping away from me.

I barely grinned at him in return. As I walked down the hall to the bathroom, I tried my best not to run. Then I was inside, I shut the door behind me, the automatic lights came on, and I was confronted with the most gorgeous bathroom I had ever been in.

It was probably larger than my whole apartment. Fabulously polished and sparkling. There was glass everywhere. The bathtub was glass too, with black marble fixtures. I was stunned into silence for a few moments and then finally managed to gather myself again.

I leaped to the mirror. It was huge too. I could see myself very clearly in it. Why was I here? Why did I accept his invitation? I should have stayed away. I should have turned him down. That way, I wouldn't have to face the embarrassment of being asked to leave now.

Feeling suddenly thirsty, I washed my face at the basin and then lapped up some of the cool water that had pooled in my cupped hands. Did I look like a mess to him? I definitely felt like a mess. I should have exercised some self-control tonight. Why did I have to strip off all my clothes at the drop of a hat?

He was my boss.

When I decided I'd been in there for too long, I stepped out of the bathroom. I could hear Duke moving around in the den. He'd put on some music too. Feeling my heart thudding in my chest, I walked to the den. This was why he'd invited me, right? So we could have sex one more time.

Duke was pouring some wine in a glass at the bar. He looked up when he heard me come in.

"Everything okay?" he asked. That handsome smile filled up his face and I wanted to just crash to the floor, curl up in a ball, and just disappear. This was more than just sex. I was attracted to him...I wanted to stay just a little bit longer.

"All good."

"You haven't touched your beer."

"I'm not really thirsty," I replied.

Duke nodded as he took a sip of his wine. He hadn't made a move toward me.

"So I guess you're itching to leave, aren't you?" he asked. There it was. He was practically kicking me out already.

"Yeah, umm, I guess I should go," I agreed. No matter what, I wasn't going to overstay my welcome.

"Or you could stay here a while longer, and we could talk?" he said.

Did I hear him right? I probably looked at him confusedly now because I couldn't believe he'd actually said those words.

"Yes, I could do that," I replied.

"I had some olives for us to snack on, but I'm thinking maybe a grilled cheese is in order. I'm starving!"

I bit down on my lip. I couldn't stop myself from smiling at that.

"Me too."

"Follow me," he said.

And I did. We went to the kitchen where Duke got busy whipping up two grilled cheese sandwiches. He knew his way around the kitchen. Not something I was expecting from him. While he cooked, we made small talk, mostly about Chicago and how long we'd both been in the city.

I was nervous around him. Nervous about making the right impression. We knew each other intimately. We'd exposed ourselves to each other in the most primal way. Twice.

But we hardly knew anything about each other in reality.

He put a plate of grilled cheese in front of me and we stood at the kitchen island, eating our sandwiches and smiling.

"Is this weird? This is weird, right?" he asked eventually. We'd been talking about Chicago for too long, avoiding the actual elephant in the room.

"What? Eating a sandwich?"

He smiled at me. "You know what I mean. You work for me. We have to pretend not to know each other at the office, but you're here now, in my kitchen."

I licked my lips. This was a perfect grilled cheese.

"It's strange, sure, but only because I've never had to sneak around like this before."

"Me neither," he said.

"Really? I kinda pegged you as someone who...a man who..." I couldn't find the right words for my thoughts.

"Who bangs every hot young thing in the office?" he asked.

That made me laugh. Mainly because he'd referred to me as a 'hot young thing', in a roundabout way.

"Well, yes, actually," I replied.

Duke sighed, licking some melted cheese off the side of his hand. It reminded me of the way he'd licked me, how explosively good it felt when his mouth was on me. I had to look away.

"You have me pegged all wrong then, Rose. I've never slept with an employee before, so I'm not sure how to deal with this exactly."

"We don't have to *deal* with anything. I'm not expecting anything from this."

"What do you mean?"

"I mean, you have nothing to worry about if you think I'm going to talk about this to other people or gossip about you, or expect you to treat me any differently."

Duke stared at me with his brows crossed now. "Okay, good, because that wouldn't be fair. For me to treat you any differently from the rest of the team. Unless you deserve it."

I nodded. "I'm glad we got that cleared up."

It was heartbreaking, to discuss our relationship in this practical way. Mechanical. Like it had meant nothing to either of us. I could see it meant nothing to him. Just sex. Either way, I wouldn't want him feeling sorry for me. That would make me sick.

Now that we'd spoken about it, my shoulders felt a little lighter. A weight had been lifted.

"Tell me something about yourself that nobody else knows," Duke said. He caught me by surprise. I was just chewing on a piece of the sandwich. I didn't know what to say. I stared at him with a grin on my face. "Come on, you can do it. You can tell me a secret. We're keeping secrets from the rest of the world already," he urged me on.

He took his plate to the sink and ran some water over it. I watched his wide, strong back. I knew what his body felt like. The thought made me tingle a little bit.

"I hate flowers," I said.

Duke turned to me. It was my turn to catch him by surprise.

"Flowers? Flowers, really? What have they ever done to you?" Duke walked back over to me, taking my empty plate away.

"No, I don't hate flowers when they're growing naturally, in fact, I love them. They're beautiful and fragrant and amazing creatures of nature. I just don't like receiving them or seeing them all cut up in flower shops. It's such a waste."

Duke washed my plate and then turned to me again with a smile.

"Okay, got it, I shouldn't ever get you a bouquet of flowers, unless it's in a pot."

I blushed. Why was he talking about getting me flowers?

"You're a flower activist," he added and I rolled my eyes.

"I wouldn't take it that far. I just admire them and think they should be allowed to bloom freely and in peace in their natural habitat."

"I agree with you, though I never considered it that way before," he said.

He came closer and I gulped. Even though I'd just had him, I wanted him again. Would I ever stop wanting him? Was I destined to always pine for him?

"Now, are you going to tell me something about yourself that nobody knows?" I asked.

Duke took in a deep breath. He slipped his hands into the pockets of his pants. He was thinking.

"I've fallen in love…"

When he said those words, my breath stopped. Could he see it in my eyes? How desperately I wanted him to continue, to explain himself. Even while I waited, in those moments, I knew he wasn't talking about me. But a girl could dream, right?

"With Ireland. I was just there on vacation. It is a beautiful country. I think I would love to retire there, someday."

I forced myself to smile.

"Come on, let's sit down," he said. Back out of the kitchen, we walked to the den. This time, we both sat on the couch together, side by side. I wanted to hear him speak. I could have listened to his voice all day long.

"Tell me more about Ireland," I said. Duke had his glass of wine in one hand. He leaned back a little so he could look up at the ceiling.

"It's green everywhere you look. There's literally grass growing through the cracks on the pavement. And the air smells nice. Fresh. Unhurried."

I hadn't realized he had this poetic vein in him. I stared at him as he spoke. Watched the way his throat moved with his words. His mouth—big and strong.

"And the people are just amazing. So warm and friendly. I really could spend the rest of my life there. I think I'm going to buy a house. In a town called Skibbereen. Well, it's basically a village. It's tiny. Just somewhere to escape to when things here become too busy."

I nodded, weaving my hands around my knee while I remained sitting beside him. There were only a few inches between us. Not nearly enough. I could still feel the strength and power of his body close to me.

"I'm sure you can't fully comprehend it, though. You're too young. You have a lot of things to look forward to in a big, bustling city."

"Just because I'm young doesn't mean I can't appreciate what you're saying," I replied.

Our eyes met. He gazed at my lips. I wanted him to kiss me again. This night was turning out to be perfect. *He* was perfect.

"I guess you're right," he said.

Duke leaned toward me and I inched toward him. He was going to kiss me again. I parted my lips while his hot breath fell on my nose and cheeks. I couldn't wait to taste the wine on his mouth.

Our lips met for a second before a buzzer rang somewhere. It was like an alarm bell ringing in my brain. I pulled away from him, startled. Duke clenched his jaw, frustrated.

"It's the reception desk calling from downstairs. I better get that," he said.

I nodded. Straightened up in my seat again. Duke left the room and I looked around. I should have tried to compose myself, but all I could really do was anticipate that kiss.

He returned a few moments later and immediately I could see a change in the expression on his face. His eyes were alert now. He didn't want to kiss me anymore.

"My sister. She's here," he said.

"Your sister?" I stood up from the couch.

"Yeah, Diane. I wasn't expecting her, but she's here now."

~

Diane, like her brother, had something about her that set her apart from everyone else. It was like an aura of some kind that she gave off. She was beautiful, no doubt. Good looks clearly ran in their genes.

She had long, silky dark hair and a tall, lithe figure. I could see hints of a resemblance between the two of them. The same high cheekbones and a square jaw. Long fingers and glittering green eyes. Except, she seemed to be a free spirit. Her clothing was worlds apart from the tailored suits and shirts that Duke usually wore.

Diane breezed through the open front door and right into the arms of her brother. From the moment Duke found out about his sister's arrival, he'd barely even looked me in the eye. He was all charged up and excited. I felt awkward standing there in the background while the two of them hugged it out.

"I've missed you, big brother," Diane spoke in a smooth, feathery voice. The voice of a singer. I connected the dots instantly. That explained her clothes.

"It's good to see you, sis. I'm glad you're here," Duke replied.

Keeping her arm around him, Diane swung around to me. She'd sensed the presence of someone else in the room.

"And who are you?" she asked, examining me from top to bottom. It seemed a bit rude, but of course I wasn't going to say anything.

"Hi, I'm Rose Johnson," I said, extending my hand to her.

Diane refused to shake it, even though she kept a smile frozen on her face. Then she glanced at her brother and I could see the guilty expression on Duke's face.

How close were they, exactly? Could Diane sense we'd just had sex here?

I took a step back and licked my lips.

"I was leaving," I said.

Diane's eyes brightened, but Duke, for some reason, ignored the comment completely.

"Grilled cheese! Would you like one, Diane? We just ate one but I could whip up another one for you," he said, drawing away from her.

"Oooh, I've been dying for one of your famous grilled cheese. Bring it on." She was beaming, and so was Duke.

"Good. Stay here. Rose will keep you company. I'll be back in a few ticks." Duke charged away like he was on a mission. All I could do was just stand there, staring after him. What did he want me to do? What was I supposed to say to his sister?

Even though I wasn't looking, I could sense Diane's eyes on me. I smiled at her. A forced, plastic smile. She wasn't smiling anymore.

"So, how do you know my brother?" Diane asked. She flopped herself on the couch while I stood to the side, nervously clasping my hands together.

"I work for his company. On the sales team."

Her eyes grew wide.

"Right. Okay. So he's your boss?"

"Yeah."

She nodded and a soft smile tugged the corner of her mouth. I couldn't tell if she was making fun of me or not.

"And what exactly are you doing here? In the middle of the night at your boss's apartment?" she continued.

Her words stung. I wanted to snap at her. Tell her it was none of her business, but I knew I couldn't. She had the upper hand here. She was my boss's sister.

"We had a few things to discuss," I said.

Diane rolled her eyes. She wasn't even attempting to hide her distaste.

"Yeah, right."

"Is there a problem?" I asked. I couldn't just stand by and take her potshots.

Diane shrugged. "Just that you seem like a nice girl. But a *girl*. You're too young for him. Maybe you don't realize you're being naïve."

"Excuse me?"

She put her feet up on the expensive-looking glass coffee table. She drummed her fingers lazily on her flat stomach.

"I'm trying to be fair to you, Rose. My brother is a highly successful, wealthy scientist and a businessman. He's also forty years old. He's a bachelor, never been in a long-term relationship in his life. Why don't you do the math and figure out what's happening here?"

She turned her green eyes to me. I saw flashes of Duke in them. Diane hated me. I gulped, holding my chin up.

"I know the details of my circumstances perfectly, but thank you for the footnotes," I said.

She arched an eyebrow.

"Oooh, snappy, are we?" she commented with a laugh in her voice.

"You're the one being deliberately rude to me. We just met. We could have kept this polite and civil," I said.

Diane looked away from me like I was boring her.

"I don't believe in pretenses. I wanted you to know something, so I said it," she claimed.

"Oh, yeah, so why did you wait to say it after your brother left the scene? Why are you bitching about him behind his back?"

Diane swung her feet off the coffee table, whipping around to face me again.

"I'm not bitching about him. I'm protecting him. I know what girls like you want from men like him."

"If you're talking about money, then you're wrong!" I snapped.

"Oh, so what is it? Love? How long have you known Duke? Five minutes?"

I couldn't believe this was happening. This conversation seemed so over the top. Just fifteen minutes ago—I didn't even know Diane existed. My shoulders heaved gently as I glared at her. She glared right back.

But before either of us could speak again, Duke had walked back into the room. He was carrying a plate with another grilled cheese sandwich.

"Do you want a drink with that, sis?" he asked, placing it on the coffee table. He hadn't noticed the intense hatred hanging in the air. Diane and I were still glaring at each other.

"I'm leaving," I said and made for the door.

12

DUKE

Rose said she was leaving as soon as I returned to the room with Diane's food. I knew immediately that something went wrong. I could see it in Rose's fiery blue eyes.

I looked up at Diane for affirmation. Her face was burning up too. I knew my sister well enough to know when she'd just had it out with somebody. I shouldn't have left them alone.

By now, I should've known—that just like Diane, Rose was completely capable of holding her own in an argument. And neither of them would shy away from one.

"Are you sure?" I asked Rose, turning to face her.

"I'm going to go," she said in a firm voice. She was already halfway to the door by the time I caught up with her.

"Hey!"

She stopped and turned to me.

"I don't know what my sister said to you but I want you to know she can come on too strong sometimes."

Rose crossed her arms over her breasts defensively. Our

kiss was interrupted. I was going to be dreaming about that kiss all night. Of what it could have led to.

"It's none of my business what your sister is like. It's clear to me now that I've overstayed my welcome here."

I wanted to reach for her hand but I got the feeling that Rose wouldn't want to be touched by me right now. I left her alone.

"I'm sorry you feel that way," I said.

She was searching my eyes for more. Maybe she wanted me to say something about Diane. To give her an explanation for her sudden arrival or make excuses for her. I wasn't going to do it.

I was well aware of my sister's flaws and I was sorry to see Rose go, but I wasn't going to take sides.

"Thank you for a lovely evening. You make a mean grilled cheese," she added. There was a hint of a smile on her face.

I nodded.

"Yes, it was a lovely evening. I'm glad you showed up."

"But this isn't going to happen again," she said quickly.

I tried to hide my surprise at that. The sex was good. We had a good conversation. I really enjoyed kissing her. I thought things were going well. How badly had Diane screwed it up?

"Okay, if that's what you want. I'm not going to talk you into doing something you don't want to do."

Rose nodded and looked away. Did I detect a hint of sadness in her eyes or was I just imagining it? Did I *want* her to be sad this was ending?

"I hope we can work normally together at the office," she said.

"I hope so too."

"I better go."

"Okay. Have a good night."

She glanced at me once and then turned away. I watched her step into the elevator and then disappear. She was gone. I would probably never see her in a dress like that again. She'd perhaps never speak to me directly again either.

When I returned to the room, Diane had her feet up on my coffee table and was chewing on the sandwich. She was pretty much lying flat with the plate balanced on her stomach.

I went over and lifted her feet off the table and swung them over to the floor.

"You're a grown woman, Diane. When are you going to act like one?"

"What's got your goat?" she said, putting her plate away.

I walked over to the bar to pour myself some more wine.

"You said something to Rose."

"Why? What did she say to you? You really shouldn't be trusting a stranger over your sister."

I turned to her, clenching my jaw tightly.

"She said nothing to me. Nothing about you, anyway."

Diane rolled her eyes.

"So what is your problem then, Duke?"

"What did you say to her?"

She glared at me with her narrowed eyes.

"You were going to ask her to stay the night, weren't you?"

"What are you talking about?" I snapped.

"I saw it on your face the moment I walked in. I was interrupting something intense."

"Well, we were on something like a date. We were in the middle of a conversation."

"You slept with her again."

"So fuckin' what?" I growled. I emptied the wine down my throat and banged the glass down on the bar.

Diane jumped up from the couch.

"That's my point. You slept with her already but she was still here. What was she still doing here? You wanted her to stay. You never do that!"

I ran a hand through my hair.

"Stay out of it, Diane," I groaned and walked past her. She followed me out of the room to the kitchen.

"She's a kid. What is she like, twenty?"

"Twenty-two," I said. I poured water in a glass from the faucet.

"She's a kid compared to you."

"It was just sex, Diane. You do it all the time. I don't come after you for it." I drank the water thirstily while she rolled her eyes some more.

"But you were looking at her differently."

"What is that supposed to mean?"

"Do you like her? Really like her?"

"I haven't thought about it. I don't have the time," I snapped.

My sister was nodding like she knew something.

"You'd be a fool if you took this any further, Duke. That girl is like every other twenty-two-year-old. There is nothing different about her. She's immature and ambitious. All she sees when she sees you are dollar signs."

I banged this glass down on the counter too.

"You're tired. Get some sleep. You know where the spare room is," I said, brushing past her. This time, Diane didn't follow me.

"You know I'm right, Duke. You know it. Don't be an idiot."

I didn't stop to respond to that. I went straight to my

bedroom so I could change and get into bed. Diane didn't know what she was talking about. I didn't *like* Rose...not in any special way. She was a nice girl. She was beautiful and sexy. We connected physically, but that was it.

Diane really had nothing to worry about.

∽

And yet, I was still thinking about Rose when I woke up the next morning. I'd dreamt about her all night. The sex was amazing. I knew I'd never been this hungry for another woman before. But it wasn't just the sex. It was something else.

We were having a good time together. It wasn't very often that I could just talk to a woman. Have a laugh. Forget about work and the company.

Diane was up making breakfast.

"Good morning, big brother," she chirped. She was back to her old self. In good spirits. She'd obviously not stayed up tossing and turning in bed fantasizing about someone.

"Morning."

I didn't want the eggs or the buttered toasts she offered me. I poured some milk into a big bowl of granola and ate that at the breakfast bar. She sat down across from me, taking a big bite of her toast.

"You still pissy?" she asked.

"Maybe we shouldn't talk about it," I suggested.

"Well, you're the one who brought it up, remember? When we spoke on the phone, you sounded worried because you slept with an employee. I was just trying to help last night."

"Help? Really? By scaring her away?"

"By making sure she didn't overstay her welcome."

I put my spoon down and glared at my sister.

"Diane, you're welcome to stay here for as long as you want. You're family. I will never turn you away, but I'd appreciate if you stayed out of my business this time."

She stopped eating and for a moment, I thought her eyes were filling with tears. I tried not to give in. All my life, I'd given in to Diane's every demand. She was my little sister. The baby of the family. Now with our parents gone, I felt solely responsible for her. Even though she was a thirty-five-year-old, grown woman.

"I don't want you being upset with me, Duke," she whispered hoarsely.

"Forget about it, okay? Let's just move on."

She nodded and breathed in deeply. "I just don't know where to go from here. I mean...the band. I don't think it's going to work out. I can't do this on my own."

"You'll figure something out. Take a few weeks off before you try getting back on track."

She wiped her mouth with the back of her hand.

"Nobody wants to hire a thirty-something singer-songwriter with no memorable songs. All these clubs want are overgrown teenagers who sing the same old songs and dress the same way."

"You'll figure it out, Diane," I insisted. I'd heard this spiel before. She went through this every couple of months until she found her next big 'break'. Another new band she attached herself to. Diane was forever chasing after her dreams.

"Thanks for letting me crash here though."

"Of course, it's no problem."

"And I just want to say, Duke, that all I ever want is the best for you and for you to be happy. I hope you know that."

"I know that," I said and stood up. "I have to go to work

now. There's a spare key in your room. You know the drill. Don't wait to eat with me. I'm pretty busy at the office these days."

She smiled as I was leaving.

"But we need to catch up soon. Like properly catch up."

"We'll have a drink together one of these nights."

"Okay."

I waved at her and then I left. I was late for the office already and had a few important phone calls lined up. Laura would be panicking.

When I reached the office, I didn't have time to think about Rose at first. There were too many things to do. Phone calls, meetings, lab work. I hadn't seen Jim the whole day either, which was good because I didn't want to look at him. Our last conversation was pretty brutal.

It wasn't until the early evening that I finally had some breathing space. No meetings and no Laura following me around everywhere. Now that I had a moment to think, my mind wandered automatically to Rose again. I knew she was somewhere in the building. Probably just a few floors down from me.

What was she wearing? What was she thinking? Would she ignore me if she saw me? But I *wanted* to see her. Just to fulfill all those thoughts I was having about her. I just wanted a look at her.

I knew it'd be too cheeky to take a stroll down to her floor. I didn't even have a legitimate reason to do it. I never went down to that floor or interacted with employees I wasn't directly working with.

But I grabbed a bunch of files from my desk and went to the elevator. Laura was looking but I knew she wouldn't follow. She was the kind of assistant who liked to keep track of every single second of my working life.

On the way down, I could feel the excitement in my bones. Just the thought of seeing Rose again was enough to make my cock jolt alive. Was there any chance of having her again?

I walked onto the floor of the sales team and some people looked up at me. Nobody expected to see me here, of course. I didn't even know where she sat. I tried to keep it casual as I walked down the aisle, gazing from the corner of my eye. Looking around until I finally caught sight of her.

She was standing next to the water cooler, small plastic cup of water in her hand and a big smile on her face. I stopped in my tracks because I saw who she was talking to. Jim. She was laughing at something he'd just said. I felt my face harden with rage. I didn't know something like this could make me so mad. I was on the verge of saying something.

But they hadn't seen me, and I wanted to keep it that way.

So I just turned and walked away.

13

ROSE

At first, when Jim came over to speak to me, I was on high alert. I was expecting him to attack me with his claims again. I could sense Monica keeping a close eye on him too. But Jim was in a different mood today.

"Free for a chat?" he asked in a skippy tone.

"I was just getting up to get some water," I replied and we walked over to the water cooler together. I wasn't going to speak to him privately. I'd made that decision already. Whatever he wanted to say, he'd have to say it in front of everyone else on this floor. I didn't care what he wanted to accuse me of, I wasn't going to let him treat me like a wounded bird.

"About yesterday, I'm really sorry if I made you feel threatened in any way."

I took a sip of the cool water.

"I'm not sure what you were referring to, but it seemed like you had something on your mind," I said. Jim looked about sheepishly and then back at me again.

"I got the impression you were romantically involved with someone in this office."

My only reaction to that was to laugh. I couldn't help myself. *Romantically involved* sounded so bizarre, it was funny to me. Jim had no idea how far from the truth he was. There was no romance involved between Duke and me.

He was smiling nervously when I settled my eyes on him again.

"Where did you get that idea from?"

"Ah, people talk. You know how it is in an office. I shouldn't have paid any attention to those rumors."

He wasn't going to confess to his eavesdropping session. I nodded.

"Yeah, people talk a lot of nonsense. It's all gossip, whatever you've heard. I can assure you, Jim, I'm not romantically involved with anybody in this office."

"And even if you are," he was quick to point out. "It is none of my business, of course. Yesterday, what I was trying to say was that you can be honest with me. But your private matter is yours alone."

I nodded. What caused Jim's change of heart? Was it the shakedown Duke had given him?

"Thank you, Jim. I'm glad you understand."

I walked away from him without giving him a chance to continue the conversation. It was too awkward as it was.

When I returned to my desk, Monica threw me a look and I shook my head. I didn't want her to worry that Jim was bothering me again. Honestly? I just wanted to get on with my work. There were too many distractions here and I was beginning to fall behind.

This was exactly why they advised you to not mix business with pleasure. I got it now.

Monica slid her chair over to me while I typed on my computer.

"What happened?" she asked.

"Nothing."

"The two of you pals again?"

"We were never pals."

"Did he tell you a joke?"

I turned to her and sighed.

"Look, Monica, thanks for your support and not being a gossip, but I really just want to move on. This whole thing with Duke Nolan. It was in the past. It's over between us."

She was looking at me strangely and then she shrugged. "Sure, if you say so, but he was here just a minute ago."

"Who was?"

"Doctor Duke Nolan." She said the name with a kind of spark in her eyes.

"He was here? On this floor? What did he want?"

"I don't know. I don't think he knew why he was here either. He looked lost. He just walked in and then turned around and left. Maybe he was looking for you, maybe he had something to say."

I gulped because my throat had gone dry.

"Well, if he has something to say, he knows where to find me," I snapped and returned to the computer screen.

I'd made up my mind. I wasn't going to let that man rule my life.

∽

I worked without breaks that day at the office. I had a lot of reports and research to get through in preparation for the new project. I certainly didn't want to let Jim down for recommending me, and I didn't want to give Duke a reason to think I wasn't good enough for the job.

By the time I caught the L back to my apartment, I could feel my eyes burning up with exhaustion. Realistically, I hadn't slept well since I bumped into Duke. Since that coffee spill and then our episode in the bar and then the evening at his apartment.

I wished I had a bathtub in my apartment because I could really do with a good soak. I needed to find a way to unwind and relax. It felt like my brain was running at a speed of a mile a minute.

I couldn't get *him* out of my head. The way he held me. His overwhelming kisses. The smell of him...and then there was Diane. The look of disdain in her eyes. She had the audacity to assume I was after her brother's money. That I wasn't capable of real feelings. What did she really know about me?

Nothing. And I didn't know anything about her either.

Hopefully, I would never have to see her again.

I dragged myself up the four floors to my apartment. I was looking forward to just crashing on the couch in front of some mindless television. Anything to keep my brain occupied away from Duke and his big strong hands.

But when I stepped on to my landing, I saw a man's figure crouched on the floor in front of my apartment door. There was a very dim light in the hallway and for a moment, I couldn't really see who it was. My heart skipped a beat.

Could it be Duke? Did he find out my address? Was he here because he wanted the same thing I did? I wouldn't feel this exhausted if I saw him again.

I took slow, short steps in the direction of my apartment. The man was standing up now, dusting his hands on his pants. That gesture was enough for me to know who it was. I stopped in my tracks.

"Will?" I said, my voice cracked.

"Hey, Rose, sorry to startle you like this," he said. He came into the light in the hallway and I could see him clearly now. It had been nearly a year since I last saw him. I felt breathless and voiceless. Every feeling of rejection and disappointment I'd felt before came rushing back again.

"What are you doing here, Will?"

"I should've texted before turning up like this, but I wasn't sure if you'd want to see me. I got your address from Felix. Please don't be mad at him. I really wanted to see you."

I stared at him while he spoke. It was like my brain had frozen and stopped working. I didn't think I'd ever have to see him again.

"What are you doing here?" I repeated.

"Can we go in?"

"We're fine here. You need to tell me why you're here."

I watched as Will ran a hand through his hair. He looked up at the bulb hanging low from the ceiling.

"I don't know how to explain this to you without coming across as a complete wuss." He waited a moment for me to respond, but I had no intention of saying anything. "I've missed you, Rose. I've missed you so much."

He reached for me but I yanked my arm away from him.

"Sorry," he said and I stepped over to my door. I opened it and waited for him to follow me in. Maybe this was a terrible idea. Maybe the last thing I should've been doing was inviting Will into my apartment—but it was too late now. He was already inside.

"So, this is the new place, huh? And I heard you have a fancy new job too."

Now more than ever, I felt exhausted. I could barely make myself go to the kitchen counter and turn on the kettle.

"I know you like your fancy coffee but I only have instant here," I said. I desperately needed the caffeine.

"That's fine, no problem. How have you been, Rose?"

I kept my back turned to him as I nodded. "Yeah, I've been good. Really good actually. Things are going great." Did I sound like an idiot? Emphasizing on the *good* too much. I didn't want to ask him how he'd been. I wasn't really interested in knowing.

"Did you hear me when I said I've missed you?" he spoke again.

I looked at him over my shoulder.

"Yeah, I heard you, but I don't know what you want me to do about it."

"I just want you to be able to look at me."

I turned to him fully, facing him head-on.

"I don't have a problem looking at you, Will. I'm not the one who cheated. I'm not the one who took you for granted."

He came toward me but I held a hand up at him.

"If you come any closer or try to touch me, I'm going to kick you out of my apartment."

He stopped in his tracks, running a hand through his hair. "Sure, yeah, of course. Whatever you want."

"So why did you really come here, Will?" I asked.

"I told you why."

"That is a ridiculous reason."

"But it's true, Rose. I've missed you. I keep thinking about you. I regret what I threw away. I miss what we had."

"What we had was based on a lie," I snapped.

Will sighed. He was staring at the floor now.

"And it was my fault, I know that. You don't have to tell me."

"You didn't seem this remorseful when I confronted you a year ago. You didn't care."

"I didn't know what I'd be missing. I was too proud to

admit my mistake. Rose, I always loved you. Even though I acted like a dick."

I stepped away from him. He followed me to the living area and I sat on the couch.

"You were cheating on me the whole time we were together. With multiple women. Everyone knew about it. All our friends. You made a fool of me. You insulted my feelings for you. Everything was a lie."

Will was standing over me now. When I looked at him, there were actual tears in his eyes.

"Will you believe me if I said I haven't been with anyone else since you left? I couldn't do it. I've been so depressed and miserable without you, Rose. I know exactly what a big mistake it was."

"What are you trying to tell me?" I asked.

He crouched down in front of me but kept his distance. He stared into my eyes, searching my face for some sort of solidarity.

"I just hope it isn't too late," he said.

"Too late for what?"

"To try again, Rose. I want to try again with you. For real this time. I'm not a kid anymore. I know how to take responsibility for a relationship. I want to be with you again."

I stood up. I had to get away from him. This was crazy. How could he even entertain an idea like this?

"Rose? Rose!" He came toward me. The kettle was boiling and whistling.

"Go away. Leave me alone!" I yelled.

"I want us to be together again, Rose, please."

"Leave! Now! Go!" I screamed. Tears streamed down my cheeks.

14

DUKE

Diane had been living with me for over three weeks now, but we rarely saw each other. It was almost like she was purposely keeping out of my way so I wouldn't ask her too many questions on what was happening with her life. Whatever, I didn't really care. I barely spent any time in my apartment anyway. Just as long as she didn't nag me about Rose anymore.

I was busy at work with the new drug, so that kept me distracted most of the time anyway. Things were really kicking up. We needed FDA approval before we could launch it publicly and the paperwork for that was filled with red-tape and would probably take several months. It was intense work but worth it. It was good work. Precisely the reason why I'd chosen this field.

At the office, I saw Rose a couple of times. It seemed like she'd smoothed things over with Jim. In fact, by the looks of it, they were very friendly now. Whenever I saw them together, they seemed at ease with each other. Rose barely ever looked at me and I only glanced at her a couple of times. Things were cordial between us, though we never really had any reason to interact with each other.

The truth was I thought about her often.

I couldn't shake off the feeling that I would have liked to get to know her better if I had the chance. This was the first time I wished a girl I slept with had spent more time with me in my apartment. Diane had cut it short. I wanted to believe it was for the best, but what if it wasn't?

I wasn't the kind of man who lived with regrets, but Rose inspired it in me all of a sudden. I also wasn't a jealous man. No woman made me feel like that before, but I couldn't help but wonder what was going on with her and Jim.

Every time I saw them together, talking and smiling and working—I wanted to grab her and pull her away from him. I wished to tell her she was mine. Remind her I had her once and it was good.

But she *wasn't* mine, and it was ridiculous of me to think that way.

So when I saw her standing at the coffee truck outside the office one morning, I knew it would be best for me to just walk past and pretend I hadn't seen her. But she caught my eye and a soft smile curled the corners of her mouth. She drew me to her without physically doing anything.

"I should probably keep my distance from you. That coffee is a weapon in your hands," I said.

Rose grinned and licked the foam at the corner of her lips.

"How are you?" she asked.

I hadn't thought about how reassuring it would be to hear her voice. I'd already made a mental note of what she was wearing. The form-fitting trousers and the blouse that stretched over her big breasts. Breasts I'd held in my hands.

There was movement in my pants and I clenched my jaw, trying to stop it.

"Busy," I said and she nodded. "You?"

"Busy, too. I'm learning a lot."

"So Jim's a good mentor?"

"He really is," she replied.

"I see you've been spending a lot of time with him."

"It's kind of necessary."

"Yes, of course."

We started walking in the direction of the building and I knew our conversation was going to come to an end soon. I didn't want it to end. I wanted to hold on to her for as long as I could.

"Are you going back to Skibbereen any time soon?" she asked. She remembered the name!

"I hope to, but I'm not sure when it'd be possible. Work's got me all caught up."

"Don't work too hard," she said.

We were at the open doors of the office building but we both stopped. Rose was looking at me expectantly, maybe she wanted me to say something. I didn't know what.

"Is it crazy that seeing you talking to Jim makes me jealous?" I asked. I wasn't planning on saying that, but it was out there now.

She was considering the statement, chewing on her bottom lip.

"Yes, it's crazy because there's nothing to be jealous of. He's my boss." I arched a brow at her and she blushed. So was I. "I'm not attracted to him, I mean."

I looked away from her.

"Not that it matters, right? There's nothing between you and me."

"No, there isn't," I agreed.

Rose nodded.

"It was just a one-time thing."

"Two times actually," I said and she smiled again. "Anyway, I'm glad we can still talk to each other without ripping our heads off."

"I told you I wasn't going to be dramatic about it."

"And I believed you," I added.

Rose was smiling again, and I wanted to say how beautiful she looked. But that would be inappropriate. We'd just established there was nothing between us. It was early in the morning, but I felt like I already needed a drink.

"I have a sales meeting. Jim's expecting me, I should go," she said quickly. Thankfully. Before I could blurt out something stupid. I nodded and she was gone.

I let her walk in first, watching her go. Her butt was tight in those pants. All I could think about was peeling every piece of clothing off her body. I hated not being able to touch her. What was the justification for that? Sexual attraction? Was that it?

"Fuck," I mumbled under my breath. I'd never felt this way for a woman I already had sex with. Twice. I should've been over her by now, but she still lingered around me. Everywhere. I hated feeling out-of-control like this, but I had no choice but to get back to work.

Thinking about Rose would just have to wait.

∽

I'd been thinking about that drink all day. Ever since the conversation with Rose, I felt like I needed one. I could've gone to the apartment and had one, but there was the chance of Diane being home. I didn't want to talk to her tonight. I wanted to be left alone.

When I finished at the office, I headed to The Dutchman. It was the bar closest to me.

Like the previous night, it was busy and the music was at just the right decibel. It felt appropriate to be here when I wanted to think about Rose. Just as long as I stayed away from the bathroom.

I went directly to the bar and ordered myself a neat whisky on the rocks. I needed something stiff tonight. Wine wouldn't do.

I gulped down the first one like it was a shot of medicine. It didn't have much of an effect on me so I asked for another one. I took it sip-by-sip with this one.

"You trying to forget someone?" I heard a voice beside me. I turned and saw a beautiful woman on the barstool next to me. I hadn't noticed her but realized she must've been sitting there this whole time.

Just like the rest of the crowd at this bar, it seemed like she worked in this neighborhood too. In one of the corporate offices around here. She was wearing a cream-colored dress with a thin belt cinched at her waist. She had her dark hair up in a bun.

"Not really. Not everyone drinks to forget," I said. That was a lie, but I couldn't admit to something that sounded like a heartache. I didn't have heartaches, as a rule.

She grinned and toyed with her martini glass.

"I guess not," she said. She was sexy. I could admit that. Rose was on my mind but that didn't stop me from being able to admire another beautiful woman. "I won't lie. I *only* drink to forget," she added.

I turned to her fully now.

"Who are you trying to forget?" I asked.

"Not who. *What*. My father passed away last week. The funeral was miserable because I had to interact with my family who I try to avoid usually. And it just hit me today that I actually miss him."

That was a lot of information in one go. I didn't ask for it, and now I didn't know what to do with it. Was she expecting consolation?

"I'm sorry," I mumbled.

It made her smile some more.

"Oops. Now I've made you uncomfortable."

"Sorry, I didn't come here for a conversation," I said.

"Okay, sure, I understand. I just thought we could have a drink together. I'll leave you alone if that's what you want," she replied. She was still staring and I was considering. Maybe it wasn't such a bad idea to have company. To talk to someone who didn't know anything about Rose or my work. And...she was a beautiful woman. I'd be an idiot to not entertain her advances, right?

"I'm Duke," I said and extended my hand to her.

"Samantha. You can call me Sammy."

"All right, Sammy, tell me about your dad."

She smiled and indicated to the bartender to get her another drink.

"We don't have to talk about my dad. I'm sorry I kinda vomited out all that depressing stuff about my family. Now that it's out, I don't want to elaborate."

"It's okay, I could really use the distraction tonight. I lied earlier when I said I wasn't trying to forget someone." I wasn't sure why I was coming clean to her. There was something trusting about Sammy. Despite her being beautiful, there was no sexual chemistry there. Neither of us was trying to come on to each other.

"You want to tell me about her?" she asked.

"I'd prefer to not talk about it."

She nodded. "So I don't want to talk about my dad and

you don't want to talk about this woman. What should we talk about instead?"

I smiled and shrugged.

"I was in Ireland recently, and it's amazing how these people can spend every night drinking in the pub together and somehow never run out of things to talk about. Without ever getting too personal about it," I said.

"Ireland? Wow. I've never been but I always wanted to go."

"You should. It's a beautiful country."

"I probably will, soon," and now she leaned to me like she wanted to whisper something in my ear. "And I'll tell you something else. My father was Irish. He emigrated here when he was just a boy. He spoke about Ireland all the time." Sammy sounded emotional and I pulled away gently from her, trying to think of something encouraging to say. But when I looked up and past her, I saw Rose.

She was standing just a few paces away from us, still in the pants and blouse I saw her in that morning. She was staring right at me, and there was a look of betrayal in her eyes. Not that there was any reason for her to feel betrayed.

There was nothing between us. I wasn't doing anything wrong. But I could see it written all over her face, I'd moved on to another woman too quickly, she thought. I hadn't. Sammy was a stranger. Just a drinking partner for the night. There was no woman I wanted more than Rose. She was drawing away from me.

I jumped away from Sammy immediately, diving into the crowd.

"Duke!" I heard Sammy call after me but I was in pursuit of Rose who was weaving her way through.

"Rose!" I yelled her name over the music but she didn't stop. Maybe she didn't hear me. I could have followed her, grabbed her hand, pulled her to myself, and kissed her. But to what end? What did I want from her? A relationship? Another one-night stand?

I had nothing to give her. So I stopped following her. She disappeared in the crowd within moments and I wasn't even sure if I'd actually seen her.

I didn't return to the bar because I didn't want to have to explain any of this to Sammy. I just went back to my apartment and hoped Diane would be asleep by now.

15

ROSE

In my bathroom, I stared into the mirror, feeling like it was time for me to call my mother. I didn't know who else I could call or what I could say. I could call Karen, she would understand, but she had so much going on in her life with Jessie and Jasper.

I was still clutching the pregnancy test tightly. It was the seventh one I'd taken since last evening. They all came back positive. I was pregnant, beyond a doubt, and now I didn't know what to do.

I'd been worried about this happening since the first time I had sex with Duke and we hadn't used protection. I kept telling myself the chances were low, but as soon as it was time for me to test, I bought as many of them as I could afford.

I just had a feeling...and I was right.

I was going to have Duke Nolan's baby.

After splashing my face with water, I dabbed my cheeks dry. My hair was damp too but that was from the sweat. I left the bathroom and went over to my bed. Thankfully, it was the weekend and I didn't have to be at the office. How would

I have walked into that building today? Knowing what I knew now.

I lay in bed for a while. Hours maybe? I couldn't picture myself as a mother.

I'd grown up in a big family with four siblings. My youngest sister was still a kid—so technically, I knew how babies worked. I wouldn't be completely new to this. In fact, I'd tried my best to help Karen when Jessie was born. But this was different. This was *my* child. I was going to be a mother. The fear gripped me with a steely claw now. I could feel the panic rising in my throat.

I should've called my mother, but she'd be so mad. She'd tell my father and the whole family would be upset with me. They had high hopes for me. They wanted me to set a good example for my brother and sister. They were so proud of me this far, and now I'd disappoint them. Having a baby so young. Single. Would I tell them who the father was? Would I tell anybody?

I didn't know how long I'd been lying in bed, but then the doorbell rang. I dragged myself off to see who it was. I wasn't expecting anybody, so I was more than surprised to see Karen. It was like she was telepathically drawn to me without knowing the reason why.

She rushed into my apartment carrying some snacks she'd bought on the way.

"Sorry I didn't text before showing up. I was hoping you'd be home. Jasper's taken Jessie to his first ball game and told me to take the day off from parenting." Karen was chirping happily and hadn't seemed to notice the look on my face.

When I didn't reply, she looked up at me.

"Rose? What's wrong? You look like you're coming down with something."

I staggered over to the couch. I needed to sit down. Even though I couldn't physically feel any symptoms of the pregnancy, it was a huge emotional weight on my shoulders.

"Karen, I'm pregnant," I said.

She was silent for a few moments and then she came up to me.

"Is it..."

"Yeah, my boss. Duke Nolan. We weren't careful when we...did it. I had a feeling this would happen. I have this horrible feeling like I *wanted* it to happen." I buried my face in Karen's shoulder while she held me. I was crying. I had no control over my emotions anymore. The floodgates were opened. Karen stroked my hair gently.

"I'm here for you, honey. You don't have to do this alone. If this is what you want."

"I'm going to have this baby, I just don't know how," I sobbed. Karen lifted my face up so I could look directly at her.

"We'll do this together, okay? Rose, you're going to be okay. Look at me! I didn't know a thing about babies when I found out about Jessie. At least you've been around babies. You kind of know what to expect."

I covered my face with my hands.

"I don't want my baby growing up without knowing its father. This is not how I pictured a family for myself."

Karen reached for me and drew my hands away from my face.

"You're going to tell him. Rose, you have to."

"He's not the kind of man who wants a family. He doesn't even want a relationship."

"It doesn't matter. You have to tell him. Remember, this is what you told me when I got pregnant. I should've told Jasper immediately. It would've been the right thing to do.

But I didn't listen to you and it was wrong. You do the right thing, Rose. Tell him."

I stared at my friend with bleary eyes. How was I supposed to approach Duke with this? How would he take it? I felt like my throat was closing up. I was going to be sick.

Karen clutched my hand tightly, staring astutely into my eyes. She wasn't going to take no for an answer. She was going to see this through to the end, and despite myself, I knew she was right.

Duke had to know. No matter how difficult it would be for me to say the words to him. He deserved the truth, even if he thought the worst of me.

∼

Somehow, I found my way to the reception desk in the lounge of Duke's apartment building. The security guard at the desk seemed to recognize me and he smiled politely as he called up.

"You can take the elevator up, Ms. Johnson," he said. I had to give him my name as before. I was relieved Duke was home. At least I could get this over and done with.

This weekend was turning out to be disastrous, but I would have to make peace with my reality at some point. Better now than never.

I stepped out of the elevator and saw the penthouse door was open. He was expecting me. Did he even want to see me? Or would he immediately turn me away? I was prepared to bear the brunt of any insult he wanted to shove in my direction for the sake of getting the truth out there. For my baby's benefit, not mine.

But instead of Duke, it was Diane who appeared at the open door as I walked to it. She stood leaning against the door frame with her arms crossed over her chest. She had a lingering smile. Like she knew something.

"I didn't think you'd be back so soon," she said.

"I'm here to speak with Duke. Is he home?" I asked. Just seeing her face made my blood boil. I could recall every word she'd spewed at me. The look in her eyes. She seemed more mellow today but I wouldn't trust her for a moment.

"He's not home right now. Gone for a run, so he'll be back soon. I can tell him you dropped by."

"I'll wait for him."

"Is he expecting you?" she asked.

"I need to speak to him, so I'll wait for him. Out here if you don't want to invite me in."

Diane rolled her eyes. "Oh, come in, will you? You sound so offended."

I probably should've stayed outside, but I followed her in. She was leading me to the den again. Just being inside this apartment made my heart race. I remembered those kisses. The way Duke held me that night. When he looked at me my body went on fire.

I hadn't seen him in what felt like a long time. The last time I did, it was at The Dutchman when he was cozying up with a beautiful brunette at the bar. I should've known he would've moved on by now. He had no reason not to. I was just passing scenery.

Diane sat down with a thump on the couch, putting her feet up on the coffee table again.

"Make yourself comfortable, Rose, I'm sure you know how to." There was that mocking look in her eyes. Did anyone infuriate me the way she did? I wanted to ask her what she was still doing here...living with her brother. Didn't she have a life of her own?

But I wouldn't say that. I wouldn't stoop to her level. I

took a chair closest to the door and pulled my phone out. I didn't want to make eye contact with Diane. I wanted her to know I was ignoring her.

"So, what do you want to talk to Duke about?" she asked.

"Do you really think I'm going to tell you?" I answered without looking up at her.

"You do realize he's going to tell me, right? He's my brother, and we are very close."

I shrugged. "If he tells you himself, that's his choice. I don't want you involved in our private conversation." I still didn't look up at her. A few moments of silence passed.

"You're not really winning any favors by being rude to me. I hope you know that," she snarled. I finally met her eyes. I wanted her to see how little she affected me now.

"I'm not here to impress anyone. Not you nor Duke. I don't care what either of you thinks of me."

"So *why* are you here?" Diane asked, her voice sizzling. I could see her beginning to lose her temper.

I just sat back in silence, totally in control this time. Maybe it was the motherly protective instinct. I didn't know what it was, but something had given me the strength and the courage I needed.

She growled angrily and jumped up from her chair. Her face had turned red and I could sense she was going to verbally attack me again. She was desperate to find out why I was here. But before Diane could say any more, Duke had walked into the room.

He was sweaty in his running gear and my body jolted like it was struck by lightning. I could see every muscle of his rigid torso underneath the thin fabric of his shirt.

"Rose!" he exclaimed. I stood up.

"Apparently, she has something to say to you," Diane interfered.

Duke looked at her and then at my face. I desperately wanted to be alone with him. I needed to tell him the truth but not in front of his sister. I was willing to beg to speak to him alone if I had to—anything to get Diane out of the picture.

"Why don't we talk outside? Do you feel like going for a walk?" he asked me. His voice was soft and polite. My heart slammed against my chest as a sudden realization dawned on me. I had feelings for this man.

I nodded silently and Duke smiled.

"Good. I feel like getting something to drink. A juice maybe. I know just the place."

I followed him out of the room and before I left, I threw a look at Diane over my shoulder.

She stood in the middle of the room with her hands on her hips, her face still a shiny dark red with rage. She couldn't protest against her brother now. The decision was made. We were going to get a chance to be alone and I knew I had to come clean to him.

This could be my only opportunity.

16

DUKE

The last person I expected to find in my apartment today was Rose. She was waiting there for me for some reason, and I had never felt this excited to see a woman in my home.

I had to take her away from Diane before my sister did any more damage. Thankfully, Rose agreed to go outside with me so we could talk in private.

She followed me out of the apartment building and we barely spoke to each other. I could sense her looking at me from the corner of her eyes. I tried not to stare. I had no idea what she could possibly have to say.

The last time a woman said she wanted to talk to me, it was to say she wanted a commitment from me. A relationship. I couldn't picture Rose asking for that. She'd already told me she had no expectations from me.

Out on the streets, we made our way through the crowd to the food truck I wanted to bring her to. I was a sucker for their juices, and it would give us some space to talk too. They usually had a few chairs put out for their customers by the side of the road.

"I'm sorry we couldn't talk at the apartment. I didn't want to ask Diane to leave because I knew she'd throw a hissy fit. My sister's a bit of a spoiled brat and I'm definitely to blame," I explained.

Rose shook her head.

"No, this is fine, we can talk here. And I'm sorry for springing on you like this. I know we kind of silently agreed to keep out of each other's way."

"We can talk, Rose, you can tell me what's on your mind."

I ordered two juices for us first and then we made our way to a small plastic table to the side. As always, this place was bustling with people. But there was something comforting about being in a crowd and surrounded by all the noise.

If I had to come clean and let her down—tell her I wasn't looking for a relationship, at least it would be out here and not in the silence of my apartment.

Rose was wearing a long dress today, something very different than what I'd seen her in before. It had thin straps that were tied around her neck like a halter. The dress was cotton and flowy in a floral print. Her golden curls were tied up messily at the top of her head. She looked carefree and peaceful today. Just as beautiful as always.

She opened her mouth to say something, but I interrupted her. I didn't want her to say something she would later regret.

"Rose, before you say anything, I want you to know that I really did enjoy our time together. I was very attracted to you. I felt like we had a connection. I've thought about you a lot since we last saw each other. But I'm a very busy man. I can't give you any more than this."

She gulped and nodded. "I know, I'm not here to ask you for more," she said.

I searched her eyes because I was confused. What else could she be here to say? Was this about work? About Jim?

I sat back in my chair. The guy at the food truck came up to us with our juices. Rose seemed disinterested in it while I gulped it down quickly. I was still waiting for her to explain but it seemed like she couldn't get the words out.

"Whatever it is, it's better out than in," I said.

She met my eyes. Hers were a light blue...calm and serene. I wished I could sit with her here all day. Even if she didn't want to talk to me, I'd be happy just staring at her face. But I had work to do. Important tasks to complete before the weekend was up.

Rose licked her lips.

"I'm pregnant," she said.

My brow furrowed. The words sounded jumbled in my ears.

"What?"

"I'm pregnant, Duke, and the baby is yours."

I stared at her in silence for a full two minutes. Rose refused to break eye contact with me. She held her chin up firmly, challenging me to challenge her.

"You're pregnant with my kid?"

"Yes. We weren't careful the first time. At the bar."

I couldn't recall what had happened. All I knew was that I wanted her with a kind of hunger I'd never experienced before. And now she was sitting in front of me telling me she was carrying my child.

I sat back in my chair. She continued to stare at me.

"I wanted to tell you as soon as I found out because I thought you should know. I don't want anything from you, Duke. I just want my baby to know its father. But you don't have to agree to it, of course. I'm not going to force you to do anything."

Rose was speaking, but her words passed right through me. Nothing settled in my brain other than the little factoid—that I was going to be a father.

I looked up at her and she had a harrowed expression on her face.

"Duke, say something. Whatever you want to say. Blame me if you have to, but I need to know that you heard me. After that, I'll walk away. I don't want anything from you." Her steely resolve seemed to be cracking. Her voice wavered. This couldn't be real. I hadn't planned for this. I never did *anything* I hadn't planned for.

But I knew I had to say something. What?

"Duke! Duke Nolan!" I heard a man's voice, so I looked up. He was approaching us quickly. The chairman of the board of directors at the Science Museum. Someone who I was supposed to be on a call with that very evening.

"Ah, Barry! How are you?" I jumped out of my chair. If there was one man in this city whose good books I had to be in, it was this guy. He came up to me with his hand extended and before he replied to me, he glanced at Rose.

"Rose, honey, what are you doing here?" he said.

What the fuck? I was confused. I stared at her while she stood up and turned to Barry Johnson.

"Hi, Daddy. Sorry I haven't called in a while," she replied.

~

I felt like I was having an out-of-body experience as I stood between Rose and Barry Johnson. He was smiling at his daughter, but Rose wasn't smiling. She'd just given me one of the most important pieces of information of her life. I could see she didn't want to be in the presence of her father.

"Where's my hug?" Barry asked. Rose smiled then, but awkwardly, and she hugged him. Her eyes were on me from over her father's shoulder. She looked like she wanted to apologize.

I still wasn't able to process all the details of the events unfolding in front of me.

Barry turned to me and slapped my shoulder in a friendly way.

"I hope you've been treating my daughter right," he said.

I panicked for a moment. Not sure of what he was referring to. He must have noticed the confused expression on my face because he tried to clarify himself.

"I mean at work, on the job."

I glanced at Rose and she spoke up.

"You're embarrassing me, Daddy."

"Right, okay, sorry," Barry said. Then, to my horror, he sat down at the table. Rose looked up nervously at me and we sat down beside Barry. I couldn't ask him to leave. My interaction with him was crucial.

"So, were you guys in the middle of a meeting? I didn't realize you work closely with each other," he continued.

Rose was trying to avoid my eyes.

"We've just started working on a project together recently," I replied.

"That's good to hear. I've always secretly hoped you'd mentor her personally. I didn't want to tell you my daughter works at your company because Rose insisted that she shouldn't receive any preferential treatment."

I smiled at him weakly.

"And I didn't realize you know each other this well," Rose interjected. I looked at her then, catching her gaze. Her cheeks were flushed. She looked so nervous. I was worried she was going to give us away.

"Duke is in the running for entry into the board at the museum," Barry explained to his daughter. Rose drank her juice like she'd suddenly remembered its existence.

"It's been something like a lifelong dream of mine, to work closely with this museum in particular," I said. It was the truth. When word got out that the museum was looking to expand its board, I knew immediately that I had to be on it. "My father brought me to the museum frequently as a kid. I believe it was those visits that spurred my interest and passion for science."

Barry grinned with delight. He slapped my back. "And we definitely need more young accomplished scientists like you on the board to guide the museum further into its coming years. We're getting too old back here."

While Barry and I chuckled, Rose remained silent. She wasn't looking at either of us.

"You okay there, honey? You look a little glum," Barry said. I noticed the way his voice softened when he turned to his daughter, the sound of concern. It was obvious that they were close. Barry loved his daughter.

And now she was pregnant with my child. How would he react if he found out what happened between us? How I got his precious daughter knocked up because I couldn't resist banging her in the bathroom of a bar. I was her boss. I was supposed to mentor her—in his eyes.

"I'm fine, Daddy, we were just in the middle of something," Rose said.

Barry looked at me, a little offended now maybe because he could sense he wasn't welcome.

"All right, sure. I'll leave you to it then," he said. When he stood up, I stood up too, reaching to shake his hand. "It's supposed to be the weekend though, honey. Watch out for being overworked," he added.

Rose hugged her father again, which seemed to calm him a little. "I'm not overworked, Daddy. It's just an unavoidable circumstance." She glanced at me then and I tried not to stare.

"I'll expect that phone call from you, Duke," Barry said before he left.

"My assistant is going to set it up this evening. Talk to you then. Great bumping into you like this."

He smiled and gave his daughter one last long look before he finally walked away. I watched him go, making sure he was safely and well out of earshot before I turned to Rose again.

She was sitting at the table, staring at the plastic cup of juice in her hand. I stood over her, feeling my chest rise and fall. "You're Barry Johnson's daughter and you never thought to give me that information?"

She looked up at me with her blue eyes burning. She was prepared for an attack, it seemed.

"I didn't realize it mattered. What difference would it have made?" she asked.

"I would have stayed the fuck away from you," I snapped. Her lips were clamped shut, her anger was rising —but so was mine. All she had to do was tell me the truth about her father. Who she really was. I wouldn't have risked my admission to the board over this. Over sex with a hot young employee. But now there was more involved than that.

It wasn't just about the sex anymore. She said she was pregnant. I had no idea how to even begin dealing with that.

17
ROSE

I couldn't believe Duke was actually reacting this way. Like it was all my fault.

I saw the look of horror and confusion on his face when he saw my father. He was barely able to hold a conversation with him. Daddy's timing was just perfect! And now Duke was trying to imply I'd tricked him. Tricked him into sleeping with me? Into getting me pregnant?

I got up from the chair and Duke stood with his hands clenched in front of me.

"This is all very messed up," he said, running a hand through his hair.

I stared at his handsome face. Those chiseled features and the sharp nose. The slight graying on the sides of his head. His intelligent face looked sullen now. I hated this feeling—like I'd disappointed him. But it wasn't my fault alone that I was pregnant. We both were supposed to be in this together. He should've been just as careful as I should've been.

"Yes, it's a mess. I wasn't planning this either."

"You could have said something. I had no idea who you are."

"You keep saying that, but I don't know how my father's identity would've made a difference in all this."

"I didn't know we were connected in any way."

"Neither did I!" I snapped.

He looked up at me with his fiery green eyes.

"I just thought you and my father were casually acquainted, and I didn't think it would've mattered. And what happened between us…it felt…it felt inevitable."

His shoulders rose and fell as he glared at me. What was he thinking? Did he wish I didn't exist? That I disappeared into nothingness? That he'd never met me?

"Do you want me to apologize to you?" I asked.

Duke said nothing, still studying me with that look of rage in his eyes.

This wasn't how I pictured my revelation to go. Didn't it matter to him that I was carrying his child? That I needed to be calm and peaceful? "Okay, I'm sorry, Duke. For everything. It looks like you want to put the blame on someone and it's going to be me."

"That is not what I'm saying," he growled.

"Then what is it? You're angry."

"Damn right I am!" He raged. I couldn't have pictured him this angry. He'd always seemed so calm and in control of his emotions.

"I didn't come here to speak to you because I want something from you, Duke. I just wanted you to know the truth. I'm going to have this baby and raise it myself, with or without your help. I just didn't want to keep a secret from you."

He rubbed a hand over his face. His eyes were pressed

close now. I needed to know what he was thinking but it didn't seem like he could articulate it.

"I need time to think about all this. Everything is messed up now," he finally said. I nodded.

"Fine. Whatever. You can think about it and let me know, whether you want to be a part of this child's life or not. Either way, it doesn't matter to me."

"I am on the cusp of a breakthrough. This new drug is going to be huge. I have a lot on my plate."

"You don't have to give me any excuses."

"And now your dad is involved. Barry Johnson. If I'd known you are his daughter, I wouldn't have involved myself with you."

His words were like little bullets piercing through my skin and body. So what he was essentially saying was that our relationship was based purely on an animalistic physical need. It had nothing to do with genuine attraction. I was just another girl to him.

"I'm going to go now," I said.

He nodded. He wanted me to leave. He wanted me to leave him alone. "And don't worry, I'm not telling my parents yet. They don't have to find out about this."

"You won't be able to hide your pregnancy and the child from your family for too long," he surmised.

I was ready to go. This conversation was over. It had been a disaster. Karen was wrong about the whole thing. I shouldn't have told him anything.

"Even if I have to involve my parents soon, I won't involve you. So you can sleep easy at night," I said. I started walking away and for a few moments, he didn't say anything. Then he was calling out my name.

"Rose!" he growled when I was already at some distance from him. I looked over my shoulder at him and his expression was that of a man who was lost at sea. "I just need some time to think!"

I said nothing and walked away. He didn't follow me. I knew he wasn't going to.

I went straight to Karen's house because it was the only place I knew I could express exactly what I was feeling.

When she opened the door, she had Jessie in her arms who was wailing, red-faced. I saw a sudden glimpse of what my life with a baby was going to be like. All the emotions and responsibilities I would have to deal with. The only difference was that Karen had help. She had a loving and supportive husband who would always be there for her. It was still difficult for her...how difficult was it going to be for me?

"What happened? What did he say?" Karen asked. She was rocking and patting Jessie, trying to calm him down.

"Everything is a mess. It's just all...wrong...and I don't know how I'm going to get through this alone," I said. I didn't want to burst into tears, not now when Jessie was crying. Karen touched my arm gently while she continued to rock her son.

"That's the thing, hun, you're not going to be alone. You will always have me and you will have your family. Your parents will be there to help," she said.

I gulped because I didn't know how true that was now. I had no idea how my dad would react if he found out the truth. I would never be able to tell him who got me pregnant.

18

DUKE

Rose was gone and now I was alone, standing in a cloud of confusion and rage. I was confused because I didn't know what I was going to do next. I was angry because I'd allowed Rose to walk away from me. I was angry with myself.

I should've held her back. I should've made her stay here and talk to me about the situation we were in. But that wasn't the kind of person I was. I wasn't accustomed to having serious, life-changing conversations with women.

So I went back home and found Diane cleaning the kitchen.

"You don't have to do that. We have a housekeeper. You know that, right?" I said, banging doors behind me as I walked through. She straightened up to stare at me.

"Talk didn't go well?" she asked. There was a laugh in my sister's voice as she spoke. She was hoping our talk wouldn't go well since she'd been left out of it.

"It was a disaster," I admitted, grabbing a carton of orange juice from the fridge. I drank straight from the box, kept drinking until my stomach felt bloated and filled with juice.

"Are you okay, Duke?" I heard Diane ask. I lowered the carton of juice and wiped my mouth with the back of my hand.

"I'm fine. I just feel very thirsty," I said and put it back in the fridge.

"I could make us some coffee. Or tea?" she suggested.

"I need something stronger than that," I declared. Diane followed me to the bar and I could already sense the scent of worry coming off her.

"Duke, you're going to have a drink in the middle of the day?" she asked. She watched me pour a whisky for myself in silence. "Are you serious? What happened?"

"I can have a drink when I want to, in my own home, can't I?" I took a sip and turned to her.

Diane licked her lips nervously, staring at me as I drank some more of the whisky.

"Sure, of course, you can do what you want. I'm just suggesting that it's probably a bit too early for a drink."

"Rose is pregnant," I said. The words came hurtling out of me before I could stop it.

Diane's face dropped and a dark cloud came over her. She stood in front of me with her brow furrowed, her jaw tightened.

"I knew it. I knew she was going to drop some bomb on you. I just got that feeling about her." She was speaking through gritted teeth.

"What are you talking about, Diane? You don't even know her." I wanted her to stop talking about Rose like she knew her inside-out.

"I know her type."

"She doesn't have a type. You don't know her. She's quite unlike most other women I've known."

"That's the thing, Duke. She's barely a woman. She's a girl! Don't you see that? A recent college graduate. Bright-eyed. Hungry for success. Ambitious."

"None of those traits belong to her. Sure, she's very young, but she's not operating on an ulterior motive," I said. Diane was following me around the den while I walked slowly about. I was restless. I couldn't keep still. I clutched the whisky glass tightly. Taking small sips from it every few minutes.

"What's happened to you, Duke? Why do you refuse to see her for what she really is? You're getting soft. You used to be able to see right through these women and their intentions earlier."

"Rose is not like everyone else!" I growled. This time, I stopped and whipped around to face my sister. Diane was eyeing me closely now, like there was something strange on my face.

"You're acting weird is all I'm saying," she said.

"Yes, of course I fuckin' am! There is nothing normal about this situation, Diane. Don't you get that? She's pregnant. By me. She's going to have my child. I'm going to be a father. What part of this sounds normal to you? How do you want me to act?" I wasn't yelling, but my voice was high and more like a roar. I hadn't spoken to Diane like this in years. Not since she was a rebellious teenager and I was the only one who could keep her in check.

She looked up at me with her lips quivering. When she was younger, at this point, she would break into a loud sob and run to her room. Our mother would try and soothe things over between us, and usually we'd end up not speaking for several days, until *I* eventually apologized.

But that wasn't going to happen this time. We were both adults now, and more importantly—I wasn't about to apologize.

Diane sucked in her breath, lifted her chin up in the air.

"You're an idiot for taking her word for it. You're right, I don't know this girl, but neither do you. How can you just believe her so easily?"

"She's not lying, Diane," I continued to growl.

She rolled her eyes and looked away from me. I could see she was still trying her best to not break into a fit of rage and tears. Her ego was bruised.

"Maybe she is. There is a big chance the baby isn't yours, even if she is actually pregnant," she said.

"Rose is not a liar," I insisted.

"And you know that based on what?"

I couldn't tell her it was a gut feeling. She would laugh at that. How was I supposed to explain it to her? I felt a connection with Rose. I'd felt it from the moment we met. I didn't need any convincing—I knew Rose was telling the truth.

"I don't have to explain myself to you, Diane," I said.

My sister's lips quivered for a moment. Her ego had turned to mulch by now. She was on her last tether.

"Fine. Don't. You've made it very clear what you want from me, big brother," she snarled. I said nothing but I knew she would continue to speak. "I'm going to pack up my bags and leave."

"You don't need to come to that conclusion, Diane. That isn't what I said. You're overreacting."

"Am I? You're making me feel like I'm a crazy person. You refuse to think rationally. You would rather trust this Rose person, practically a stranger, over your own sister."

Well, my sister had this unique ability to make everything about her. The truth was I could do with some space. I wanted to think about the future for me and Rose and the child she was carrying. Our child. I was going to be a father. But none of that mattered to Diane.

"So I'm going to go," she added.

Maybe she was expecting me to ask her to stay, but I'd had enough with her. I wasn't going to do it. I needed some peace around here.

Diane came up closer to me as I emptied the whisky down my throat.

"You are willing to throw your life away—everything you have—based on what a twenty-something claims?"

"I am not throwing away anything, Diane. I'm just going to give Rose the support she needs from me."

"This is not you. This is so not you!" she shrieked. I could see defeat in her eyes. She wasn't happy about that.

"Diane, I don't care what you think of me, but I'm not going to abandon my child."

"What if it isn't your child?"

"It is."

She rolled her eyes and finally walked away from me. I watched her leave the room. I couldn't hear her in the spare room, but I could only hope she was packing up her stuff.

I was well aware Diane had nowhere to go. She wasn't the type of person who'd bought herself a place to stay, or even rented. She just floated around from place to place, usually crashing at people's homes or renting rooms in cheap motels. At one point, I used to worry for her.

But not anymore. We were both grown-up enough to be able to live our lives on our own terms. I wasn't going to tell her what to do, just like I wouldn't let her tell me what to do either.

At least half an hour later, she showed up in the den, dragging her bags behind her.

"I hope you're happy, Duke. I'm leaving now. You can be alone again. Or maybe you'll ask Rose to move in with you," she snapped.

"Maybe I will," I said and she rolled her eyes again. She didn't think I was capable of that. I didn't think I was capable of that either. Asking her to move in would be taking it too far.

19

ROSE

I called in sick at work the next day even though I felt just fine. It was still early days of the pregnancy, and as it turned out, I was one of the lucky ones who didn't feel extreme pregnancy symptoms.

However, I couldn't drag myself out of bed and turn up at the office today. I didn't feel like facing Jim or Monica or any of my other colleagues. Neither did I want to worry about the chance of bumping into Duke. He would probably avoid me too, but the whole situation just left me with a bitter taste in my mouth.

I wished I hadn't gone to see him. Then we wouldn't have bumped into my father either.

Duke didn't want to have anything to do with the baby. Just as I'd predicted. He wasn't interested in a family, he didn't want a child, and by revealing the truth to him—I'd only given him a burden.

So, I decided I would stay away from him. The last thing I wanted was for him to assume I needed something from him. The pregnancy was an accident, a mistake, but I wasn't going to let my baby feel like they were a burden to their father. Like they were unwanted.

Karen promised to help out as best as she could, but I knew she had her hands full with Jessie. Eventually, I would have to tell my family. They would never forgive me if I kept the pregnancy a secret from them. But I wouldn't tell them about Duke. I didn't have the courage for that. Also, my father was fully capable of taking some strong action against him. Making him pay for what he'd 'done' to me.

And Duke seemed very passionately determined about his membership to the board at the museum. I didn't want him to blame the baby or me if he didn't get in.

I stayed home from work but didn't end up doing anything productive. I was pretty much brooding all day. The only sensible thing I did was take a long shower and carefully blow-dry my hair. This usually made me feel better. It calmed me down, but I wasn't rid of my anxiety completely yet.

When the doorbell rang, I thought it was Karen. She said she would try and stop by later in the day if she got a chance. So I was still in my bathrobe when I went to the door.

To find Duke on the other side made my heart bounce. I wrapped an arm around my waist, making sure the robe was still securely in place. He scanned me quickly before settling his gorgeous green eyes on my face. I should've hated him, despised him for his behavior, but I couldn't help but melt every time he looked in my direction. The father of my child. I wished I was stronger.

"Laura helped me hunt down your address. Sorry for turning up like this," he spoke. For a moment, I allowed his deep voice to seep through me. It was lusciously thick and comforting. Like a big warm hug.

"Why are you here?" I asked him. Thankfully, I was able to put up a show. I didn't want him to see how easily he melted me.

"I thought I'd get a chance to talk to you at the office, but then I was informed you didn't come to work today. I wanted to check on you. Are you doing okay?"

"I just needed a day off. I'm fine." I walked away from the door, leaving it ajar. Duke took a few moments before he eventually followed me into my apartment.

I went to the kitchen section and turned on the kettle for tea. Anything to keep my hands busy. So I wouldn't have to stare at him the whole time.

"This is a nice place. It's cozy," he commented.

"It'll do." I wanted to add it would be very cramped with a newborn, but I didn't want him to think I was asking for something.

"But you can't keep living here when the baby comes," Duke said. Had he read my mind? I whipped around to look at him with my eyes burning. He was standing by my couch with his arms firmly planted across his chest.

"I'll figure something out in time," I replied.

He was staring at me. There was something on his mind. I could tell he had something to say.

"Or you could come live with me," he said.

The words hung in the space between us like they were floating in air, moving toward me, but I couldn't accept them in—because I didn't believe what he was saying to be true. Had I imagined it?

"I know it sounds like a ridiculous idea right now, but think about it. Do you really want to parent a newborn by yourself? Without any help?" Duke spoke proudly. Sure of himself. He'd come over here having made up his mind already. He wasn't asking me to move in with him. He was telling me.

"I won't be alone. I have friends, and I have my family. They won't let me do this by myself. I'll have the support I need to raise this baby without you."

He nodded and then took a step toward me.

"But I'm offering you a chance to raise this kid with its father. Why wouldn't you take it?"

"Because I don't need anything from you. I don't want anything," I said. It just sounded so wrong—being forced to and forcing him to live with me when we weren't actually together. This wasn't the environment I wanted our child to grow up in, as much as I wanted the presence of a father.

"I'm not offering this to you for you. I wouldn't do it if I had nothing to gain too."

I waited for him to explain. What was that supposed to mean?

"Your dad. Barry Johnson. I can't piss him off. If he finds out I'm the father, which he eventually will, at some point—I will never be accepted to the board at the museum. Even if I'm accepted now, he'll kick me out as soon as he finds out about the baby."

My brows were crinkled. Was he serious about this? I opened my mouth to speak but Duke held up a hand to stop me.

"I know what you're going to say. You won't tell him who the father is. But how long will you keep it a secret? Months? Years? Will you keep it a secret from the kid all your life? It will come out, and wouldn't you rather do it now than later?"

I stared at him, stunned. He wasn't making sense but I was curious to know where he was going with this. Duke came closer and I remained stuck with the kitchen counter digging into my back now.

"Why don't we just tell everyone now? Tell your family the truth about who the father of this child is. You move in with me, and we can pretend like we're giving it a shot."

"Giving what a shot?" I blurted.

"Being married, having an actual family. Giving this child a home and parents."

"But we'll only be pretending."

"Yeah, sure, but who cares? That way, you'll have the support you need of a father for the first few months of a newborn's life, and your family won't hate me for not claiming the child."

The words were stuck in my throat. He'd actually thought this through...he really believed this was a good idea. I couldn't help but picture a life with him. Living in his apartment. Playing with our baby together. Duke rocking our child to sleep.

"And what happens after those first few months?"

"We can pretend like we're separating, getting a divorce, whatever. It'll look legitimate and nobody can blame us for not trying."

He came closer and I tipped my face up to look at him.

"I...I...don't..." I couldn't get the words out. This plan still seemed so ridiculous to me. Duke placed his hands on my shoulders, slowly beginning to stroke them. It was like he had me magnetized with his stare.

"Come on, Rose, you know you want to do this. It would be stupid of you to not take up this offer. You won't have to be pregnant alone, you won't have to be alone when this baby is born. Sure, you'll have your family and friends, but it wouldn't be the same as having me, would it?" Duke was peering into my eyes as he spoke in a clear firm voice. He was so sure of himself, so confident, that I was slowly beginning to see his point of view. Maybe he was right, maybe this made sense. Why wouldn't I want to give my child a chance to bond with its father?

"What do you say, Rose? Will you marry me? Temporarily?" he asked, a smile growing on his face.

I gulped, my throat was dry, but now the words came to me clearly.

"Yes, okay. Yes, I will."

~

Duke seemed stunned when I said yes. Maybe he didn't expect to convince me this easily, but then he quickly wiped off that look of surprise from his face and smiled.

"Sorry, I don't have a ring," he said. This time, with some effort, I managed to slide away from him. I needed to put some distance between us. I needed some breathing space. What did I just agree to?

"I don't need a ring," I managed to say. The kettle had boiled and now I stared at it like my life depended on it. I couldn't look at Duke. I started pouring boiling water in a cup. I could sense him standing behind me, watching me.

"Look, Rose, I know you're weirded out by this. It's strange for me too. But this is the best thing to do for us now, don't you think?"

He was speaking but all I could think about was how this was not what I imagined my wedding proposal to look like. There was no romance here. No ring. No promises made of loving each other forever. This was more like a contract, a contract of convenience.

"I guess it is. You definitely get what you want out of it," I said. It was just hot water in a cup, but I sipped it like it was tea. The taste didn't matter. I wasn't actually focused on what I was drinking. I just needed to do something with my hands.

"It's a mutually beneficial arrangement. You can move into my apartment as early as tonight, if you want."

"And what about the wedding? Are we actually going to have one?" I asked.

Duke shrugged. "We can just tell your family we got married at City Hall soon after we found out about the pregnancy. We wanted to do the right thing. I'm sure they wouldn't want to see any official documents." He was grinning as he spoke. He looked like a man who was proud of his recent accomplishment. I had to look away. My cheeks were flushed with embarrassment and frustration.

I was embarrassed because I couldn't stop picturing what a real marriage proposal from Duke Nolan would look like. Why did I want that? We weren't in love...I wasn't in love with him!

"Sure, yeah, that works for me," I said, clutching the hot mug harder. He took a few steps toward me again.

"This will be good. This'll work out great. In nine months, we'll be parents, I'll be on the board at the museum, everything will be perfect—and then we can take the next step."

"The next step?"

"Once you're comfortable with looking after the baby on your own, we can fake a divorce."

My stomach turned at the thought. Was this really how I wanted my child's life to begin? Surrounded by a bunch of lies. Duke snapped me out of those thoughts by clapping his hands together loudly.

"So. When would you like to move in? You can pack your

bags now and we can go. Don't worry, Diane doesn't live with me anymore."

I gulped and shook my head. This was too much of a shock to my system. I couldn't do it right now.

"Not tonight. I want to spend the night here, in my own apartment."

"Okay, fair enough. How about over the weekend? That'll give you enough time to get comfortable with the idea, don't you think?"

All I could do was nod. He actually seemed excited by this. Like we were going on some big adventure.

"Maybe we should meet up with your parents too. This weekend. Give them the big news as a couple."

I stared at him, trying to read his mind. He was so handsome there, with his hand in the pocket of his pants, his shirt collar open and revealing just a triangle of his sturdy, muscular chest. What would my parents think of the situation? They would be in shock, no doubt. He was much older than me. Way more successful. He was rich and out of my league. Now I was pregnant. Would they see right through this?

"Okay, I'll call them. We can have lunch at the house," I suggested.

"Good, that's great. The sooner we get things settled, the more time we'll have to get comfortable. I'm glad we're on the same page," he said.

Were we?

"I think I need to lie down. I feel very tired now," I said. I wanted him to go. Having him here, talking to him about marriage and meeting my parents, was giving me a heartache.

"Yes, you should rest. I'll give you some privacy. Rose,

you don't have to come in to the office if you're not up for it. Don't worry about it," he said.

"I'll be at the office tomorrow. I don't want any preferential treatment, please," I said. At least my work was the one shred of normalcy I could still cling to. He stared at me for a moment and then nodded.

"Okay, if that's what you want."

I moved toward the front door, indicating to him that I now wanted him to leave. Duke thankfully got the hint. He followed me there in silence.

At the door, we stood staring at each other for a few moments and then I opened it.

"Email me when you've spoken to your parents. I'll clear my weekend," he said. I nodded, and then he was gone.

I shut the door behind him and leaned against it, my forehead knocking against the warm wood. I pressed my eyes closed. I couldn't believe this was happening, that I'd actually agreed to his plan. It sounded like a trick somehow. It was going to be a lie. I would lie to my parents, lie to my baby. Was this the right thing to do?

But there was something drawing me to him. I couldn't say no. Somehow, I couldn't resist this opportunity to be with him. Live with him. Have him in my baby's life. Why?

The answer stared right at me but I couldn't look at it. I didn't want to admit that I had real feelings for him. That would be crazy. Impossible. The only thing it could lead to was heartache.

20

DUKE

The thing that astounded me the most was the fact that I couldn't wait for the weekend to arrive. Now that we'd fixed a plan, Rose was moving into my apartment and we were going to meet her parents—this was all I thought about.

It affected my work, my ability to focus on lab work, my attention span during meetings or important phone calls. I was aware it was only pretend. It wasn't like I would actually have a family or a wife with a kid on the way. But I couldn't stop thinking about it. Playing house.

Rose was at the office. Laura had informed me of the same, but we kept out of each other's way. I didn't want to publicly embarrass her until we'd decided what we were going to do about our relationship at work.

Eventually, she emailed me about lunch on Saturday at her parents' place. I emailed back, saying I would pick her up and that she should have her bags ready to move into my apartment that day.

I even got the spare room prepared and ready for her. Just because we were pretending to be married didn't mean she would want to share the room with me. And it might be better if we stayed away from that option.

But would I be able to *resist* her? Would I be able to keep my hands off this woman I found irresistible? When I thought about it, I still wasn't fully sure why I'd made this suggestion. Why I asked her to move in and came up with this plan?

I wanted to impress Barry. I wanted to be in his good books—but not this desperately.

The truth was this arrangement had nothing to do with her parents and everything to do with this baby. But I couldn't admit that. Not openly to her.

I wanted to be a part of this baby's life. I wanted to bond with my child, even if it was for a few months. I wanted to lay down a sturdy foundation of a relationship between us. A part of me wanted to get to know Rose a little better too. She was going to be the mother of my child. I wanted her to be a part of my life too.

But how? Until I could figure all of that out, this was the only way to proceed.

∼

Rose was waiting for me at the entrance of her apartment building with one hand on her hip. Her bags were on the steps beside her.

She was in a pretty pink cotton dress and sandals. Her golden curls blew in the breeze as I pulled up. I jumped out of the car to bring her bags in first. Rose barely looked at me. It seemed like she still wasn't quite sure of our arrangement maybe.

When she sat down beside me in the car, I decided to bring it up.

"Are you having second thoughts about this?"

She was gazing out of the window.

"No. I've decided it's the right thing to do. You were right about everything. This is the best way to go about our situation."

I knew Barry's address, so I knew where to drive to. Rose sat beside me with her hands clasped together in her lap. I wanted to reach out and hold her hand but that would've been inappropriate.

"I haven't told my family anything, so we'll be making the big announcements today. Both of them."

I pulled up to the side of the road, swerving quickly into a parking spot. Rose squealed in surprise, holding on to the door.

"What are you doing?" she asked, whipping around to me in her seat.

"I wanted to give you something before we met your parents. Sorry, I had to pull in when I saw the spot." I reached for the box in my jacket. Her eyes grew wide when I pulled it out. It was an engagement and wedding ring set. I had a matching one in my pocket.

Rose said nothing when I opened up the box and showed them to her. I'd bought her the biggest diamond I could find in the city on such short notice. But it didn't seem like she was pleased. She just continued to stare at the rings.

"I can't accept that," she said.

"Why not?"

"It just...it just feels wrong."

"How can we pretend to be married without a ring?" I asked. Rose looked up at me. Her blue eyes were wide and stormy.

"You should have got something less...expensive, I guess."

"That isn't something you need to worry about," I said and picked up the rings, waiting for her to hold her hand out to me so I could slip them on. But she didn't. She wasn't going to do it because it was fake. The one thing I was beginning to find out about Rose was that she valued honesty.

I dropped the rings in her lap instead and she eventually picked them up.

"Let's go," she said in a weak voice and I started up the car again. My gaze went to her belly. I pictured my child growing in there and I felt something inside me. A strain of longing. I never pictured myself as a father before, but now I couldn't stop imagining it.

∽

Mr. and Mrs. Johnson greeted us at the door together. They were clearly watching out for our car in the driveway. Behind them, I could hear the sounds of kids. I was embarrassed to realize I didn't even know how many siblings Rose had.

"I was surprised to hear Rose invited you along for lunch, Duke," Barry said as he shook my hand. "Pleasantly surprised, of course."

Mrs. Johnson was smiling at me as she hugged her daughter, but there was a look of curiosity there too.

Rose drew away from her parents nervously and then turned to me...as though for support. I could see how difficult this was for her. She wasn't a natural liar, and lying to her parents was probably even harder.

I reached for her hand before she was forced to say something. I held on to it tightly and gently tugged her to myself.

"Well, we wanted you to find out from us before you heard it elsewhere. We should have probably come clean to you the other day when you bumped into us, Barry," I said.

Their eyes grew wide. Maybe they were suspecting something already, but seeing it in person was different.

Mrs. Johnson looked at her husband.

"Shall we go in?" Rose turned to me. I saw that her cheeks were burning red.

"Rose!" A little girl, no older than ten or eleven, had made her way through her parents. I had no idea Rose had a sister as young as this.

"Hi, Lizzie, honey. How are you?" Rose embraced her sister. Two others came up to the door. A boy who seemed like a young teenager and another girl who was closer to Rose's age. "Flora, Oz," Rose said and she reached out to hug them too.

I stood back, watching in surprise as I realized how big Rose's family was. Barry and his wife were staring at me. They hadn't been able to properly react to the news.

"Okay, let's go in," Mrs. Johnson finally said.

"Is that your boyfriend?" Lizzie asked, hanging on to Rose's arm. "Daddy said you were bringing your boss to lunch."

"Hush now, Lizzie. Help me set the table, will you, honey?" Mrs. Johnson tried distracting Lizzie, but the kid had already trained her eyes on me.

"Are you Rose's boyfriend?" She marched up to me now while we took off our jackets.

"Lizzie, go help Mommy, please?" Rose insisted. I couldn't ignore Lizzie and her million-dollar question. We needed to tell everyone the truth at some point. We were both wearing the rings which nobody had noticed yet. I glanced at Rose, who suddenly looked deathly pale. Was she chickening out?

I smiled at Lizzie, stopping down to her height. "I'm her husband," I said.

Those were not words I'd ever imagined saying aloud. I was somebody's husband. I was Rose's fake husband.

There was a loud gasp behind me. It was Mrs. Johnson. Her hand covered her mouth now.

"What?" Flora squealed. I couldn't tell if she was delighted or just shocked.

"Rose, what is going on?" Mr. Johnson turned to his daughter now. Lizzie started giggling.

"Sorry, Daddy, we should be explaining this better. I didn't mean to tell you like this," Rose remarked. She glared at me now like this was my fault.

"Well, it needed to be said. That's the reason we're here now, isn't it?" I drew closer to her.

She gulped.

I took her hand and she then turned to her parents again. Looking like she'd seen a ghost.

"I can explain," she said.

"You're married now? When? Why didn't you tell us?" Flora was on a mission to interrogate her sister. Oz stood to the side, looking confused. Mrs. Johnson still wasn't able to formulate her words, while Barry glared at both of us like he could kill us.

Maybe I could have dealt with the situation more sensitively, but how?

"Flora, you need to give me a chance to explain instead of attacking me," Rose snapped.

"You got married and didn't invite us? Didn't even tell us you were dating your boss!" Her sister continued to argue.

"Flora...stop, that's enough," Mrs. Johnson finally spoke up.

"It all happened very fast. I was going to say something but then..." Rose was trying.

"But then what? He gave you that huge diamond ring and you were blinded? You couldn't pick up the phone and call one of us?" Flora was on attack-mode. I stood beside Rose, holding her hand, and every bone in my body wanted to do something to protect her. I hated seeing her in this position.

"Flora, stop it!" Barry growled at his daughter. Lizzie looked frightened. She was hiding behind her mother now.

"Have you seen the ring on her finger?" Flora asked with a laugh in her voice.

"You need to give your sister a chance to explain herself," Barry said.

"Explain what? That she thinks she's blissfully in love with some new man and she can ignore her own family?" Flora continued. Funnily enough, she reminded me a little bit of my own sister.

Rose's eyes were raging. She was throwing daggers at her sister, but this wasn't going to stop. I turned to Flora fully, blocking her view to Rose a little.

"I am as much to blame in all this as your sister," I said. The others fell quiet now.

"Duke..." Rose tried interjecting.

"So have at me. It's my fault too that you guys didn't find out sooner. She wanted to say something but I wanted to keep it a secret. I was thinking of my reputation. I was an idiot."

Flora's eyes dimmed a little. She looked at me and then at her sister. Her shoulders were still heaving up and down with anger, but it seemed like she was beginning to calm down.

Mrs. Johnson took this opportunity to step in.

"Why don't we all sit down and have a cup of coffee? Shall we? Please, talk about this calmly?"

She came closer to us, nervously reaching for her daughter. I let go of Rose's hand so she could go to her mother. Mrs. Johnson wrapped an arm around her shoulder and then gently led the way to the kitchen. We all followed. Barry and I trailed at the end.

I could sense he was itching to say something to me. I wanted to give him the opportunity to say it. I was in his home. I'd knocked up his daughter. His oldest precious daughter. He didn't know this yet, but he would find out soon enough. Maybe their whole world would be rocked and I'd be at the center of it.

"Barry," I said and hung back. He turned to me with fire in his eyes.

"You could've said something at some point. We've been on phone calls and meetings in and out with each other for months."

The truth was I didn't even know of Rose's existence until about five weeks ago.

I clenched my jaw and nodded.

"Yes, I should have said something, but I didn't. I hope you can forgive me."

21

ROSE

I followed my mother to my parents' bedroom. She'd managed to take me aside while the others were setting up the table for lunch. I didn't know where Duke was. I guessed he was with Daddy.

This wasn't going as I planned. I actually didn't have a plan at all. I thought we'd go with the flow, tell my parents together calmly. Instead, Duke had decided to take the lead and now everything was a mess.

Mom shut the door behind us and I whipped around to her.

"I was going to tell you sooner…"

She came to me and pulled me into her arms.

"First of all, Rose, congratulations. You're a married woman now, and even though I missed your happy day, I'm still happy for you."

She was holding me at arm's length, peering into my eyes. I could barely bring myself to look at her.

"Thank you, Mom. I thought you would be so mad."

"I'm mad because you didn't tell me, not because you did it."

"So you're in support of this marriage."

"Well, honey, I don't know Duke Nolan at all. Whatever I know of him, I've heard from your father and read about him in the news. He seems like a good man, and I trust your instincts. Do you think you've done the right thing?"

It was so hard to lie to her. I'd never lied to her before. Not even when Will and I broke up. I told her the whole truth, as embarrassing as it was.

"Yes, I think so. I love him and he loves me," I replied.

She pulled me in and hugged me tightly.

"See, that is all I wanted to know. It's all I care about, your happiness."

But I wasn't smiling. I was afraid of what I was about to tell her next.

"But why the rush? Why did you get married so quickly? Without telling anybody?" she continued. She was searching my eyes again, trying to figure it out. Maybe she'd guessed it already. All I could do was hang my head. I didn't want to be ashamed of my baby.

"I'm pregnant, Mom. About five weeks pregnant."

There was silence in the room for a few moments, and then there were loud thumps on the door.

"Rose? Mom? Let me in!" It was Flora.

"Give us a minute!" Mom snapped. She rarely ever spoke this way. Her eyes were watering now as she stared at me.

"You're about to have a baby? By him?"

"I really didn't want to tell you like this, Mom. I wanted to properly explain, but we thought it would be best if we made it official first. You know, to give this baby a normal family life. I didn't want to keep this a secret from you guys."

I didn't know whether she would burst into tears again. Her lips were quivering.

"You're going to be a mother?"

I was silent. She knew the answer. It was a rhetorical question of disbelief.

"Oh, Rose, honey! This is such great news!"

Mom lunged at me and I burst out in sobs while I rested my head on her chest. "Are you sure, Mom? You really think this is great news?"

"You will be such a good mother, Rose. You've practically been a mother to Oz and Lizzie all their lives. It comes naturally to you. And now you'll have a baby of your own." Mom was stroking my hair as she spoke.

"I thought you guys would be angry with me," I murmured.

"Well, your father won't take it lightly. He'll probably need some time to get used to the idea, but he'll come around eventually."

I looked up at her and she was smiling again. "I'm so relieved that you're doing the right thing. This marriage is a good thing. See, I knew Duke Nolan is a good man. Responsible and reliable. Your father will see that."

I licked my lips and nodded. Duke's plan was working already. Our fake marriage was passing the test.

There was a bang on the door again. Flora was growing impatient.

"Okay, come in," Mom shouted for her. Flora threw the door open and found us standing, huddled together.

"What happened? What is going on?" she asked, rushing to us.

"Rose is...she's pregnant, honey. You're going to be an aunt," Mom said.

"What!" Flora shrieked. She jumped at me, hugging me too. She was laughing and now Mom laughed along with her. They couldn't stop hugging me and telling me how happy they were. I hadn't expected them to take the news so well. I thought they'd come up with a million reasons why this was going to lead to disaster, but they didn't.

I loved my family for their support, and it made me feel even sicker now, knowing I was lying to them about my relationship with Duke.

~

We all sat silently around the dinner table. I wasn't sure if she'd done it on purpose, but Flora seated Duke between Lizzie and Oz. They were both staring at him, making eyes at each other...being kids. While Daddy stared at me. Mom was holding his hand that lay on the table.

Flora sat next to me and she was the only one eating.

"Daddy, you should eat something," she said. Nobody had said a word since Mom gently broke the news of the pregnancy to him.

"Yes, Barry, honey, eat something."

"I don't know if I'm hungry," Daddy said. He couldn't take his eyes off me and I kept my head hung. I hated the way he was glaring at me. It made me feel sick. Would he hate my child too?

"Yes, you are, Barry. We can talk about all this after dinner. When things have settled a bit. Huh? How about that?" Mom was trying to be as gentle about it as she could, despite Daddy looking like he was about to burst into flames.

"You got her pregnant?" Daddy turned to Duke now. Unlike me, Duke was able to hold his gaze.

"Yes, there is no other way to put it."

"So you married her because you got her pregnant?" Daddy continued. I could feel a wave of nausea rising in my stomach. Our plan was going to fail. Daddy would see right through this, and then what? What would my family think of me then?

"I'm in love with your daughter. This marriage isn't just about the pregnancy," Duke said. All eyes in the room were on him now. I stared at him with my mouth hanging open. He was so convincing. He had a look of trustworthiness on his face. He was handsome and as my mother said—reliable.

"This should be a celebration, Barry. We should be happy for them, shouldn't we?" Mom added.

"You're much older than her. You do realize that, don't you?" Daddy growled at Duke.

"Of course. I am very well aware of it. But that doesn't change how I feel about Rose and about this baby to be born."

Daddy glared at him but there wasn't really much he could say to that. Duke had him cornered now. So he swung his head over to me.

"How did you let this happen, Rose? I thought you were more responsible than this!"

"I wasn't trying to make this happen, Daddy. This wasn't a part of the plan. But we're here now and..."

"And it's going to be good. It'll be great. We're in love. We're married. We're having a baby. We're building a family. What is wrong with that?" Duke interjected. All eyes turned to him again. My cheeks flushed. It made me jittery to hear him speak about me like this.

"Maybe you should stay out of this," Daddy snapped.

"Hey!" I cried out to him just when Duke stood up. He walked around the table to my side and held out his hand.

"Okay, let's get out of here. We can come back when your family's had some time to think this through."

I stared at his hand in front of my face.

"You don't have to do this…" Mom said, standing up too. Daddy said nothing. It didn't seem like he was going to crack easily.

I looked up at Duke, straight into his eyes and then I took his hand. He helped me up, even though I didn't really need his help. Mom, Flora, and Oz were all talking to each other and us. Trying to convince Daddy to say something to make us stay. But their voices seemed to drown out. The only thing I could focus on was my hand in Duke's. He was leading me out of the house.

I looked over my shoulder when we were at the door. Through the kitchen door, I could see the rest of my family shouting at each other. Mostly shouting at my father, who continued to sit in his chair, staring straight ahead with anger in his eyes.

Duke and I didn't speak until we were sitting in his car.

"Rose, I'm very sorry about this. I shouldn't have blurted it out. We should've gone in there with a better plan of action."

I turned to him, searching his eyes.

"If Daddy doesn't come around and accept this marriage or the baby, then your chances of entering the museum board will be over. So what is the point of all this?" I asked.

Duke looked away from me, out at our house. Nobody had come to the door yet.

"Right now, my priority is to make sure you and the baby are in good health. You being caught in the middle of that emotional family drama can't be good for either of you. I needed to get you out of there."

"But your plan was…"

He cut me off. "I remember what my plan was, and I'm hoping Barry does come around. I'm going to do my best to make him see sense, but if he doesn't, he doesn't. I want the baby to be well and healthy, and for that, you need a calm and peaceful environment."

I wanted to hug him. I wished he would just take me in his arms and hold me. This was strange for me, because I'd never felt this safe or peaceful with anybody other than my family and Karen. Not even with Will.

He looked at me again and this time he was smiling.

"I'll help you move in today. You get some sleep tonight, and tomorrow we can worry about your family again."

He started the car and we sank into a comfortable silence. But I couldn't stop staring at the glittering diamond ring on my finger. Would I have to give it back now? Did this mean our fake marriage was over? Just when it had begun, just when I was getting comfortable with the idea.

I glanced at Duke's profile as he drove. Strong, handsome, sexy, intelligent...a man who could have any woman he wanted. And yet, he was stuck with me because I was the one having his baby.

22

DUKE

Rose didn't have many bags, and within an hour of arriving at my apartment, she had officially 'moved in'. The lunch hadn't gone according to plan, and her father was stubborn, but I didn't want to think about that now. I was concerned about the effect it would have on Rose and the development of the baby. I wasn't lying when I said I wanted them to be at peace.

Rose said she wanted to nap and I left her alone in the spare room, which she'd moved into, and I decided to get some work done. In my home office, at the other end of the penthouse, I couldn't focus on work. I couldn't focus on anything.

There were two rings on Rose's finger and one ring on mine. Even though it officially didn't mean anything or have any legal standing, we'd already declared to her family that we were married.

I sat at my desk, repeating the words in my head —*married man*. I was a married man. But more real than that was the fact that I was going to be a father. Something had changed in me. I wasn't thinking about work all the time. My research and the new drug were both far from my mind. I was picturing a nursery, a cot, a baby sleeping swaddled in the middle of it, a baby opening its eyes to see my face peering down at it. A baby smiling.

I jumped off my chair and paced around the room. A few weeks ago, I would have reached for the bottle of Scotch stashed away in the back of the drawer. Not today. I didn't crave a drink, I felt alive enough already.

I pictured Rose as a mother. Her beautiful smiling face as she held a baby out to me. The look of pride in her eyes as she watched me rocking the baby in my arms. She would make a good mother. She was strong and smart, beautiful and gentle. Would the baby have her beautiful big blue eyes? I hoped it would.

Maybe now I could buy the house in Skibbereen. For the baby. For my family? Were we a family now?

I snapped out of my thoughts when that word rang around in my brain. *Family*.

Did Rose want to be a family with me? Why would she?

She was so young. She had a whole life ahead of her. Why would she want to be tied down? And with a man she didn't actually have feelings for. After all, wasn't it just sex? The baby was an accident. The result of our carelessness. The baby wasn't the result of actual love.

How long would we actually be able to keep this up?

Was it even necessary if Barry wasn't going to give me the board nomination anyway?

My phone buzzed. It was the reception desk calling. They said Barry Johnson was here to see me and with my heart pounding in my chest, I went to the door.

Rose was still asleep in her room when her father stepped out of the elevator. I was there to greet him at my door.

"Is Rose here?" he asked. His voice was less gruff than it was in the afternoon.

"She's taking a nap. She needs her rest," I said. I would've done anything to stand in his path if he was going to start up a fight with her again. But it looked like I didn't have to.

"Okay, good, I'm here to see you," Barry said.

I invited him to my den, where he looked around sheepishly and then went over to stand by one of the windows. I hadn't bothered offering him refreshments because it seemed like he didn't plan on staying long.

"I've had a chance to think about all this, and while I'm still in shock, I also don't want to push my daughter away. She needs to be with her family. I want to be a part of her life and my grandchild's."

I nodded. "Good, I'm glad you see that."

Barry's eyes were wide. He glared at me, and at one point, I thought he'd lunge at me.

"But if I ever find out, even if I get the hint that you're hurting my daughter in any way, I'm going to make sure everyone finds out about it. Everyone who matters in your circle." He spoke through gritted teeth.

I tried to remain calm. This conversation was crucial. "Why would I hurt Rose? She is going to be the mother of my child."

"And as long as I've known you, Duke Nolan, and the better acquainted we got over the years—I have known you are not a man to be tied down. Nobody ever predicted you would get married."

"Things change, Barry, people change."

"Rose changed you?" He grunted.

"You underestimate your daughter," I replied.

He clenched his jaw and looked away from me, shaking his head.

"She is too young and a little naïve. Headstrong, sure, we raised her so she'd always be able to look after herself, but I can see how easily she could've fallen for you. She hasn't known you as long as I have."

"We don't really know each other, Barry," I said.

"I know enough."

I took in a deep breath and then slid my hands into my pant pockets. "Look, if you've come over here just to fling insults at me in my own home while your daughter is asleep, then you can give it a rest now. You've done your job. You have successfully insulted me."

Even though he was still glaring, I could see him visibly trying to calm himself. He stared at a painting on the wall, trying to avoid eye contact with me.

"I'm here to tell you that I want Rose to be happy. I want my grandchild to be happy and well taken care of."

"They both will be, I can guarantee that," I said.

He drew toward me and I stretched my hand out to him. We shook hands like we were making a deal. The words were unspoken—my board nomination, but I could see it in Barry's eyes. He was going to nominate now. I was his son-in-law, after all.

"Daddy?" Rose's voice interrupted us. She was standing at the door of the den. Her eyes looked a little droopy with sleep and her hair was a little tousled. Evidence of sleep. I was glad she got some rest.

"Come over here," Barry said. He threw his arms open and beamed at his daughter. A smile grew on Rose's face as she ran to him. I watched them hug tight, eyes pressed closed.

I could feel something of what Barry was feeling right

now. This was how I would hug my child. This was how desperate I would be to keep my own child safe and happy.

"Don't you worry about me anymore, you hear?" Barry said as Rose looked up into her father's eyes. "Duke and I had a good chat. We understand each other now."

She looked at me, and I was smiling too. Trying to reassure her it was all right.

"And I'm sorry I reacted like that."

"You were in shock," Rose said.

"Yes, I was. I still am. I didn't expect to become a grandfather this soon, but now I can't wait to meet the baby. I want you all to be happy."

Slowly, Rose drew away from him and came closer to me. I held a hand out to her and she took it. Within moments, she was in my arms. I could feel the softness of her body against mine. I wanted to kiss her. Kiss her mouth. Take possession of her again.

But I couldn't. All I could do was stare at her while she spoke.

"I am happy, Daddy. I'm happy with Duke."

I was shocked to realize that a part of me wished this was true. That there was some truth to this scene. But instead, everything was a lie here. Nothing except the baby was reality. Rose didn't love me. She wasn't happy with me. She was doing this so her life could be a little bit easier. She was doing this for the sake of her child.

I glanced up at Barry, a strained, plastic smile stretching across my face. I nodded.

"Yeah, we're very happy. Our life is perfect," I lied. Slowly, I let my arm drop away from her body. I needed to put some distance between us.

23

ROSE

Monica and I were having lunch together at the staff cafeteria. I wasn't wearing the rings Duke had given me because we still hadn't talked about it—what we were going to tell everyone else at the office. I assumed the ruse applied only to my family.

"You're living with him?" She was in shock. I'd kept her out of the loop for a long time now, but I decided I needed someone to talk to. Someone who knew the whole picture, knew Duke, someone I could trust.

"In the spare room. We're not sharing a bedroom or anything like that," I said.

Monica's eyes were wide. She hadn't touched any of her food.

"You're living with Duke Nolan?" She hissed through her teeth, trying to keep her voice down.

My cheeks were flushed and I wasn't looking at her. I didn't know whether to be giddy with excitement or embarrassment.

"And you're having his baby?"

"Yes. I'm six weeks pregnant at the moment, so it's still

early days, but everything seems to be on track. Baby is healthy."

Monica reached for my hand on the table just as I reached for a juice box. She was holding it tightly.

"Hey, how are you doing, Rose?"

"I'm good."

"No, seriously, you can talk to me. Tell me if something isn't quite right."

I met her eyes and smiled. "I'm good. I really am. My family knows now, so I'm relieved. They've been very supportive through the whole thing."

"But you're still in shock, aren't you? With this pregnancy and then moving in with Duke Nolan and pretending to be married to him. I mean, that's a lot of drama for one person to handle. One *pregnant* person."

I took a bite of my sandwich and chewed slowly. It gave me some time to think about what Monica was saying. Then I shook my head.

"Right now, the only thing I can think about is this baby growing inside me. My situation with Duke is awkward, but I'll get over it."

"So you're not actually in a relationship?"

"It's a relationship of convenience. The marriage never happened. We're both gaining something from this," I said.

Monica's nostrils flared and she sat back in her chair and sighed.

"Yeah, sure, he's gaining something from this. He gets to look like a hero. What are you gaining?"

I snapped up to look at her, but she said nothing more. I was about to open my mouth to say something. To explain the situation to her. I was gaining the chance for my child to have a relationship with its father. That was invaluable. I was doing this for my baby.

But Jim interrupted us.

"Hi, guys. Everything okay here?" He sat down at our table before either of us could respond. Things between Jim and me were back to their usual professional self. Nonetheless, I didn't exactly want to spend my lunch hour with him.

Monica looked uncomfortable, too, as she sat there, smiling politely.

"Yeah, everything's okay, we're just having a chat over lunch," she said. I continued with my sandwich, keeping conversation to a minimum now in the hopes that he would get the message.

But he didn't. He sat at our table, sipping his coffee and trying to make small talk. The only thing he really had to talk about was the new project. Neither Monica nor I were interested in that at the moment. We had other things on our minds.

Eventually, when Jim started noticing we were not really contributing to the conversation, he gave me a long hard stare.

"Anything on your mind, besides work?"

Monica shifted in her seat—a dead giveaway!

I turned to Jim with a smile and shrugged.

"Nothing really. Work's keeping me busy," I replied, and instinctively, my hand went to my belly. I stroked it gently, just when I noticed Jim's eyes being drawn to that gesture. Why did I do that? Why couldn't I just be cool about it?

"How have you been, Jim?" Monica asked. It was her attempt at distracting him, but he couldn't take his eyes off me.

"Are you feeling ill?" he asked, still looking at my stomach. If nothing else, it was highly inappropriate!

I grinned at him, beginning to get nervous now. "I'm fine. Why would you think that? I'm perfectly fine."

Jim glanced at my face and then at Monica. "Oh, nothing. It's just a feeling I got."

I felt the desperate urge to ask him to leave. Just to leave me alone. He had no right to come here and ask me these questions. Even though he was my manager. He had no right!

"Rose is fine. I'm fine. We're both perfectly healthy," Monica interjected again. "In fact, we were just going to go for a walk."

She stood up and glared at me, trying to convince me to stand up and go too. But Jim didn't move from his seat and neither did I. I could feel a rush of anger rising up. Who did he think he was?

"I'm so grateful for your concern for my well-being, Jim," I said. I was practically hissing with anger.

"Yes, of course I'm concerned. You're an invaluable member of my team, and now you have the responsibility of a huge project on your hands."

Monica stood behind him, trying to catch my eye, but now I was riding this rollercoaster, I couldn't get it to stop.

"It doesn't matter, Jim, you need to fucking back off." The words escaped my lips before I could stop them. I had suddenly turned into a big grizzly mama bear.

Monica's eyes widened and Jim's face turned all shades of red.

"Excuse me?" he hissed.

"You heard me the first time. I don't appreciate your advances. Frankly, it creeps me out. So please, keep your concerns to yourself or I'll have to report you to HR." I looked up at Monica. "I have enough witnesses, so you can't turn this around on me. I hope you understand."

Jim licked his lips like he'd tasted something bitter. I could see how pink the tops of his ears looked now. Was he going to say anything more? What *could* he say now?

"There you are! I hoped I'd find you here."

I heard Duke's voice behind me and within moments, I felt his hands on my shoulders. I craned my neck to turn and look at him from my chair but he was already stooping down. His face was inches away from mine now, and then his mouth was on my lips. We were kissing. My breath was caught in my throat. I felt a heavy load dropping away from my arms. What was happening?

He drew away but kept his hands on my shoulders.

"Enjoying your coffee there, Jim?" he asked.

Jim and Monica weren't the only people in the cafeteria who were staring at us now. In fact, there wasn't a single person in that place who wasn't. My body burned with nerves. I didn't know what to say or how to react.

"Ummm....yeah. Sure. It's good coffee, Doctor Nolan." Jim managed to murmur a response. Duke didn't move away from behind me. He remained glued there to the back of my chair.

"I'm glad. I just wanted to pop down and check in on my wife."

"Wife?" Jim's voice nearly broke. I didn't know how much longer I could bear this public scrutiny.

"Oh, honey, didn't you tell him? Yeah, we got married over the weekend. So you were right all along, Jim. Rose was most definitely in a relationship with someone in the office."

Jim stood up now. It seemed like it was physically painful for him to keep sitting.

"Congratulations. Yeah. Ummm. Congratulations! I should get back to it. There's a report I need to get to."

"Yeah, of course, you wouldn't want to get behind on

that," Duke said. Jim hurried past us. Monica hadn't made a single move. The others in the cafeteria slowly began to talk to each other in whispers. I wished they would just stop staring at me. I felt like a clown. Like a caged animal to be pointed at.

Duke came around to face me. I hadn't seen him since the morning at the apartment, when we said courteous good mornings to each other in the kitchen.

"You okay? Was he bothering you again?" he asked me now. Monica had turned away. She was taking herself out of this private conversation. Didn't he realize we were in the middle of our office cafeteria? That all eyes were still on us?

I noticed the ring on his finger now. He was wearing it. We hadn't discussed this. What was going on? Why wouldn't he tell me what was going on? I felt the pricking of hot tears at the backs of my eyelids.

"Duke. Can we talk?" I snapped, standing up with a jerk.

"Sure, we can go to my office," he said.

∽

Laura left us alone this time, even though Duke and I walked past her desk and I could see her eyes growing wide with curiosity. When he shut the door behind us, I gaped at him.

"You're wearing the wedding band."

He walked over to his desk and just stood there, leaning against the side with his long arms crossed over his chest.

"Yes, gotta wear the ring to make this look real."

"Look real to whom? The whole office? I thought we were just pretending for the sake of my family."

"And your father has connections everywhere in this

industry. Word gets out. If he finds out nobody else but him knows about our marriage, he's going to get suspicious."

I stood there, licking my lips nervously.

"And why aren't *you* wearing the rings? Are you ashamed of our arrangement?"

"It's exactly that. An arrangement. It's not a real marriage. Those rings don't have any actual significance. I didn't think it would matter." We were both glaring at each other. This wasn't a calm conversation. Duke clenched his jaw and took in a deep breath.

"You do realize, Rose, that I'm not *making* you do this. You're free to break off this arrangement any time you want. I thought we were both gaining something from this."

I saw a flash of the way he'd kissed me back there in the cafeteria. How his arm was protectively wound around me. Now the blinds were dropped. We didn't have to pretend anymore.

"I didn't realize we'd have to keep this up at the office too."

"I've already told Laura. I'm sure she'll spread the word to everyone else who needs to know," Duke continued.

I took in a sharp breath and tried to not shudder.

"I just wish we'd spoken about this before you started spreading it."

Duke picked up a pen from the desk and tapped it repeatedly. Then he sighed, as though he was thinking about something very grave.

"Fair enough. I should have spoken to you about it. We should discuss the finer points of our relationship, make these decisions together," he said.

"Yes, I am as much a part of this arrangement as you are, and if we're going to make it through the next few months, we need to be on the same page."

"Yes, I agree. You're right," he said.

"I don't like being surprised, and it seems like you have a knack for it. You did it at my parents' house and now in the office…"

"I'm not used to making joint decisions with a spouse," he said. Now he was grinning. That was all I needed to melt. One handsome grin coming from him and I was toast. "So why don't we have dinner together? Tonight? So we can discuss this, the finer points."

I gulped because what I was picturing now was a date.

"Okay, yeah, that sounds good."

"Great. I'll cook."

I remembered the grilled cheese. Duke sure knew his way around a kitchen.

"Okay," I murmured.

"Let's say, eight? In the apartment? I'll see you then."

I nodded.

"Good, you'll have to excuse me now. I have to get to the lab," he said firmly. That was it. I was dismissed.

∽

The lunch hour was over by the time I returned to my cubicle. Monica was sitting at her desk but I got the sense she hadn't actually been working. I could also feel everyone else's eyes on me. They were talking about me and Duke. I knew it!

When I sat down, Monica pushed herself in her chair over to me.

"Are you okay?" she asked.

I turned to her and gulped.

"I don't know. We decided we need to talk about it… about everything. So he's cooking me dinner tonight."

"Wow!" She couldn't hide the look of excitement from her eyes. She chewed on her bottom lip now. Then she placed a hand on mine. "Rose, I'm really happy for you."

"For what? Because I'm having a baby?" I asked in a low voice.

She shrugged and continued to smile. "Because you're having *his* baby, I guess. I mean, this isn't something anyone expects from a man of his position. He could've just chucked money at you and expected the problem to go away. He could've denied you and rejected you completely. Instead, he's taking responsibility for you and the baby. The way he acted today toward Jim was purely because he felt protective."

My throat was dry. Was that really what was happening? Was Duke taking responsibility?

"Like you said, he's gaining something from this too. He gets to be my father's son-in-law. His entry into the museum board is practically guaranteed now," I said.

Monica sighed. "Yeah, maybe that's a part of it, but something tells me he genuinely wants to be a part of this baby's life. He wants to be a father. Maybe he's trying out marriage for size too?"

Now she'd planted the seed in my head. I stared at her hopefully. Was there a chance that our marriage could turn into something real? Would Duke ever want something like that? Would I?

I swung my head around to the computer. I had a mountain of work to get through and I didn't know how I'd manage.

"What you need right now is to not stress. I'll help you with your workload, okay?" Monica said.

"Thank you…for everything," I told her and she smiled at me. I was glad I decided to open up to her. I really needed a friend around here because I was sure nobody would treat me the same anymore. Not now that they believed I was married to Duke Nolan. And things would take another nosedive when they found out I was also carrying his child.

"Don't worry, Rose, it'll all work out in the end. For you and the baby," Monica said.

24

DUKE

I took off early from work so I could get back to the apartment in time and cook us dinner. Garlic parmesan mashed potatoes, tortellini salad, and a creamy chicken lasagna. It took me a whole of two hours to prepare and by the end of it, I felt fulfilled. I hadn't had the motivation to cook dinner like this for a long time. Not even for Diane when she was around.

Was I trying to impress Rose? Yes.

Did I miss cooking an elaborate meal? Yes.

I wanted her to feel welcome in the apartment—for the benefit of the baby and herself.

She arrived a little before eight. I heard her use the keycard to open the door. Her heels clicked on the marble floor as she made her way to her room. I got the food arranged on the table in the dining room. There was sparkling grape juice for both of us to accompany the dinner. The bread pudding was cooking in the oven for later.

Fifteen minutes later, Rose emerged, changed and

looking comfortable. She took my breath away each time I saw her. Maybe now that I knew she was carrying my child —she had more of a startling effect on me.

She was just in a pair of sweatpants and an oversized shirt. She'd washed off her makeup and tied her hair up in a messy bun again. Her golden curls fell around her beautiful face. She licked her glossy pink lips and a smile grew on her face.

"Oh, my God. I could smell this from the front door. I just didn't expect it all to look this good!"

I held a chair out for her and she sat down.

"Sorry, I just wanted to get comfortable. I feel like I'm not dressed for a fancy dinner like this," she said.

I pushed the food in her direction while I took a seat across from her.

"It's not fancy at all. Just a simple home-cooked meal."

Rose served herself the parmesan potatoes first and took a bite. The smile grew. I loved watching her eat and enjoy the food I'd cooked for her.

"You saw my family. It's a big family. We ate a lot of one-pot meals and casseroles while growing up. So this definitely looks fancy. Where did you learn to cook?" She was wolfing down the potatoes and taking intermittent sips of the grape juice. I was glad to find we could actually just sit down and have a regular conversation. I didn't want to argue.

"From my dad. He was a chef, and he loved to experiment at home. Cooking in our house was always a big affair. A major part of our upbringing."

Rose smiled at me and then looked away.

"You definitely seem skilled. This is delicious."

She helped herself to the salad and the lasagna next. I

realized I loved watching her like this. I would've enjoyed cooking for her every day. Knowing she was also nourishing the child growing inside her.

"You don't cook at all?" I asked.

Rose shrugged.

"Not really. Other than cup noodles and boiled eggs." We both laughed at that. "I've never felt the need to. Mom always cooked for us and I never felt the need to include myself in the process."

"You guys seem close," I said, even though I knew this was sensitive territory. There was a good chance this conversation could take a sour turn once we started discussing her family. But Rose smiled and nodded.

"Very close, yeah. Especially to my siblings. Flora and I practically raised Oz and Lizzie. Mom got very sick after Lizzie was born and we had to take over the household. Daddy tried to help but he's pretty useless around babies. He knows how to love them but he wouldn't be able to care for one. Flora and I had to grow up pretty quickly."

I noticed the way she kept her head down as she spoke about her family now.

"They seem very happy about the baby. Especially your mother."

She nodded. "Yes, she is. They are. I knew it would come as a shock to them. They weren't expecting it. I'd never expressed any interest in having a child this young. But they will love and care for this baby fiercely. That much I know."

I wanted to reach for her, to hold her hand. I wanted to tell her I would love and care for this baby fiercely too. That I couldn't wait to be a father.

She looked up at me and spoke again. "How did Diane take the news? I assume you told her about the pregnancy."

I took a big bite of the lasagna. "Not well, if I'm being honest."

I could see Rose trying hard not to roll her eyes.

"I'm not sure of exactly what was said between the two of you, but I get the feeling it was intense," I added.

Rose played with the glass of juice in her hand. "Your sister doesn't like me. I think she feels like she knows me. Or knows my type. She thinks I'm after something. Your money or your things. I don't know."

"Diane can be pretty strong-willed. The thing is she's fiercely protective of me, even though I'm the older sibling."

"She feels the need to protect you from all the female piranhas circling you?" Rose said with a cackle.

I shrugged.

"She's not been completely wrong in the past."

"Is that what you think of me too?" she asked.

"No."

We stared at each other. She was studying me, like she was trying to decide if I was honest.

"I wouldn't have invited you to live in my home or kissed you in my office cafeteria if I thought you had an ulterior motive," I said.

Rose seemed to sit up straighter in her chair now. She turned her face to her food, toying with her fork.

"*Why* did you kiss me?" she asked.

Wasn't the answer obvious to her?

"Because I wanted everyone to know you belong to me."

She put down her fork and I saw the way she pursed her lips now. "But I don't really...belong to you, I mean."

"That isn't the story we're selling to everyone else. For all intents and purposes, you belong to me. You're my wife. The mother of my child. I have every right to kiss you."

I left out the part about the fact that I *wanted* to kiss her. That I was burning up to do exactly that.

Rose's cheeks flushed deep red. Her name suited her. I watched as she gulped nervously like her throat had gone dry.

"It's just that I'm not very good at pretending. I'm not a good liar or an actor."

"You don't have to act," I said. She looked up at me, peering into my eyes.

"What are you talking about, Duke? This whole thing is an act."

"No, it is not. You're really pregnant and we're having this baby. We slept together in order to make this baby. We couldn't keep our hands off each other at one point, remember?"

Rose stood up from her chair with a jerk and I realized I'd said something wrong.

"What?" I asked. She swung away from the table.

"I need some air."

"Why?"

"I need some space from all this."

I stood up too and followed her out of the dining room.

"Rose. Stop."

She was hurtling away from me. This dinner was a mess now.

"What the fuck did I say?" I growled. I wanted her to stay and explain, but I wasn't going to chase her out of the door. If she wanted to leave, she could leave. I couldn't make her stay against her wishes.

She stopped in her tracks and whipped around to me.

"Nothing. You said nothing."

I took in a deep breath, squaring my shoulders as I faced

her directly. "Look, Rose, the only way we can make this work is if we stop playing games with each other."

"I'm not playing any games."

"Then why the fuck are you storming away from me?" I took a few steps toward her and she followed me with her eyes. "Tell me what is on your mind. This evening was supposed to be all about us talking, being honest with each other."

"...and it is."

"You need to tell me what is going through your head instead of walking away from me."

Rose looked into my eyes. She was watching me closely now. When she parted her luscious mouth, I knew I wanted to kiss her. I always wanted to kiss her.

"I don't like to be reminded of our mistake. Of the circumstances that led to us conceiving this child. I don't want to be reminded that this baby is a mistake." She spoke in a soft voice and I moved toward her. When I reached for her, she didn't move away. I touched her hair, her beautiful golden curls first, then the side of her face. The backs of my fingers grazed the softness of her cheeks. Then I explored the shape of her perfect bow-lips. Because her lips were parted, I could slip a finger in between them easily. I felt the soft flicker of her tongue on the tip of my finger.

A bolt like electricity ran through my body. This girl was irresistible. What was I doing? This wasn't a part of our agreement, but I couldn't stop it now.

It wasn't just me, she was drawing herself closer to me too. I could feel the warmth of her body against mine. The rise and fall of her generous breasts.

"This baby is not a mistake," I grunted in a deep voice. I realized I could barely speak. My need for her was like a fire burning inside me. Consuming me. My cock pumped hard between my legs. Growing. Demanding.

Rose looked up at me from under her deliciously heavy lashes. Her blue eyes were shining bright. She opened her mouth wider so my finger slipped deeper into her. She sucked on it. Giving me a taste of what it would feel like to have my cock there. I wanted her.

With my other hand, I grabbed a clump of her hair at the back of her head. She was pinned to me now. No escape. I pulled my hand away from her mouth and touched her neck. It traveled down her breasts until I found the end of her sweatshirt. I touched her skin underneath it. Her stomach was deliciously warm, scrumptious. A baby was growing inside and this was the most beautiful body I had ever possessed.

Rose leaned backward, arching her back and my hand traveled down her pants until I felt the wet warmth between her legs. She gasped and I found my way underneath her panties. It was sticky and delicious in there. I was hungry for more.

"Does this feel like a mistake to you?" I asked. She stared at me for a moment and then shook her head no.

"Good, because it's not. It's very, very right. This is exactly how it should be between a husband and wife," I said, slipping a finger into her. She arched her body again, gasping for air as she swung in my arm. My thumb found her clit as I slipped my forefinger in deeper in her depths.

She clutched me tightly, digging her nails into my back.

"Duke...please."

"What, Rose? What do you want? Tell me what you want."

"More."

"More what?"

She stopped for a second. Her breathing was still ragged, her cheeks were flushed, and her blue eyes narrowed with desire.

"More of you. I want more of you," she said.

I plunged my finger into her deeper, stroking her clit at the same time. I wanted to watch her come.

25

ROSE

Duke's finger was inside me and he was stroking my clit, making me feel like I could explode any minute. With his big strong body, he pushed me, but he was gentle now. He was moving me toward the wall behind us. He pinned me up against it while his finger took possession of me.

His mouth was on my neck, exploring my skin. My hands were on him. I was clinging to him, holding onto him for dear life. I wanted him to devour me. Did he know I wanted to give myself to him?

While his fingers worked their magic on me, bringing me to the brink of my orgasm—the only thing I could think about was what it would be like if this was for real. If this was the sex we had as a real married couple. If he was really my husband.

The thought took my breath away. That and the fact that he knew exactly how to touch me. He pumped his fingers into me. My clit was swollen and tender, just waiting to explode. His mouth was on my neck, then nibbling my ear, then on my lips.

We were all over each other, pressed up against the wall, pressed to each other, until I couldn't hold back anymore.

"Oh, my God..." the words came rushing out of me like a tremor. Duke knew exactly what was going to happen so he pounded me with his finger even harder. He wasn't going to stop until he got what he wanted and I came. My orgasm took over me. His finger slid in smoothly with the sticky juices of me. There was so much of it, filling up my panties. Warm and intense.

I moved against him uncontrollably. I breathed raggedly, like I would lose my breath. I couldn't help it...I sank my teeth into the tough muscles of his shoulder but he didn't say a word. Did he even feel it? Was he made of steel?

It took several minutes until I was finished. He slipped his hand out of my pants and I felt totally raw and exposed.

Duke took a step back. I could see his fingers glistening with my juices but he didn't rub it off. My chest heaved. I was out of breath but I wanted more. I wanted him to feel the way he made me feel. It was only fair.

I lunged at him before he could move away. I was on my knees in front of him and his fingers were in my hair. I got a whiff of my own scent. I felt sexy. Suddenly very powerful. We both still had all our clothes on but I'd never felt this intimate with anyone else before. How was it possible?

I unbuckled him. Unzipped him. Duke stood in front of me. Over me. His legs wide apart like two solid tree trunks. His hands were holding me in place. Keeping me still. My mouth was wide open while I worked his cock out of his pants.

I knew what to expect and still, he nearly took my breath away. So big and strong. Just like how I felt, his cock was powerful. He had the power to possess me. To make me dance to his whim. Did he know that?

He was erect, throbbing hard as I took him in my hand. I didn't know why my mouth watered. That wetness between my legs hadn't gone anywhere. I was ready for him again, but this was about him.

I opened my mouth wide while I rubbed his cock. Slowly and then fast. I looked up at him while I brought my mouth closer to him. I watched how his face turned dark. He knew what was about to happen but it looked like he was about to hold his breath. I felt the smooth tip of his cock on my tongue. I tasted the salty strength of him and I gulped.

What was it about Duke that made this so much sexier than it ever was before? His perfect bone structure? His chiseled abs? The way his hands had a hold of my head? The control he had on me that made me act so irrationally?

His cock filled my mouth and then dove deep down my throat. I gagged but only gently...only because he was so big. And then I was sucking him. Devouring him. I grabbed his balls and stroked them gently too. I saw the way his eyes pierced me. His jaw was clenched. Duke Nolan had no control over anything right now. I was the one sitting on the throne here, and it felt good.

I sucked and slid my tongue over his cock until I knew he was about to come. He growled like a wild animal, letting go of me. He threw his head back while his body shuddered, pulling his cock out of my mouth and then he came all over my face. His cum dribbled down my neck, down my shirt. Warm and rich and belonging to him.

I remained on my knees, watching him jerk his cock until he'd emptied his last drop on me. We glared at each other then. I needed him to say the first word because I didn't know what came next. Would he take me into his arms? Nuzzle me? Do what any other loving husband would?

Love...

That wasn't going to happen.

Duke gulped and his shoulders fell. He gave me a hand to help me off my feet.

"You should clean up. I'll clean up in the kitchen," he said curtly. The moment had passed. I licked my lips and nodded.

When I was about to walk away, he stopped me. Just hearing his voice was enough.

"I want you to get some rest, Rose. For the baby."

I went to my bedroom and shut the door behind me. I tried to catch my breath before I went to the bathroom to clean myself. Did this really happen? Would it happen again? Would we ever stop? I knew I couldn't. I couldn't resist him. He had me hooked.

∼

It was complicated, to say the least. Our relationship was unique and every time we had tried to discuss it, we'd failed. So how were we supposed to act around each other now? What were we supposed to say to each other at the office? Were we going to continue to have sex?

These questions whirled in my mind and I couldn't find the answers to them because Duke hadn't helped.

At the apartment, we barely saw each other unless we happened to be in the kitchen or the living room at the same time—which didn't occur frequently. Other than that, it felt like he was avoiding me. Or maybe he just always worked late and at odd hours.

The housekeeper took care of the house and most of the

meals. So basically, I didn't need to lift a finger around the place. At the office, I didn't see him either. Jim barely spoke to me and Monica was my only support.

"Do you have another doctor visit coming up?" she asked me a few days later. We were having our lunch together at the cafeteria.

"Yes, this time I might actually get to see a baby. The last time the scan didn't show anything really. We could hear a heartbeat though. It was amazing."

Monica smiled.

"Is he going with you?"

I shrugged. "He's welcome to if he wants. I've told him about it. I want him to be involved in the baby's life."

"And how are things between the two of you at home?"

I didn't know how to explain it to her so she'd understand. I was worried she'd judge me for how weird the situation was.

"We had sex. It wasn't planned. It just happened."

She put her spoon down and stared at me.

"Is that what you wanted?"

"I always want him."

"I can imagine why," she said with a grin, but I wasn't grinning. It was an actual problem for me.

"But it needs to stop. I mean, it isn't a good thing. Sex only complicates matters." I didn't realize I was toying with the rings on my finger as I spoke. Monica was watching them. Then she sighed and nodded.

"Yeah, I hate to agree, but it does. It stops you from thinking rationally."

"And that is exactly what I need to do right now, for the sake of my baby. I can't keep sleeping with a man who doesn't want me...or at least doesn't want anything more than sex."

"But you're living with him. You're having a child together. You're pretending to be married to each other."

"So you're saying it's a natural thing to do?" I snapped.

Monica shrugged. "I'm saying I'm not surprised. But you're right. You need to make more of an effort to keep your hands off each other."

I gulped guiltily. The truth was if Duke walked into the cafeteria right now and asked me to follow him to his office so he could kiss me, I would do it right away. I would do more.

I cleared my throat. Monica was watching me steadily. Trying to read my mind.

"Hey...you wanna tell me what you're thinking?" she asked finally. I met her eyes. I was so afraid she'd see it there. It was obvious, wasn't it? I was falling for him. The last man in the world I should've been falling for.

"Nothing. I'm okay. I'm alright."

"Rose, you can tell me. I want to help. It's not good for the baby to keep things bottled up like this."

I looked up sharply at her. "I'm doing everything I can to make the right decisions for the baby."

"Yes, I know you are."

"I'm trying my best, Monica."

"You are." Her voice had softened. She was looking at me kindly. I sucked in some air and looked away, trying to get a hold of myself.

"Sorry. I'm sorry. It's all the baby hormones. Making me a little wonky."

She smiled but only sympathetically. On the table, my phone beeped with a new message. I lunged at it, unable to hide my bubble of hope that maybe it was an email from Duke. Maybe he wanted to see me.

But it wasn't. It was a text. From Will. I gulped as I stared at his name flashed across the screen.

"What is it?" I heard Monica ask.

"A text from my ex."

"What does it say? Are you going to open it?"

I didn't know if I wanted to know what Will had to say. I'd managed to push him out of my mind for so long. Even after he came to see me. But curiosity got the better of me.

Rose, can we talk? Please? You weren't at your apartment last night. I need to see you. Please? I just want to talk to you.

I looked up at Monica. It seemed like she was holding her breath in anticipation.

"He wants to see me. He wants to talk," I said.

"What are you going to do? Isn't this the guy who cheated on you?"

I nodded and put down my phone again.

"I don't know what to do. I don't know what the right thing is. I always thought Will doesn't deserve a second chance. But maybe he does deserve a right to explain himself."

"Rose..." Monica was on the brink of saying something but I interrupted her.

"I'm going to get back to my desk. I have a lot of things to get through today. Thanks for listening." I got up and left before she could add anything else. I just needed to be alone right now. I felt claustrophobic and helpless. The baby deserved better. The baby deserved a mother who had a hold on things, and not a blubbering mess like me. The Queen of bad decisions.

26

DUKE

I was peering into a microscope but thinking about Ireland. About Skibbereen. About the calm and peace I'd experienced during my stay there. Would I ever experience it again?

"Doctor Nolan?" It was Laura. Her voice cut through my thoughts and eventually, I pulled my face away from the microscope. How long was I standing there? Trying to work but not getting anywhere.

"Yes?"

"Jim's here. He says he needs to speak to you urgently. He's been waiting for you to finish up in here but I thought I'd come in and check with you."

"You can send him in."

Laura left the lab. She was barely speaking to me these days other than the bare essentials needed to get the job done. I got the sense she'd taken offense to the surprise I'd sprung on her. I was married. To Rose Johnson of all people. In her eyes—a nobody.

I kept my lab coat on but took off my working glasses just as Jim walked in.

"Sorry, Doctor, I didn't want to interrupt anything."

"What is it, Jim?" My patience was running very thin with this man. I wanted to fire him but needed a legitimate reason for it. Or did I?

He stood with his hands clasped to his front.

"I just wanted to clear the air between us."

"You think it needs clearing?"

"It was inappropriate of me to talk about your...umm... wife to you like that. If I had known it was you..."

"You wouldn't have proceeded to insult her?" I snapped.

Jim clenched his jaw. I could see the anger building up on his face, and him trying his best to keep it in check. Maybe he was aware he was walking on very thin ice. Maybe he knew I was just looking for a reason to fire him.

"I wasn't trying to insult her."

"But you did. You made a judgment on Rose's character and ability to perform at this job based on her personal life. What would you call that?"

Jim stared down at his feet.

"I was trying to keep you in the loop. To bring matters of importance to your notice, Doctor Nolan," he said.

"Why would anybody's personal life be a matter of importance to me? I don't need to know about anybody's love life and neither do you."

"I was just..." he tried to say but I raised a hand to stop him.

"You know what? We've had this conversation too often. I don't want any other woman in my company to be subjected to this kind of treatment or judgment from a manager."

"Doctor Nolan..."

"Pack your things. You're fired. You can sue me if you

want for this, but you won't win. There is too much evidence against your behavior."

Jim's mouth was hanging open.

"Tell Laura on your way out so she can get started on the paperwork. Get out of my lab."

Maybe he would've said something else but he didn't. He stood there, quite still, for a few minutes more, and then left. I felt good. This was good. I didn't want Rose to have to see his smug face ever again. Just the thought of him thinking about Rose made me clench my fists.

The thought of any other man thinking about her...

Laura entered the lab just when I thought I would explode.

"You fired Jim?" she asked, a little aghast.

"Yes. Take care of it."

"Doctor..."

"He has misbehaved toward Rose, and who knows how many other women at this company."

Laura stood in front of me with her hands clasped together. She stared disapprovingly at me. My temper was still stretched thin.

"What?" I snapped.

"I just want to make sure this isn't all about your wife. About the people she's had problems with in this office."

"Are you insinuating something here, Laura?" I growled.

She had her chin thrust up and she looked indignantly at me down her sharp nose. I'd known Laura for many years. We worked well together. I liked to believe she knew me well and therefore she had the liberty to talk to me this way. In a way nobody else would dare speak to me.

"Things are changing around here," she replied.

"Yes, I'm a married man now, and soon I will be a father.

I will have a family. Things are going to be different. It's inevitable."

Laura's eyes grew at the news and I realized I'd slipped up again. I'd given Laura the news about the pregnancy without consulting with Rose first. Fuck that.

I couldn't quite tell, but it seemed like Laura was on the verge of a smile. The news of a baby solved everything.

"You're having a baby?"

"Rose is pregnant."

Her hands rose up to her mouth and she tried to contain her excitement. This was the sort of reaction I was hoping for from Diane.

"Congratulations, Doctor Nolan!"

"Thank you, but Rose doesn't want everyone to know just yet, so can we keep this between ourselves?"

Laura nodded, although I wasn't sure she would actually be able to keep her mouth shut.

"So now you know why I feel protective toward her. Toward my family."

She nodded her head vigorously.

"Of course, Doctor, you did the right thing. Jim had to go."

"Good. Okay. Take care of it. I need to get back to work."

Laura was still smiling when she left me. I was alone in the lab again. I was thinking about Rose and what it would feel like if I returned to the apartment and she was waiting there for me. In lingerie. On my bed. Ready to give herself to me.

But that wasn't going to happen. This was all just pretend.

When I returned to the apartment, Rose would be in her room, probably already asleep and I wouldn't see her until the next morning and we'd hardly say a few words to each other.

How did I land up here?

∽

Barry Johnson came to see me the next evening at the office, toward the end of the day. Laura was just on her way out when she came in to tell me he was waiting outside. I told her to send him in.

Barry came into my office and I stood up to greet him. He wasn't just a man I did business with anymore, he was also apparently, my father-in-law.

"I wanted to see you at a time when Rose wouldn't be around."

"She left at five. You're in the clear," I said and we both sat down.

Barry hadn't been in here before. Usually, I met him at the museum when we had a meeting. So he was looking about the place curiously.

"You seem to keep things simple," he said, commenting on my minimal décor.

"I'm a simple man, Barry," I replied. He had a grin on his face and he nodded.

"I thought we should talk, after our strained conversation the previous few times we've met. My wife has made me see the light. She's been able to convince me this is a good thing. Rose is happy. We should all be happy for her."

"I'm glad to hear it," I said.

Barry remained silent for a few moments.

"You know, I'd always pictured Rose's wedding as a fabulous affair. No expense spared. I wanted her to have her dream wedding. God knows she deserves it."

"As far as I know, she didn't want the fuss."

"And you seem to think you know her better than I do?"

"That isn't what I said. We came to a decision together, to have the wedding this way," I insisted.

"At City Hall? With a bunch of strangers as your witnesses? No family or friends around? I don't know why I find it so hard to believe."

This man was smart. He was relentless. It wasn't as easy as I'd thought to convince him. I stared at him, holding his gaze.

"It was unconventional, I'll give you that, but our circumstances were unconventional too."

"We aren't a bunch of prudes here. I'm aware accidents happen. We would've been happy to plan a big wedding for her even if she told us she was pregnant."

I took in a deep breath and shook my head. Things were beginning to get out of hand. I leaned forward on my desk, weaving my fingers together.

"I'm sorry your daughter didn't do what she was supposed to, or live up to your tailor-made expectations of her, but I'd hoped we would be able to convince you we are happy together. We are looking forward to the birth of our child."

There really was no more I could say. It was all a lie, and even though I had a pretty decent poker face—I wasn't sure I could keep lying to this man. All he really wanted was the best for his daughter and I was manipulating him.

Maybe it was time to own up to him. Tell him the truth.

Barry tapped his finger on the desk.

"You're right. We needn't talk about this. If Rose wants something else, she can tell me. She can always come to me. That's how I thought I'd raised her."

Biting words. Barry was a good man who deserved to know the truth.

"Anyway, I didn't originally come here to rub any more salt on open wounds. I came here with the intention of congratulating you. I'm nominating you to the board."

I stood up from the chair, lunging at him with an outstretched hand. This was exactly what I needed to hear. I was relieved now that I hadn't blurted the truth out to him seconds ago.

"Thank you very much, Barry, you will not regret your decision."

"No, I don't think I will. There's just a short approval process involved with the rest of the board but that shouldn't take long. It should be relatively painless too. Nothing to worry about."

"This has been a lifelong dream of mine," I said, pumping his hands tightly.

Barry was standing now too. We smiled at each other.

"I know how much you've wanted this."

"I want to do some good work for the museum. I believe in it strongly."

"We look forward to receiving your contribution and your ideas."

I walked him to the door of my office now. I was beaming and a little giddy with excitement. This was the best news I could've received today.

"I'm glad to keep this in the family."

Family. He truly believed I belonged to the family now. I kept the smile on my face but my eyes were beginning to burn.

"Yeah, family," I commented.

"I'm sorry for taking my time to come around."

"Hey, you're a father. Soon, I'll be one too and I'll experience the feeling first-hand. Nothing and nobody is good enough for our kids," I said. Barry was smiling now. He thumped my shoulder affectionately before leaving.

When he was gone, I returned to my desk. I wanted to give someone the good news. Somebody who would understand. Maybe Diane?

No. She wouldn't get it. Not only was she still mad at me, but she'd also just ridicule me for my science-ey interests. The only person I could think of texting was Rose.

Your dad came to see me just now. He's nominated me to the board.

She must have checked the text immediately because she replied within seconds.

Congratulations, Duke. This is exactly what you wanted.

She was right. This was exactly what I wanted, but there was something else I wanted now which wasn't going to be a reality. A life with her. I was falling for Rose. I couldn't get her out of my mind, but all she was doing was pushing me away.

For now, I had her exactly where I wanted her, but it wouldn't last long.

27

ROSE

Will said he wanted to meet at a bar, so I invited him to the Dutchman so I could easily hop over there from the office. I still wasn't sure why I'd agreed to meet with him. Maybe a part of me felt sorry for him.

I sat at a table in the corner, nursing a cold glass of orange juice that was sweating in my hand. He went to the counter first and brought a beer along with him.

"You look beautiful, Rose," he said as he sat down across from me.

"I'm here now, Will. What do you want to say?"

"It's nice to see you too."

I looked away from him, choosing to stare at a rowdy group of drinkers close to us. I much preferred to stare at them than at him at this point.

"Okay, sorry. Shall we start over? It's great seeing you, Rose. I'm so glad you agreed to see me."

"I was afraid you'd randomly turn up at my apartment again."

"Yeah, sorry about that. I just needed to talk to you. Where have you been?"

"It's none of your business, Will," I snapped. The truth was I didn't actually have a reason to be this mad at him. Whatever happened between us was in the past and I'd moved on a long time ago. But I was taking out my other frustrations on him.

"Okay, fair enough, I don't need to know. I just want us to have a decent conversation like grown-ups."

"About what? What could we possibly have to talk about?" I glared at him challengingly. The more I stared at him now, the more I found it unbelievable that I was ever attracted to him. That I ever thought I could love him and build a life with him.

This was all Duke's fault. He'd ruined me. Now I compared everyone to him and it was unfair. It wasn't like I was going to build a life with him either.

"About anything. Whatever you want to talk about. We used to be friends once, remember? We used to be able to talk to each other." Will searched my eyes. I couldn't keep looking at him because I was on the verge of bursting. Just blurting it all out to him.

When I held my silence and kept my face turned squarely away from him, he stood up. He'd chugged his beer like it was going to disappear. I assumed he wanted to go get another one.

"Another screwdriver?" he asked.

"Excuse me?" I snapped at him.

"Your cocktail. Isn't that what you're drinking? That's what it looks like to me," he said.

I stared at my glass for a moment.

"No, it's just orange juice," I said.

Will had a confused look on his face. "Why?"

I licked my lips and kept my face on the glass. It would be so easy to lie right now. *I have a big day tomorrow and I don't want a hangover...I've given up alcohol because I was never much of a drinker...it's none of his business what I drink.*

Instead, I looked up at him, holding his gaze.

"I can't drink because I'm pregnant," I said.

Will said nothing for several moments. Moments that seemed to stretch like a rubber band. Would he ever say anything? What did he think of me? Was he relieved?

He sat back down in his chair, still keeping his eyes on me like he was afraid I'd disappear.

"Wow. That is insane."

I took a sip of my orange juice. It tasted disgusting for some reason, so I pushed it away.

"Yeah, it kinda is," I said.

"Do you know who the father is?"

"Of course I do!" I snapped.

"Sorry, I didn't want to make any presumptions. Who is he?"

"You don't need to know that. I've told you too much already," I said.

Will gulped and I could sense him tapping his foot on the floor. He always did this when he was agitated, feeling a bit clueless.

"Okay, Rose, you don't need to tell me anything you don't want to say."

"Well, I'm not going to."

"How far along are you?"

"Twelve weeks," I admitted.

"Wow. Okay. This is crazy! You're going to be a mother! This is truly insane."

"Will you stop saying that? I know how *insane* that is. You don't have to keep reminding me!" I was snapping at him, hissing with rage. I felt so helpless and angry because I felt like I was losing control of my life. I was having a baby and falling in love with the father of my child. A man who was using me to get what he wanted. A man I was using too. How messed up was all this? How could I ever explain it to anyone?

Will stood up and came around the table. When he was standing over me, I kept my face turned from him. I felt him place a hand on my shoulder and I shuddered.

"Rose, I'm here if you want to talk to me. No judgment. I really want to help. Talk to me, please." The voice I heard was that of a guy I used to know when I was much younger and more naïve. A boy who I thought was the love of my life. I felt weak now when I looked up into his eyes. He had a concerned expression on his face.

"I'm a mess," I said.

He dropped down in the seat next to mine. His arm was around my shoulder and now I had no choice but to rest my head on him. I needed the comfort. I needed the support and for the first time, Will was actually there for me.

"You have every right to be. You shouldn't have to go through this alone," he said.

I closed my eyes and rested my head there for a while. I wasn't alone. Not technically, but I knew I would feel alone all my life if I didn't have Duke.

～

Will and I were sitting together, barely talking. He said he was happy to just sit beside me for the moral support if I needed it.

I needed it.

I dropped in bits of information to him as and when I felt strong enough to.

"I'm living with him now but it's only a temporary arrangement," I said. He said nothing, just nodded. I could see him trying his best to not make a comment—some judgmental statement. He'd promised not to.

"You can tell me what's on your mind. I'm giving you permission to," I said finally. He clenched his jaw and then sighed.

"It's not my place to say anything, not after everything I've done to you, Rose, but I feel like you're punishing yourself."

"How?"

"By keeping yourself this close to him. I mean, it's great you want the father to be a part of this kid's life and of course he deserves it, but why do you have to live in his home?"

"Because I need the support. Do you know how difficult it is to raise a baby? I wouldn't be able to do it on my own. And the first six months are crucial bonding time in a baby's life. I want my child to bond with its father."

Will took in another deep breath and looked away.

"I just feel like you're complicating matters. I mean, look at you, you admitted it yourself—you're a mess."

"It is not my baby's fault that I don't have a handle on my life."

"Rose, you're going to be a twenty-three-year-old mother. Nobody expects you to have a handle on your life yet."

I stared at Will. When did he wise up? Or was he always like this? He reached for me and tucked a stray curl behind my ear. Maybe I should've stopped him but I didn't.

"It seemed like a good idea at the time. Moving in with him. He said he would take care of everything."

"*Is* it a good idea? You said you're not in a relationship with him, yet you guys are playing house."

"I don't want to burden my family. Mom will tire herself out over this if I move in with them. Lizzie and Oz drain her, Flora tries to help as best as she can. I don't want to add a pregnant daughter to the mix. Daddy will be helpless... besides, they're so happy right now. They think it's the perfect situation."

Will rolled his eyes.

"This way, Rose, you're not honest with anybody. Shouldn't you be honest with this baby?"

"I want to be. I will be. When the time comes. When they are old enough to understand."

We stared at each other for a few moments in silence. I wasn't expecting this from him but Will had truly stepped up. It seemed like he'd grown at least a decade in the last year we were apart. He was like a completely different person now. More like the man I'd always wanted him to be.

When he reached for my hand on my lap, I let him have it.

"I think you should leave."

"Leave?"

"Him. The guy who knocked you up. The loser who isn't willing to commit."

"I haven't given him the choice to commit." Why was I defending Duke? The thought of an actual commitment had probably never entered his mind.

"He shouldn't wait for you to offer it to him. He's having a kid with a beautiful young girl. He should be jumping at the opportunity to build a life with you, Rose. I know I would."

He was holding me firmly now and all I could do was stare at him. There was something comforting about the way he was looking at me. My heart was beating fast. What did I want Will to say? What did I want to hear?

"I'm still willing to do it," he continued.

My brow furrowed. What was he talking about?

"I want to build a life with you, Rose. I always have."

"It's impossible now," I said.

"Why?"

"I'm having another man's baby!"

"And why should that matter? This baby will still belong to you. You are its mother and maybe I can be its father. Maybe we can give it the family we deserve together."

Every other voice and noise in the bar was drowning out while he stared into my eyes. This was unreal. Was he seriously offering what I thought he was?

"Will..." I didn't know what to say.

He took his hand away from my lap and placed it gently on my belly. I let him keep it there. He was smiling now.

"I seriously didn't know what to expect from our date tonight, but I definitely wasn't expecting this," he continued.

"Date?" I tried interrupting him.

"But this is exactly what we need. A fresh start. A chance to have what you always dreamed of having. Remember? We were going to buy our own place. Build a life. We could still have that, Rose."

My throat was dry. Will's hand on my belly was beginning to feel heavy. It felt wrong. I didn't want to hear him say all this to me. It wasn't making sense anymore.

"Tell me you'll think about it, Rose."

I opened my mouth to protest but didn't get a chance to get the words out.

"Get your fuckin' hands off my wife and my baby before I knock your teeth out of your mouth."

Will and I both heard Duke's deep animal growl in front

of us. I looked up and saw his enraged face. The way he was looking at Will looked like he could kill him.

Will swiftly moved his hand away from me.

"Who the fuck are you?" he asked, standing up.

Duke took a step forward, pointing his head toward Will like he was ready to head-butt him.

"I'm the father of her child," he said and Will turned to look at me. I didn't know what to say.

28

DUKE

Whoever this guy was, he had no business touching Rose or the baby growing inside her. He was standing over her like he owned her, like he needed to protect her against me. I wanted to shove him away, but one look in Rose's direction stopped me. If I was violent toward him, I could see Rose would be upset by it.

"And who the fuck are you?" I growled at him.

"Rose and I were together, not too long ago," the guy replied. He glanced at her again and now she was beginning to stand up.

"Okay, the two of you need to calm down," she said.

"Calm down? How am I supposed to be calm right now? This guy was groping you in the middle of a crowded bar!" I raged at her.

"He wasn't groping me, Duke," Rose said.

"I have every right to touch her. Rose would tell me herself if I wasn't allowed," the guy spoke up now. Rose wedged in between the two of us. Maybe she was afraid I would end up hitting him. Maybe I would. I was very close to doing it.

"Try touching her again. Go on. Do it," I barked at him. Challenging him with my eyes. He glared at me but I could see he wouldn't dare touch her now.

"Duke!" Rose placed a hand on my chest. Her touch calmed me. It was like the rest of the world disappeared around us and she sucked me in. I stared into her eyes—her big, blue, pleading eyes. "Please, just calm down. Will is an old friend. He wasn't stepping over any line. He isn't Jim." I watched her speak, her beautiful pink lips moving. I wanted to pull her in and kiss her. I wanted Rose to be in my arms.

"Who is Jim?" this guy asked. Neither of us bothered to reply.

"He shouldn't be feeling you up like that," I said in a lower voice now. Things were starting to make sense in my head again. We had rings on our fingers, but none of this was real. I didn't actually have any claim over her. She wasn't really my wife.

"He wasn't. He was just touching the would-be bump. Lots of people are going to try and do that over the course of this pregnancy. You can't beat up all of them." When she spoke, she was calm. At this moment, it was difficult to tell she was nearly twenty years younger than me. I was the one behaving irrationally, immaturely. I wanted to take her face in my hands and kiss her forehead.

In that instance, I got the same sense of peace I'd gotten in Skibbereen. Serene. Unconfused. I'd never felt like that with anybody before. She had a strange effect on me.

"Duke? Are you listening to me?" she spoke again. I was staring at her and finally, I blinked.

"I'm fine," I said and glanced quickly at the other guy.

"So am I. So is the baby," she said.

I nodded. I ran a hand through my hair. What was happening to me? Why did I react like that?

"I came in here to get a drink but I think I will skip that," I said.

Rose licked her lips, watching me closely still. "I think I'm going to go."

I felt a little embarrassed. I'd behaved like a violent, arrogant bastard who thought he had any right over this beautiful woman. She was strong and independent and knew how to take care of herself. The truth was that she didn't need me at all. I was the one who needed her.

"Okay, yeah, I think that's a good idea," she said. She didn't offer to go home with me. She was going to stay here and talk to her friend. What were they going to talk about? Me? How ridiculous I was? Immature for my age?

I didn't look at her again as I stormed quickly out of the bar. The chaos, noise, and music started to fade behind me and I just kept walking. I was desperate to get out of there. Put some distance between Rose and me. She was like a magnet pulling me back but I had to get away.

Outside in the cool night, I filled my lungs with the air. The fresh air and oxygen in my body had an immediate dizzying effect on me. My car was still parked at the office. I would have to walk back to it so I could drive home. I didn't want to drive home. I wanted to run.

I started jogging through the crowd in the direction of the apartment. I was jogging in my suit. I loosened my tie. Was I losing my mind? Was it Rose? The baby? What was making me act this way? Like I had everything to lose and no means to hold on to it.

It would take me a long time to jog back to my apartment but I had a lot of time on my hands. Nowhere to be.

Rose had her family, she had her friends. I didn't even feel like I had my sister anymore. She hadn't called since she left Chicago, and neither had I. I had my work. I had the money. I had my face splashed on the front cover of scientific journals. But what did that mean?

It made me feel nothing. The only time I truly felt alive was when Rose was with me. When she smiled at me. When I kissed her. When she told me she was having my baby.

∾

I was surprised to find Diane in the lounge when I finally arrived at my apartment building. I wasn't expecting to see anyone, least of all my sister. She got up from the couch when she saw me walk in through the revolving glass doors.

"What happened to you?" she asked. She had one backpack that slid off her shoulder when she stood up. I was out of breath, dripping sweat, and feeling like I was going to spontaneously combust any moment. I was pretty sure I was even hallucinating when I saw her.

"I jogged from the office," I said, touching my hair. It was completely soaked in sweat. I needed a shower. "What are you doing here?"

"I felt terrible about the way we left things the last time. I couldn't stop thinking about it and I knew I needed to see you."

Thankfully, the lounge was empty and nobody could overhear us. I stood in front of my sister, trying to catch my breath. She was watching me closely.

"Are you all right, Duke?" she asked.

I rubbed my temples with my fingers.

"Yeah, I'm fine. I'm just tired. It's been a long day."

"And you jogged here from the office."

"Yeah, there's that too."

"Can we go up to the apartment? I was kinda hoping you wouldn't mind if I crashed here for a few days."

I wanted to ask her what the real reason was for her to show up out of the blue. I knew Diane loved me and cared, but she was also very stubborn and egotistical. She would never be the first one to offer the olive branch at the end of an argument.

"Rose is living with me now," I told her. When I caught her eye, I added, "In the spare bedroom."

Diane nodded and licked her lips. "Cool. That's cool. I can take the couch."

"I'm not sure how wise it would be to have the two of you living under the same roof," I said.

"I'm your sister, Duke. Are you really going to turn me away? What do you want me to do? Go to some motel?" She hooked her hands on her hips and glared at me. I recognized the look on her face. She would soon burst into tears if she didn't get her way. Not much had changed since we were kids.

"You're my sister and she's going to be the mother of my child," I said.

Diane gulped, shaking her head as she looked away from me, like she was in utter disbelief.

"So, it's actually happening to you too. You're going to forget about family, about everything that matters, because of some girl?"

"Rose is pregnant. I have a duty of care toward her, Diane!"

"And what do you think I'm going to do to her? Eat her alive? What kind of a monster do you think I am? Or has she fed you some insane lies about me?"

"She has told me nothing. I still don't know what the two of you argued about."

Diane gave me one long stare and relaxed her shoulders.

"Okay, to tell you the truth, I have nowhere to go. Okay?

When I left your apartment, I spent all my money on hotel rooms and trying to score some new gigs around town."

"You've been in Chicago all this time?"

My sister nodded. Her eyes were beginning to redden. I could expect a loud sob from her any moment now.

"What's going on with you, Diane?" I asked, taking a few steps toward her. I didn't have to do anything more. She collapsed into my arms, hugging me tightly to herself.

"I don't know, Duke. I really don't know what to do with myself. I feel so lost. I'm trying to find my footing here but I just can't. Maybe I'm just too old for all this. I don't know. All I know is I don't want to be alone anymore." She gazed up at me now with her bleary eyes. This was the girl I knew when I was a boy. We'd grown up together. She was my flesh and blood. I knew I couldn't turn her away.

"You can take the couch, as long as you promise to stay out of Rose's hair. I need her to be calm and healthy and comfortable, for the sake of my child."

A smile spread on Diane's face. She was nodding vigorously. "Trust me, you won't even know I'm there!"

"I highly doubt that," I said. Together, we started walking to the elevator. She was back to being in good spirits again. I knew I would talk to her soon about working out the intricacies of her life. She couldn't live with me forever. Not now that I was going to become a father and had new responsibilities on my hands.

"So, the two of you...Rose and you...are you guys, you know? Boinking?" Diane was grinning wide as we entered the elevator.

I gave her one long hard stare.

"Stay out of it, Diane. I've told you this already."

She held up her hands.

"Sorry, just asking. I just want to be clear on the dynamics of your new household."

"There is no dynamic. We're having a baby together. I've invited her to stay with me until the baby is born and things are under control."

Diane breathed in deeply and nodded, like she was totally supportive of me. Then her eyes traveled over me and finally rested on my hand. I realized what she was looking at. Fuck! I should've taken it off.

"No dynamic? Is that so? Then why do you have a wedding ring on your finger?" she asked just as the elevator doors pinged open before us. "You fuckin' married her?"

I heard the accusation in her voice. I stepped out and she followed me.

"Duke!" she called after me as I rushed into the penthouse.

"It's a temporary, fake arrangement, all right? That's all you need to know. Now stop asking any more questions and just leave me the fuck alone."

29

ROSE

"Are you sure you want to return to the apartment to him?" Will asked as we walked out of the Dutchman, a little over two hours after Duke had stormed out of the place.

"I have no reason to be afraid of him, Will," I replied. He shrugged, digging his hands deep into the pockets of his jeans.

"I dunno. He just didn't seem like a guy with things under control." He had a smirk as he spoke. I knew he thought he'd won this round. Duke was pretty volatile back there. I knew he had a temperamental streak in him—I'd noticed that from his behavior with Jim too. But tonight was over the edge. I was sure he would've hit Will if I hadn't intervened and managed to stop him.

"Duke angers easily, but I have nothing to worry about," I said. I knew I was right. We walked a little distance from the bar. I was going to stop a cab, but Will was holding me back.

"Hey, tonight was really great. Despite the interruption."

He proceeded to gently try pulling me into his arms but I resisted. I managed to draw away from him.

"Yeah, it was nice catching up."

"We should do this again sometime," he added.

I stuck a hand out to stop a cab but the streets were busy. Friday night.

"Rose...Rose, come on, don't leave like this." He wasn't touching me but I had no choice but to turn and look at him now. I'd already spent too much time blabbering to him. He pretty much knew everything about my situation now. I couldn't just walk away from him.

"I'm tired, Will. I just want to go home and rest my feet."

"You don't have to go back to his place. You can come back with me. I'll massage your feet, run you a bath if you want. Rose, you know I can take care of you. Better than him." He was pulling me to himself and I didn't resist.

It wasn't the same with him. I didn't feel that fire burning inside me the way I felt it with Duke. However, there was something comforting about Will at the same time. He was familiar. I knew him. I didn't know Duke, not really.

When he was peering down at me, bringing his face closer and closer like he was going to kiss me, I knew it was time to go.

"I'll talk to you later. Thank you for listening to me," I said.

I was grateful that a cab stopped right then in front of me and I got in before he could say anything. I didn't look back when we drove away. I wasn't even sure if I'd ever see him again.

When I returned to the apartment, the one thing I knew was that I didn't want to see Duke tonight. I needed some time to gather my thoughts.

It was nearly midnight and the place was dark when I made my way in. Like most other nights, Duke was going to keep to himself. It was the most sensible thing to do at the moment.

My heels clicked the marble floor as I made my way to the kitchen. I needed a drink of water. It also reminded me that I needed to hang up my heels. My ankles and calves were beginning to swell and hurt in dainty shoes. I needed something more comfortable.

When I walked into the kitchen, I found Diane sitting at the breakfast bar. She was eating a bowl of cereal in the middle of the night. I startled to a stop and she looked up at me with a smile.

"Congratulations are in order," she said.

I felt an immediate rush of anger. This wasn't what I'd signed up for. I didn't agree to live with Diane.

"Thank you," I said in a quiet voice. She was smiling while she watched me fetch a glass of water from the faucet.

"I know you're dying to know what I'm doing here," she said.

"This isn't my home and you're not my sister, so no, I'm not interested in knowing what you're doing here." I didn't really want to stand here chatting with her, but Diane wasn't about to let me escape this easily.

"Maybe not, but you're married to my brother now," she said. I wasn't sure what Duke had told her and I toyed with the rings on my finger. Diane stood up and came closer to me, eyeing the rings.

"That's a pretty big rock. For a fake marriage," she said.

"I think I'm going to go to bed now. I'm tired. I'm sure your brother will fill you in on all the details."

I tried walking past her but she stopped me again.

"Rose, I don't want to fight with you. Especially not if we're going to be living together."

"I'm not going to be living here for long."

"I'm trying to make amends. Give me a break," she said. We stood facing each other now. I didn't know what to say to her. I'd had a pretty rough night already.

"Okay, so what do you want me to say?" I asked.

"That we can try and start over again. Will you try? I'm going to be an auntie soon and I don't want to fight with you."

I stared at her while she spoke. I didn't know whether to believe her. Everything she said I took with a pinch of salt.

"We can start over," I replied.

She smiled.

"Good. Let's talk properly tomorrow. You get your rest now. Duke will kill me if he finds out I kept you up when you should be resting."

She was smiling but I couldn't. I couldn't trust her just yet.

"Goodnight," I said and walked to my room.

∽

I couldn't really sleep that night. I was wide awake by six in the morning, having hardly slept at all. I'd spent most of the night lying on my back, staring up at the ceiling, thinking.

In the morning, I decided I needed to speak to Duke before he left.

The apartment was quiet when I stepped out of my room. Diane was probably still asleep. I tiptoed my way to Duke's room and knocked on his door.

"What?" I heard him snap. I could hear the anger in his voice. Was he still pissed off?

"It's me. Can I come in?" I spoke softly. Moments later, Duke was at the door.

He was wearing a pair of dark navy tailored pants and was shirtless. My instant reaction to that was to gulp. I hadn't forgotten how sexy he was, but seeing his chiseled torso in front of me now made me reel. His waist was narrow, his biceps bulged as he stood before me. He was getting ready to leave.

"I wanted to catch you before you left."

It didn't matter that it was a Saturday, I knew he'd have somewhere to be. He looked freshly shaven now and I got a scent of his rich aftershave. His dark hair was neatly combed back and his face was clear. He looked well-rested enough.

"Come in," he said in a softer voice and stepped aside. "I don't know if you know, but Diane is here. She's sleeping on the couch for a few days. I'm sorry about that."

"I know, I bumped into her last night," I said.

Duke's room was big and well lit. He kept it neat and clean, and there wasn't a stray piece of clothing in sight. It seemed like he'd just stepped out of the shower.

"I would've warned you, but I wasn't expecting her," he said. I watched as he walked over to his closet to pick out a shirt. I'd lost my train of thought. "Did you want something from me?"

"Umm...not exactly, I was just hoping we could talk."

"About last night?"

"Yeah."

Duke threw a shirt over himself and started buttoning up. His naked torso was beginning to disappear and I was disappointed. I had to look away because I was afraid of drooling.

"Do you want me to apologize?"

"Not if you don't mean it."

"I reacted the way I did because I saw a red flag. Who is he?"

I gulped. I'd walked over here with a lot of confidence, hoping to put him in his place and remind him of his actions—but it didn't seem to be working.

"He's my ex. We've known each other for a long time."

"Why did you break up?" Duke asked. He was looking at himself in the mirror now, fixing his tie.

I cleared my throat and tried to keep my head up. "He cheated on me. A lot. I broke up with him when I found out about it."

I caught him glance at me over his shoulder.

"And this is the guy you were entertaining last night? After what he did to you?"

"I don't know what you mean by that, but we were just catching up. Either way, I don't need to justify myself to you."

Duke flipped around to me. His eyes were stony and harsh.

"Then what are you doing in my room at six in the morning, Rose?"

"I was actually hoping you *would* apologize. You reacted way over the top."

"He was touching you. Trying to get close to my baby. I did what I thought was the right thing to do."

"He was being friendly."

"Is that what you would say Jim was doing too?"

"So you're blaming me for the way these men behave around me?" I asked through gritted teeth. Duke clenched his jaw and slowly shook his head.

"If you knew me at all, Rose, you wouldn't think something like that. It isn't the person I am. I thought I was looking out for you."

"I don't need anyone looking out for me."

"For all intents and purposes, you are my wife in public. Another guy touching you like that isn't very convincing for our relationship."

"There wasn't anyone at the bar we know."

He grunted and brushed past me. At the dresser, he started putting his cufflinks on.

"I'm not going to apologize for being protective of my child."

"Will is not a danger to anybody!"

"So you came here to defend your lying cheating ex, is that it?"

I went up to him. Too close to him. He was fully dressed now. I was still in my pajamas. Once again, I was reminded of the world of difference between us. We were never going to be on the same page, were we?

"I came here hoping you would feel sorry for your actions," I snapped. I was about to walk away, but he grabbed my wrist and pulled me back. I fell on his chest, losing balance. When I gasped and looked up at him, Duke was bringing his face down toward me.

I felt a sudden sharp tug between my legs. My mouth parted, anticipating him. Our lips touched and he moved his tongue in, taking possession of my body. I clung to his chest while he kissed me deeply. His arms were tight around me, holding me in place—not that I was going anywhere.

I had my eyes pressed closed. The only thing I could do was sink into this moment. I'd been dreaming of this. My hips thrust into him as I tried to mold myself to him, but as suddenly as he'd kissed me, he was pulling himself away.

The kiss ended. I was out of breath and in shock.

"This is the real reason why you came in here, Rose,

because you know as well as I do that we can't keep our hands off each other."

Duke took a step back from me. Could he see my erect nipples poking through the thin material of my pajama top? To say I was embarrassed would be an understatement. I wanted to melt into him again but he was glaring at me now.

He'd just proven some kind of point.

"I'm going to leave now before I'm late for another meeting because of you. You and Diane, try not to kill each other today."

And just like that, he walked out, leaving me alone in his bedroom. I still felt like I was spinning out of space.

∽

I didn't know what I'd done to drive Duke away. Was it because I'd asked for an apology? Why did he kiss me then? Did he want me? Did he hate me?

That kiss felt like something. Like it *meant* something, but maybe he was just proving a point? Whatever it was, I knew I couldn't hang around in his room forever—even though his big warm bed looked very tempting right now. I would've fallen asleep in it instantly. But I needed to leave before I did something stupid like climb in there. Duke wouldn't appreciate that, I had a feeling.

Something didn't feel right as I returned to my own room. Duke was gone. I'd heard the front door close earlier. Diane was asleep somewhere in the apartment, probably in the den. But there was a sharp pain in my abdomen now that felt very unnatural. I hoped it was just because I felt sick over Duke.

I closed the door shut behind me and got back into bed. I just wanted to curl up and go to sleep. I guessed I was just very exhausted from not sleeping a wink that night. But each time I shut my eye and tried to go to sleep, I felt that pain in my stomach again.

I stroked my belly.

"Hey, baby, you okay in there?" I said aloud. I decided I would have to go and check, so I went to the bathroom.

But then I saw blood. I was bleeding. It was just a few drops, but enough to make me scream like the house was on fire. I panicked. My first thought was that there was something wrong with the baby.

There was a banging on the bathroom door but I couldn't think.

"Rose? What's happening? You okay?"

It sounded like Diane, but I could've been wrong.

I just stood in front of the mirror, pacing back and forth, flapping my arms in the air like I'd touched something hot. That sharp pain shot through me again and I screamed once more.

"Okay, I'm coming in."

It was Diane. She burst through the door. She was still wearing what she wore last night but her makeup was all smudged. She'd clearly just woken up.

"Rose? Are you all right?"

I was doubled over on the floor now, clutching my stomach, tears streaking down my cheeks.

"My baby...I don't know...there was blood."

"Blood? You're bleeding? We need to take you to the hospital."

I had no idea how Diane got me to stand up. She must've forced me to lean on her and guided me out of the bathroom. We were sitting in a cab at one point and I didn't know how. All I saw was a haze. The world was a blur. The shooting pain had stopped. I didn't know if I was bleeding anymore, but it felt like my heart wasn't beating anymore.

Diane helped me out of the cab. She forced my arm around her shoulder so she could lead me into the hospital.

"Help us! Someone help us! She's pregnant. She's bleeding!" Diane was yelling when we'd barely even made it through the door. Somebody in scrubs came rushing to me.

"Are you all right, miss? Do you want to sit down? Sarah, get the wheelchair." The woman was trying to pull me away but I didn't want to let go of Diane. She was holding on to my hand tightly. I looked into her face and saw how deathly pale she looked. She was worried, but then she managed to smile weakly at me.

"Rose, you're going to be okay," she said.

They forced me to sit down in the wheelchair. Then they were wheeling me away somewhere.

"Immediate family only, sorry," the nurse said.

"Diane!" I called out for her in a panicked voice.

"Everything is fine. It's just a false alarm. You'll see," she called after me.

"I want her here. I want her to come with me. Please!" I begged the nurses while they wheeled me away.

"Miss, we need you to calm down. Please? We need to get you examined."

"I want her to come in with me."

Diane shoved her way in through the doors of the examination room with us.

"I'm sorry, you can't be here," one of the nurses said. Diane ignored her and knelt down by my wheelchair and took my hand.

"It's okay. We're related. She's my sister-in-law," she said.

I looked up at the nurse and nodded.

"Yes, she is and I want her here with me."

"What's the problem? Get a doctor to look at her. That is what's important right now," Diane snapped at the woman. I felt her tighten her grasp on my hand and I sucked in my breath.

She knocked her head against mine. "You will be fine, Rose, it's nothing."

"Will you text Duke, please?" I asked.

She nodded and we looked at each other. This wasn't how I pictured this morning to go, but she had no idea how glad I was she'd turned up at the apartment last night. I was lucky she was sleeping on the couch, that she'd heard me scream. I was usually strong and calm, but I didn't know how to handle this situation. I felt completely lost. I wouldn't have been able to do this alone.

Diane typed on her phone and then the doctor entered.

30

DUKE

I sat at the head of a long boardroom table. Someone was making a presentation but I wasn't listening. The only thing I could think about was Rose and our kiss this morning. When I opened my bedroom door and saw her there, I wanted to pull her in and tumble into bed with her. I knew I needed to focus on this presentation. It was about the new drug and it was supposed to be important. Rose and the baby were affecting my work—my life's work. Was this a bad thing?

I felt my phone vibrate on the table. It was turned screen-down so I couldn't see what the notification was. Good. I didn't need any more distractions.

The presentation droned on and I zoned in and out of it like I was in a dream.

If this was the effect Rose had on me already, what was going to happen once the baby got here? How much more was my life going to be turned upside-down?

I'd gotten what I wanted, didn't I? Barry said I was as good as in. Maybe it was time to put some distance between Rose and me? I would give her whatever she needed for the baby, of course, but harboring feelings for her just wasn't an option for me right now.

Not when I still had so many important things to accomplish.

Laura interrupted the meeting by walking in unannounced. I had no idea how much time had passed. I noticed the look on her face—she had something to tell me. It usually meant bad news.

The guy giving the presentation stopped for a moment while Laura came up to me.

"Doctor Nolan, it was your sister on the phone just now."

"Diane? What did she want?" I snapped.

"It's your wife, she's in the hospital," Laura said. She spoke in a whisper but it was loud enough for me to know I had to get out of here.

∽

Diane had tried to get in touch with me a few times apparently, but I'd ignored the notifications on my phone all morning. So by the time I got to the hospital, Rose had been there for over an hour already.

I was running down the corridors in search of the examination room. My mind was spinning and I couldn't seem to find my way. Eventually, a helpful nurse pointed me in the right direction and I burst in through the doors.

Rose was lying on her back on a hospital bed. There were two other people in the room. Diane—who was holding Rose's hand. The other was a woman operating a machine for the ultrasound. Rose's belly was exposed and our baby was on the black and white screen beside her.

All three of them looked up at me and I could see tears in Rose's eyes.

"Are you okay? Is the baby okay?" I asked.

A soft smile spread on the doctor's face.

"She's fine. The baby is fine too. There is nothing to worry about, a little bit of bleeding isn't cause for concern in this case. We examined her thoroughly."

Diane slipped away and I took her place beside Rose.

"That's our baby," she said and we turned to look at the screen together. I could just about make out a head and ten fingers. The baby was moving, kicking its tiny feet as it floated about in dreamland.

"The baby is okay?" I asked again. Rose nodded. "I'm sorry. I was in a meeting. I didn't check my phone. I should have been here sooner."

"Diane was here with me. I wasn't alone, and it was nothing —I just panicked unnecessarily," she said in a soft voice.

"Nothing is unnecessary. You did good to come and get checked out. It could have been something more serious, but it's not," the doctor spoke again.

I looked up at Diane who was standing by the door now, arms crossed over her chest, head leaning on the wall. She looked relieved. I was glad she was here. This was the sister I knew and loved. The sister I could always rely on.

I was also glad Rose got to see a slice of that today.

"I'm really okay. You don't have to be here. You can go back to your meeting if you need to," Rose said.

"I can take her home," Diane suggested.

The doctor was printing pictures out of the ultrasound machine and she handed them to me. I stared at the image of my child. In black and white, but as clear as it would ever be. This was all too real and I didn't know how to feel.

Emotional? Worried? Afraid?

Rose reached for them and I handed the photos to her.

"Isn't it amazing? There's a human being growing inside me," she said.

"It is absolutely amazing and you're doing a tremendous job," Diane replied. I didn't know why I couldn't say anything.

Rose and Diane smiled at each other like they'd been best friends all along.

"I think I will go back to my meeting, if everything is fine here," I said and straightened up. Rose nodded but she looked away from me. Did she want me to stay? It was so hard to read her. "Can I talk to you, Diane?" I added.

I thanked the doctor and walked out of the room, followed by my sister. When the door closed, she turned to me.

"Are you seriously going to leave her right now? After the morning she just had?"

"What? Isn't that what she wants? You said you'd take her back," I said, confused.

Diane rolled her eyes.

"For one of the smartest men on this planet, you can be a pretty big idiot sometimes," she said, shaking her head like I was a complete moron. I had no idea what I was supposed to do next.

∽

On Diane's command, I took Rose back to the apartment. My sister said she had some stuff to do around the city and would be back later. I was pretty sure she was just trying to give us some time to ourselves.

Every time I offered Rose my arm to lean on or a hand

for support, she turned me down. Apparently, she could take care of herself perfectly fine. I didn't argue with her. She was the one carrying the baby.

In the apartment, I helped her get comfortable on the couch.

"I'm going to make you some soup," I suggested. I couldn't think of what else I could do to help her.

"Really, I'm fine, I just had a false scare. You can go back to the office," she protested.

"The meeting wasn't important. I wasn't paying attention anyway," I said.

In the kitchen, I spent over half an hour preparing an elaborate cream and pea soup. I served it up with some rustic bread and butter. When I brought the tray over to Rose, she looked like she'd dozed off. I was about to leave the food on the coffee table in front of her and go, but she woke up.

"You must be hungry," I said, holding the soup bowl out toward her as she sat up on the couch.

"I'm actually starving, thanks. This smells really good. You didn't have to go to the trouble of making this. I'm sure there was something in the fridge I could've made do with."

"You need something fresh and healthy."

I pulled up a chair close to her as she started eating. There was silence between us. A lot had happened in the span of just one morning. Eventually, Rose looked up and broke the ice.

"Diane made you bring me back, didn't she?"

"I wasn't sure what was appropriate. You seemed like you wanted to be left alone."

"We're only fake married, remember? You don't have to go out of your way to help me."

"This isn't out of the way. You're carrying my child. This is the least I can do."

Rose brushed her curls away from her face. She was still in her pajamas, and just like this morning when I kissed her, I couldn't help but admire her simple beauty. Those flushed red cheeks and deliciously pink lips.

"I hate to think that you're doing all this because we made a deal."

"I'm doing this because it's the right thing to do."

"That's very noble of you," she said.

"I wasn't looking for compliments."

She put down the bowl of soup on the coffee table and met my eyes.

"Duke, about this morning…"

"We don't need to talk about it. You have to rest."

"No! I want to say something. I need to get it out of my system."

I waited for her to continue. There was a renewed fire in her eyes and I knew I wouldn't be able to stop her from saying what she wanted to say. I didn't want to hear it. It all felt way too complicated to me.

"I shouldn't have barged into your room like that, early in the morning, looking for an apology." She gulped and I said nothing. Where was she going with this? "And you shouldn't have kissed me."

We stared at each other in silence for a few moments.

"Well? Aren't you going to say something?" she asked.

I clenched my jaw tightly. "What do you want me to say, Rose? I told you already, I'm not going to apologize. I did what I thought was right. From where I was standing, it seemed like that guy was getting too cozy with you. You said it yourself, he is a lying, cheating bastard."

"But he is a friend of mine and he didn't deserve that reaction from you."

I stood up from my chair.

"Look, Rose, I don't want to get you worked up...with the baby and all, but I honestly don't know what you want from me."

"I want to set some ground rules, I guess. We should've done it a long time ago."

"Okay, what kind of rules?"

"We need to stay out of each other's personal lives. This is a fake marriage of convenience. We're having a baby together. Once it's born, we can move on with our lives. We can figure out a way to efficiently co-parent, but that's it."

"You're telling me to back off?" I asked. I had my fists clenched by my sides. Rose looked up at me with her lips parted—the most beautiful woman I had ever seen.

"I'm telling you to give me some space. If I need your help, I'll ask for it. In return, I won't show up at your door at odd hours of the day. I don't want us to complicate matters anymore."

"By kissing or ripping our clothes off each other, you mean?"

She paused for a moment and then nodded.

"Yes, because that would just mess up everything. Our working relationship."

"So, I'm supposed to act like a husband and be the model father with no other benefits in return?" I grinned as I spoke but only because I had an anger building inside me. She was ordering me to keep my hands off her and I didn't know if that was possible. But of course, I would do it.

"That is a ridiculous thing to say..." She was beginning to protest but I'd heard enough.

"Hope you feel better soon. I'll leave Diane's number in

the kitchen. If you need anything, you can call her. I have to go back to the office."

She clamped her mouth shut again and I stormed to the door. Then I stopped and turned to her.

"Oh, and I got a visit from your dad. I'm on the board at the museum. So, thanks for that. Looks like I don't need you anymore."

31

ROSE

Duke said it himself, he didn't need me anymore. After he left, I remained sitting on the couch, trying to eat some more of the soup, but he'd left a bitter taste in my mouth. I couldn't eat it. All I wanted to do was bury my face in the couch and cry.

I told myself it was just the pregnancy hormones, but the truth was that it hurt me to hear Duke say those words. He got what he wanted from me, and what did I get?

A chance to get close to him. A chance to spend more time with him, thereby falling for him even harder.

Feeling useless and helpless, I did the only thing I thought would help. I texted Will and decided to meet him at a café nearby.

He was waiting for me when I got there, smiling wide and looking way less complicated than Duke did. He stood up when I approached him and touched my arm gently.

"You have no idea how happy I was to get that text from you. I really hoped we'd be seeing each other soon," he said.

"I...I had kind of a scare this morning. With the baby. I had to go to the hospital."

"Are you okay now?" he asked, looking concerned. I nodded and he reached a hand over the table to hold mine.

"I wish I could've been there for you, Rose," he said.

A part of me wished he was there too. Maybe I would've felt better to have him there instead of Duke. How had Duke helped? He only made me feel unwanted.

"The next time something like that happens, you call me all right? Was anyone there to take you to the hospital?"

"Yeah, Duke's sister."

"And what about him? Where was he?"

"At a meeting. He came by later."

"On a Saturday?"

"He's a busy man."

"Maybe you should stop making excuses for him, Rose. He's going to be the father of your child," Will said.

I gulped as I stared at him. I knew he was right. Since the first moment I met Duke, all I did was make excuses for his behavior. I always gave him the benefit of the doubt. And look where that landed me!

Will was smiling again.

"Anyway, everything is okay now and you can start thinking about what I said before."

I looked at him quizzically, and he continued.

"About giving me a chance to look after you."

"I don't need..."

"Looking after, I know. But you know what I mean. Give me a chance to rebuild the life we'd dreamed about. With this baby. This is exactly what we always wanted, right? To have a family of our own."

I couldn't believe this was actually happening. That I was actually entertaining this bizarre idea. Will wanted to raise another man's baby with me. What would that look like?

"You don't have to decide right away. Don't worry. I'm not going to pressure you into doing something rash. Take your time. You still have a few months before the baby comes."

"Raising a child is not an easy task, Will. I don't think you realize the kind of responsibility you're asking to take on."

He brushed his hair and grinned handsomely. "You're right, I don't know the first thing about babies—but you do, and I'll be there to help you. I want to be there for you, Rose." He reached for my hand again.

Was this why I'd texted him? Was this why I wanted to see him?

Because a part of me wanted to give this plan a shot? As crazy as it sounded.

I gently tugged my hand away from his and sat back in my chair.

"There are a lot of things I need to sort out first," I said.

"Of course, like I said, take your time. I'm not going anywhere. In fact, I have another surprise for you."

"A surprise?"

"I'm putting down the deposit on a house. Well, an apartment, if I'm being honest. It's in Wheaton, really nice neighborhood for a kid to grow up in. Gated community, safe..."

I couldn't believe what I was hearing. I never expected Will to suddenly turn into this ultra-responsible person.

"How..."

"After you left me, the only thing I wanted to do was work hard at my job and save up so I could try and give you the life you always wanted."

My heart thudded in my chest.

"I wanted to show you I can be the man you expected me to be. The man you thought I was. Of course, I never planned on starting off with a baby, but this is going to be great. This baby will bring us closer together. You'll see."

I stood up from the chair with a jerk. I felt like my thoughts were all over the place.

"Will, I need some time to think. To straighten things out. This is all very overwhelming for me." I was making to go. He stood up too.

"I'm not going anywhere, Rose. You'll see this time. I'll be right here, waiting for you."

He was smiling at me and I had no choice but to smile at him weakly too.

"I'll call you."

"With good news, I hope?"

A part of my mind was beginning to convince the rest of me that this was an excellent idea. That this was just what I needed to move on with my life. Forget about Duke who didn't need me anymore. To raise my baby comfortably.

"I hope so too, Will," I said and walked away from him. Thankfully, he didn't follow me out or he would've noticed the deathly pallor of my skin. The look of panic and confusion on my face. Could I really start afresh with Will? Was it always my destiny to be with him? Maybe it was.

∼

I met Monica at a burrito truck she'd suggested. She'd already ordered two of them for us when I got there.

"You realize you're starting to show a little, right?" she said with a smile, glancing at my belly. We hugged before we sat down, but I was too flustered to remain calm.

"I'm so sorry for springing on you on a Saturday, I just didn't know who else to call. My close friends are all busy and I didn't want to trouble them with…"

"Hey, Rose, it's okay. I wasn't doing anything important. Do you want to tell me what's going on? Are you okay?"

I took in a deep breath and then blurted everything. What happened last night with Will and Duke, Will's plan, our history, Diane being at the apartment, our trip to the hospital, and then what Duke told me before he left.

"Wow! You've had an eventful twelve hours. All I did was eat a pint of ice cream by myself and watched *Sex and the City* reruns."

Monica was smiling and I couldn't help but smile at that too. I sighed aloud and she tipped her head to the side sympathetically.

"Well, first of all, I'm glad you texted me. I'm glad you didn't spend any more time talking to Will or entertaining his grand ideas."

"He's only trying to help," I said. What was it with people beating up poor Will? Was it only me who saw him in a different light? Maybe it was because they didn't actually know him.

Monica rolled her eyes.

"He's trying to help by enticing you to move in with him so you can go back to doing what you always did—take care of him while he's living his best life."

I stared down at my lap. "He's changed. He really has. He's even buying an apartment. He never would've saved up enough for that before. Not without me pushing him."

"That's the thing, he realizes he needs you in his life. After you dumped his ass, he saw what he was missing. Of course, he'll do whatever it takes and say whatever he needs to. You're a wonderful, beautiful woman, Rose."

Monica's eyes had softened and she was leaning toward me, making sure she held my gaze. She spoke firmly, like she wanted to make sure I had no doubt in my mind about the truth in what she was saying.

"Any man would be lucky to have you, and Will knows that. He was a cheater and probably still is. He lost you through his own mistakes. It wasn't just one mistake, Rose, he cheated on you repeatedly."

"I know that! But it's in the past. People deserve second chances, don't they?" I snapped.

She sat back in her chair.

"Sure they do, if they come clean themselves, if they acknowledge their mistakes. But he didn't. He kept you in the dark for years, let you believe you had a healthy relationship. If you didn't find out about him when you did, he would never have owned up. He would've let you continue to live a lie."

I glared at Monica, wondering where she was going with this. Was she seriously taking Duke's side on this? I shook my head.

"And you think the alternative is better? You think Duke's behavior is excusable?"

"I'm not trying to excuse Duke's behavior or actions, but the one thing about him is he's honest. He has been from the beginning, right? At least with him, you know where you're standing."

"Yeah, alone, on the edge of a cliff," I said, rolling my eyes.

Monica grinned.

"Maybe that's what it feels like, but wouldn't you rather know the truth?"

"That he wants to have nothing to do with me. He got what he needed from me. Yeah, sure, I know the truth."

"But you told him you wanted him to stay away from you."

"That isn't exactly what I said. I tried to make him see we couldn't get...intimate...without complicating things between us."

"That sounds a lot like rejection to me, Rose," she stated.

Monica and I peered into each other's eyes. I was trying hard to find fault in what she was saying. She had to be wrong! But she knew she wasn't, so she started smiling.

"It's obviously his defense mechanism. You rejected him, pushed him away—so he snapped back at you. Don't you see that?" she continued.

I had my lips pursed together, my chin held up in pride.

"He meant what he said. I could see it in his eyes," I said.

"You're being stubborn and so is he. The two of you are quite similar to each other in a lot of respects."

I looked away from her, shaking my head.

"I would rather be with someone who wants to be with me, no matter what they did in the past."

"But Will is capable of hurting you again. How do you know for sure he's changed?"

"And Duke is hurting me *now*!" I hissed.

I hadn't touched my burrito. In fact, I'd barely eaten anything since the morning. I had no appetite. When I started standing up to leave, Monica stood up too.

"Rose, I'm sorry, I didn't mean to upset you. Why don't you eat something? Let's talk some more?"

"Thanks for your help, Monica, really...I'm sorry for snapping at you...but I think I just want to rest." I softened my voice. I didn't want to make her feel like her help wasn't appreciated, but this wasn't what I wanted to hear.

I wished someone could just tell me definitively what to do. I wasn't capable of making logical decisions anymore because my heart wanted something else...for Duke to want me the way Will did. But that was impossible. We didn't have the same history or even a relationship.

I rushed away from the food truck and I knew Monica was staring after me, worrying. But I was wrong in meeting up with her and Will today, hoping to find some answers from them. The only person who could make this decision was me.

32

DUKE

"Don't worry, she's asleep," Diane said when she found me tiptoeing around the kitchen that night. I said nothing and just poured myself some milk in a glass and picked out a cookie from the jar on the counter. Diane was working on her laptop and she shook her head.

"What?" She'd tempted me to snap at her.

"You're like such a child in so many ways, Duke. It's ridiculous," she said.

"A child? Me? Are you kidding me? Look who's talking."

Diane sighed. "I don't know what you said to her, but you were supposed to comfort her and make her feel safe when you brought her back from the hospital. You do realize that, don't you? Instead, the two of you are walking on eggshells around each other now."

I dipped my cookie in the milk and took a bite.

"We had a mature adult conversation and came to the conclusion that things are too complicated between us to play happy families. We need to keep our distance from each other, that's all."

Diane cocked her head to the side.

"Is that what she said or you?"

"Does it matter, Diane? How long are you staying this time?" I snapped.

She closed her laptop and glared at me.

"I could leave tomorrow, I have a new gig lined up in LA, but I think I'll stick around. For Rose's sake. She could use the extra help around here."

"Since when did the two of you become best friends?" Even though I was trying my best to show I didn't care, there was a part of me that was pleased they were finally getting along.

"Since I realized I actually care what happens to my little nephew or niece."

I nodded. "Well, you can stay here as long as you want, sis, but just keep out of my way."

"Are those the exact words you used with Rose too?" she asked with a smirk. "No wonder she's so happy to be here."

"I'm going to bed. I don't need to explain myself to you," I snapped. Diane rolled her eyes and I walked away from her, carrying my glass of milk with me.

Things were too complicated as it was, without my sister breathing down my neck too. I was supposed to go directly back to my bedroom, but instead, I meandered over to Rose's room. She had a way of always drawing me to her. Surprisingly, I found her bedroom door slightly ajar.

I stopped in my tracks because I caught sight of her lying in bed.

She was right on the edge, turned to her side to face me. She was asleep and her eyelids fluttered. Even from the distance, I could see the shape of her face and body. Her shoulders gently rose and fell under the covers as she slept. The table lamp beside her was left on and her golden curls glowed under the bright light of it.

There was something so angelic about the way she slept. So peaceful. While my baby grew inside her, safe and warm.

I felt an intense wave of emotion rush over me. My instinct was to rush to her, throw my arm over her, protect her…to let her sleep as long as she wished.

But that wasn't what *she* wanted.

She told me to stay away from her. That I shouldn't kiss her anymore. It was going to be difficult with her living in the same home as me. Maybe it was time for her to move out? Maybe I could buy a separate apartment for her and the baby? But she wouldn't agree to it.

Rose had her pride. I knew that much about her.

A hand fell out from under the covers then and I noticed the diamond ring glittering on her finger. There was something reassuring about the fact that she was still wearing the rings I'd given her.

The marriage was fake but there was nothing fake about those rings. It was what she deserved. Did she know that? She deserved to have a happy family with a man who could give her what she wanted. This child deserved to grow up in a happy home too.

Maybe she was right. This situation was too messy. I never should have suggested it and complicated things between us.

Rose stirred softly as she slept. I drew closer to the door. I could have stood there staring at her forever. But then her eyelids fluttered again and before I could move away, she was opening her eyes. She was facing me directly and our eyes met.

She looked a little surprised at first, but then her gaze relaxed. She just continued to lie there in her bed, staring at me while I stared back at her through the gap in the door. A few moments passed and then she started to sit up in bed. It seemed like she was about to say something.

I turned away from her and I heard her say my name softly, like it was choking her throat. Maybe I just imagined it.

She shouldn't have caught me staring. What did she think of me now? That I creeped on her when she slept every night?

I went to my room and shut the door behind me firmly. I was half expecting her to knock moments later. I *wanted* her to knock on it. But there was complete silence in the apartment. Not even Diane made a sound.

I forgot about the glass of milk. I changed and brushed and got into bed, even though I knew sleep wouldn't come easily to me tonight. I was going to spend the rest of the night dreaming about Rose and how different my life would look if she was in love with me too.

33

ROSE

Two months later

I was five months pregnant and now when I looked at myself in the mirror, I didn't seem to recognize this person anymore.

My belly was rounding up, protruding through the dresses I wore to flaunt my bump. I was proud of it. Proud of the way my body was nourishing and growing a child. I loved the way women looked at me admiringly on the streets, the gaze of respect in men's eyes when they saw my belly. I was going to become a mother and I'd never felt more beautiful before.

At the apartment, we had managed to fall into a working relationship too. Thank God for Diane! I didn't know what I would have done without her. She went above and beyond the call of duty to make me feel comfortable and forget about the awkwardness that still existed between Duke and me.

We rarely saw each other at the office and hardly ever bumped into each other in the apartment. I wasn't the one trying to avoid him, so it had to have been him trying his best to stay out of my way.

Diane was the one who kept me company, sometimes picked me up from work to go grab dinner together. She was the one I went shopping with and bought stuff for the nursery. She kept insisting her brother wanted this baby to have everything, while all I wished for was that Duke would make his presence felt a little more.

I couldn't help but think about what Monica had said—over and over again. Did I reject him? Was I too harsh with him after that kiss? Maybe he was doing what he believed was the right thing to do. Maybe this was all my fault?

On the other hand—I'd been avoiding all of Will's phone calls and texts for two months now. I told him I needed time to think and that was exactly what I was trying to do.

Today after work, I found Diane in the lobby of the office building again. She was smiling, standing there in her cowboy boots and her red hair flying everywhere. If she wasn't Duke's sister, someone would have politely asked her to leave the premises by now. Diane didn't exactly fit in with the uptight corporate scene of this place.

"I thought we could go check out that Thai place I was telling you about?" She hurried over to me, threading her arm around mine.

"That's a lovely idea, but Diane, seriously, you don't have to keep me company all the time. I'm sure you have your own stuff to do."

"What could I possibly have to do here? This isn't my town. I hardly know anyone here, besides, I *want* to hang out with you."

We were smiling at each other as we walked out of the building. The Thai place wasn't too far away so we were going to walk there. These days, I was starting to walk slower. I could feel my hips swinging in full force with every step I took. This pregnancy was changing my body.

"So how was dinner with the folks last night?" she asked as we made our way together.

"Good. Really good. They're all very excited about the baby, you know?"

"And Duke? Don't they wonder why you keep turning up for family dinners without the precious husband?" She had an eyebrow raised as she spoke. I tried not to meet her eyes.

"They know he's a busy man, and they don't ask too many questions."

Diane sighed.

"The two of you need to talk. How long are you going to keep avoiding each other? It's been a shit lotta time already. Pretty soon, the baby is going to be here and…"

"I'm a guest in his home. I don't want to make things awkward for him in his own home."

"You're going to be the mother of his child, Rose, it doesn't matter whose apartment it is."

"Why are we discussing this right now? Can't we just forget about it? Enjoy our dinner?" I snapped.

We were standing at the doors of the Thai place now and Diane had a pleading look in her eyes. I knew instantly that she'd done something she wasn't supposed to.

"What? Spit it out. What did you do?" I hissed at her. She reached for my shoulders, squeezing them affectionately.

"I'm sorry, sweetie, I just feel like you two should talk. Outside the apartment. It's been so strained for so long, it's driving me nuts!"

"What?"

"Diane?"

It was Duke's voice. I heard it loud and clear behind me and I whipped around to find him standing there with his hands deep in the pockets of his thick dark coat.

His green eyes were narrowed, his jaw clenched. We hadn't run into each other in several days and now he looked me up and down. I noticed the way his gaze settled on my belly for a few moments and his face immediately softened.

"I'm sorry, this is all my fault. You guys need to talk. The food is great in there and the vibe is really good...it'll be fine. Trust me. Just talk." Diane was pushing us both in through the doors. Neither of us struggled much against her because that would be childish.

I looked at her over my shoulder and she gave me a wink.

"Now, be gentle with each other," she said quickly and then she was gone.

"Table for two?" A hostess showed up, smiling and offering us menus. I glanced at Duke, half-expecting him to storm out of the restaurant immediately. Refusing to entertain Diane's devious plan. But he scowled at the hostess and nodded. We were going to have dinner together. In public. For the first time.

I followed them to our table and silently sat down. Duke ordered a drink for himself and I dared not meet his eyes. What were we going to talk about? I didn't know what to say to him. I wasn't prepared for this.

After the woman was gone, he turned to me again, fixing his cold hard stare on me in silence.

It looked like neither of us were about to make the first move.

"How are you, Rose?" he finally asked. I looked up at him and found him staring at me. The same way he did that night when I woke up to find him at my door.

"The baby is doing great. I'll find out the gender at my next appointment in a few weeks."

"I would like to be there for that, if it's okay with you."

"If that's what you want, you're welcome to come with me. Diane said she'd be there."

"I'm glad to see my sister and you getting along now."

"Yeah, we had some teething troubles at the start, but we're doing well now."

I toyed with the glass of water on the table. I couldn't look away from him. Once again, I was mesmerized by him. Maybe because I hadn't seen him in some time. But I'd dreamed about his handsome face often. I saw him in my sleep. I pictured us kissing every time my mind drifted. The truth was I couldn't get Duke out of my head, no matter how seldom I saw him. He wasn't like Will. I couldn't just forget about him with a click of my fingers.

"You said the baby's doing good, but how are *you* doing, Rose?"

"I didn't think you cared."

"You told me to stay away from you."

"I was trying to make things simpler for us."

"Things are never going to be simple between us."

"But every time you kissed me, or touched me...or things got heated up between us...it just confused me." I was blubbering. Maybe I sounded like a complete fool now. I could barely look at him. I knew my cheeks were flushed.

"I didn't mean to confuse you, Rose. I don't want to hurt you."

Duke was speaking in a low, deep hum. It was soft and

gentle. I'd never heard him speaking like this before. My heart seemed to soar.

"You've never hurt me. If anything, I've hurt myself with all the stupid decisions I keep making," I said.

We were looking at each other in silence when a waitress showed up to take our orders. Duke ordered Pad Thais for us without looking at the menu. He just wanted the woman gone.

"Yeah, I guess we made some rash decisions," he continued once she left. I watched as he weaved a big, strong hand through his dark hair. Did he have more gray hair now? Or was I just imagining it? "And now we're having a baby and I feel grateful for that. I don't know how you're feeling, but I'm looking forward to meeting this person."

I couldn't help but smile. I felt a little relieved. I was worried he resented me now, but it seemed like he didn't.

"I am excited too. I can't wait. I can feel the little kicks and flutters these days and it's amazing."

Duke took a sip of his drink and smiled.

"Good. I'm glad to hear you're in good spirits. And I just want you to be rest assured that I won't be pouncing on any of your friends again."

I gulped. I felt a little guilty because of the things Will had said.

"I haven't seen him in two months," I said.

"It doesn't matter. You can see him as often as you like. It's your personal life and I'm going to stay out of it."

My heart sank again. What was he trying to tell me? That he would be okay if I got together with Will? That he wanted me to move on with my life and have a relationship? I stiffened up immediately but he didn't seem to notice.

"I went to my first meeting with the museum board. I don't know if your dad told you," he continued.

I nodded because Daddy had. I tried to smile at him. I could see the genuine delight on Duke's face now. He cared more about the museum and the board than he did about me. I could tell from the level of excitement in his manner.

"The whole thing has been a dream come true. I can work toward taking the museum to greater heights, reaching its potential and all that. I couldn't have done it without you, Rose."

"You mean you couldn't have done it without fake-marrying me? Because I haven't really done anything else." Could he sense the sour tone in my voice now?

Duke grinned.

"Something like that, but I'm happy things worked out for the best."

Best for whom? I wanted to ask. Just when I saw a flicker of hope for us, it was gone again. Duke had shown his true colors.

Our food arrived in that instance and he started eating immediately. My appetite was gone. I had that sinking feeling in my stomach—the realization struck me that things would never work out between us. I was a fool for holding on to that hope every day. What was I even doing living with him? I gained nothing from him, except be in his way.

"I think I should move out," I said.

Duke looked up at me, his chopsticks half suspended in the air.

"Excuse me?"

"You got into the board. That was the whole reason we were doing this, right? It's done now. Like you said, you don't need me anymore. I think it's time I move out."

Duke put the chopsticks down and dabbed the corners of his handsome mouth with a napkin. His face was darkening again. That smile disappeared, and his mood was changing.

"I'm not going to fight you on this, Rose, neither am I going to hold you prisoner. The door is open. You can walk out any time you want."

∽

"You what?" Diane followed me around the room as I tried to hurriedly pack things in my bags.

"You heard what I said. I'm leaving."

"But, Rose, you can't. This dinner tonight was supposed to make amends, not dig a deeper hole."

"A deeper hole in what? Our relationship? Wake up, Diane, It doesn't exist!"

I had my back turned to her while I tried to zip up the bags. They were stuffed with clothes now and I couldn't manage. Diane came over and gently nudged me aside.

"Here, let me do it."

I stood with my hands on my hips, huffing and puffing as I watched her start folding the clothes neatly and arranging them more evenly in the bags. She shook her head.

"This wasn't supposed to be how it worked out. You were supposed to talk and make peace."

"Nothing is going to change, Diane," I said.

"You're moving out! Everything is changing."

"It'll finally give all of us a chance to move on, start making space in our lives for this new baby...separately."

"And where will you live? With your parents?"

"I can't tell them yet. They think we're happily married. Newlyweds. I can't do this to them right now."

Slowly, she zipped up the bags and turned to me. Her eyes looked watery. Was she going to cry? I licked my lips, trying to rein in my emotions. She came up to me and gave me a hug.

"My brother is a pig-headed stubborn bastard. That's what he is."

"I didn't give him much of a choice. This is what I want too."

She was peering into my eyes like she didn't believe me for a moment.

"Where are you going to go, sweetie? Let me come with you. We can get a place together. Make Duke pay for it?" she suggested with a smile.

"My friend Monica offered me a room in her apartment, so did my friend Karen, but I don't want to impose on her and her new family. So I'll stay with Monica for now, 'til I find my own place."

Diane nodded. "Don't you for one second think of not letting Duke pay for stuff for the baby. It's not charity. It's his duty as the father. You hear me?"

I smiled weakly, but I wasn't so sure of it. I didn't know yet the extent to which I wanted Duke involved in our lives from here on.

"Is this about Will? About his offer?" she asked. I'd told Diane about him when we started talking to each other more openly. This baby brought us closer. I was happy to see she didn't judge me, not even for the sake of her own brother.

"No. I haven't seen or spoken to him in two months. You know that," I said.

"My brother is an idiot!"

"Your brother is a successful rich man who gets what he wants," I said.

She rolled her eyes. "You're right. What more can we expect from him?"

Diane asked me to wait just fifteen minutes so she could get ready. She made me promise to let her help me move into Monica's place that night. While I waited in the living room with my bags, Duke walked in. He looked surprised to see my bags at first, like he'd forgotten our conversation just a few hours ago.

"You're leaving tonight?" he asked.

"I don't want to delay it."

"Where are you going?"

"To my friend Monica's place."

"Monica from the office?" he asked and I nodded.

Duke took in a deep breath, his shoulders squared and he remained by the door. He was a tall and foreboding presence. I was attracted to him. I may have been in love with him. I wasn't sure anymore. Or rather, I didn't want to admit it to myself.

I just wanted to leave so I could be in control of myself again.

"Things turned out pretty messy for us, didn't they?" Duke said. He was watching me intently from under his sheepish eyelids. His eyes green were glittering bright.

"We shouldn't have done this. It was a stupid idea."

"You think so?" he asked.

I proceeded to remove the rings from my finger. "Don't think I need these anymore."

"What about your parents?"

"It doesn't matter what they think. It's not like they can kick you out of the board now. It's done. Either way, Daddy is going to retire in a few months. You won't have to deal with him for much longer."

Duke took a few steps toward me. I thought he was

coming forward to kiss me. A fire burned in the pit of my stomach. I wanted him to hold me. To kiss me—even though I'd categorically told him not to.

But he stopped just a few paces before me.

"I don't care how bitter things turn between us, Rose, I will always make the right decision for the sake of our child. I will always do what is best for him or her."

When I looked into his eyes then, I knew I believed him. This man loved our baby, even though he might not have known exactly how to show it.

"Rose?" Diane was at the door now. We both turned to look at her. She rolled her eyes at Duke. I had a feeling she was going to give him a piece of her mind later. For now, she was focused on me.

"There's a cab waiting for us, let's go."

I didn't look at Duke again as I walked out with Diane. I didn't want to know if I'd see regret in his eyes or not. Did he even care? Was he relieved I was leaving? Now he'd have his apartment back. His life back.

Diane kept an arm firmly around my shoulder as we left the building. She carried most of my bags for me.

"Just focus on the baby for now, sweetie. Nothing else matters," she said.

34

DUKE

The next few weeks after Rose moved out of the apartment passed slowly. Diane was obviously pissed off with me. We had one big blow-out argument where she blamed me for not making Rose stay. I insisted I wasn't going to force her to do something against her wishes. Diane claimed I didn't know what I was talking about—and matters ended sourly.

It resulted in her moving out of the apartment too. She said she'd found a job in Chicago, working evening shifts at a bar that hosted Live Music sessions. She'd also found a place to stay, close to where Rose was living with Monica so she could visit her often.

Even though I wouldn't have admitted it to Diane; I was glad of this arrangement. This way, I was sure Rose was being watched by someone I trusted. That I would find out if she ever needed anything.

So it was back to me living alone in my apartment and working twelve-hour days every day of the week. Even though Rose and I barely interacted with each other while she was living here, I missed her presence now.

Sometimes, I walked into the kitchen and hoped I'd catch her shy glance at the table where she might be sitting with Diane, chatting over a cup of tea. But I was the only one here.

I didn't see her at the office either. Monica had replaced her on the sales team which was working closely with me on the new project. I wasn't sure what everyone else at the office thought of our relationship. I still wore the fake wedding ring in order to field off questions from Laura or anyone else.

Eventually, I received an email from her, giving me the date of her next doctor's appointment. I wasn't going to miss it no matter what. I had Laura change around my schedule so I could attend it in the middle of a busy day.

Diane and Rose were sitting in the waiting room when I arrived.

"Oh, you're here!" my sister exclaimed like she was totally expecting me to not turn up.

"I'd appreciate if it was just the two of us for the scan this time, Diane," I told her. Diane humphed and then after squeezing Rose's shoulder, she walked away, claiming she was feeling like a coffee anyway.

Finally, we were alone again. I sat down beside her. I'd already noticed how different she looked. Just a few weeks had changed in a lot of ways. Her skin glowed, her eyes looked brighter, her belly looked bigger and so did her breasts. I wished I could tell her just how much more beautiful she grew every day. Maybe it was the distance from me that did the trick.

"Thanks for coming," she said, smiling as she turned to me.

"You don't have to thank me for that. I would've been here whether you invited me or not. Although my sister seems to think you need protection from me." We both grinned at that.

"Yeah, I don't envy your position. I was once at the receiving end of Diane's wrath. I know what that feels like."

I watched as she played with a golden curl on the side of her face. She was doing it unconsciously and it made me think about how young she looked now. Would she be ready for the responsibilities of being a mother? What about the rest of her life? Her plans for the future? Were they all disrupted now?

"I'm going to say this now because I'm not sure when I might get a chance to see you again," I began. Her eyes seemed to grow as she watched me. "I am open to taking full responsibility of this child if that is what you want."

Her cheeks seemed to lose their color for a moment. "What is that supposed to mean?" she asked.

"If you don't think you can do this, you don't have to. You will of course always be a part of the baby's life, you will always be its mom, but I can take over."

"You want me to give my baby to you?"

"You're saying that like I'm a stranger. I'm the baby's father."

"And I'm its mother. I'm going nowhere. If you want to fight me on custody for this baby, you better talk to my lawyer."

"Do you have one, Rose?"

She blushed again and I wanted to do nothing more than kiss her right now.

"I will get one. I will fight you on this. You may be used to always getting what you want but..."

I interrupted her now. "Always getting what I want? Is that what you think of me?"

She licked her lips angrily. Her nostrils were flared. She was about to say something but she looked away.

"I've worked hard for everything I have. I don't come from money. I wasn't looking for success. Everything I've achieved so far has been because I tried to find solutions to medical conditions and help people."

"I know that..." she said softly, meeting my eyes again.

I stood up from the chair.

"I wasn't trying to take this baby away from you, I was just trying to offer you some help. For the sake of *your* life and your future."

"Rose Johnson?" A nurse had come into the waiting room with a clipboard in hand.

Rose stood up and started following the nurse. I followed her. But then she stopped in her tracks and turned to me, causing me to almost bump into her.

"I don't need rescuing from my life, Duke. *That* is not what I need."

"Okay, so what do you need?" I asked.

Her shoulders drooped and it almost looked like she was about to admit defeat—tell me what was on her mind exactly.

"Nothing. I need nothing. I have everything I want."

∾

"Congratulations, guys, you're going to have a wonderful healthy baby girl," the doctor said.

Rose and I watched the screen intently. Our baby was floating and kicking, clenching and opening her little fists. When I heard the words the doctor said, I jumped off my chair. I fist-pumped the air before I could stop myself.

It resulted in the doctor and Rose staring at me like I'd

lost my marbles. Neither of them was expecting that reaction from me.

"I was secretly hoping for a girl," I said. Rose smiled at the doctor and nodded.

"Thank you," she said.

"Yes, thank you. This is great news."

The doctor was wiping the gel off Rose's belly and I helped her off the bed. I wanted to hold her close, hug her... celebrate in some way. She was beaming too, but we were both on edge around each other.

"I'm sure you guys want to go celebrate, so I won't keep you. You're good to go," the doctor said.

"So the baby is healthy?" I asked again.

"Absolutely, I see every indication of good health and growth."

"And Rose? She's doing well too?" I asked.

The doctor smiled. "Yes, perfect, you have nothing to worry about, Doctor Nolan." The way she said my name sounded like she'd recognized me. Sometimes I liked to forget that my every word and action were scrutinized in public by people who recognized me.

While we were talking, Rose had managed to dress quickly.

After a swift exchange of goodbyes, we were walking out of the examination room. Despite the awkward conversation we had just before we entered, I couldn't help but feel elated right now.

"Have you thought of names?" I asked her, holding the door open for her.

"I have a short list. I'll let you know when I've made the final choice," she said. It was obvious she didn't want my opinion, and honestly, I didn't care. I would love this baby girl with all my heart and soul regardless of what Rose decided to call her.

Out in the waiting room, Diane was back. She jumped up when she saw us.

"It's a girl," Rose said. I watched as the two of them hugged. Diane looked just as excited as me. She even smiled at me cautiously.

I wanted to suggest some way for us to go celebrate, but I had a feeling Rose would turn me down.

"Do you wanna go get pizza and ice cream somewhere? We could call Monica over too, I'm sure she's dying to find out," Diane said, beating me to it. Rose nodded. She glanced at me and my sister sighed.

"Why don't I go get a cab for us and you follow me out?"

Rose and I stayed back. I felt like she had something to say to me.

"Congratulations, big brother," Diane said, giving my shoulder a quick nudge before she walked out.

We watched her go and then Rose turned to me.

"I would invite you for pizza but maybe the other two will be uncomfortable with you around."

"It's fine," I said. "I'm used to being left out of my little sister's cool group."

That seemed to make her smile. Rose brushed her hair with her fingers.

"Today is a good day," she proceeded to say.

I nodded.

"It's a great day. Today is the day I found out I'm going to be a beautiful little girl's daddy."

"I'm sorry about what I said earlier. If I gave you the impression that I think any less of you—it isn't the case. This girl is going to be very lucky to have a daddy like you."

Of all our conversations, this was probably the nicest

thing Rose had ever said to me. Lately, all we did when we saw each other was inflict pain.

"And she's going to have an amazing mother. I wouldn't want to separate her from you. You have nothing to worry about as far as custody is concerned," I said.

Rose smiled.

We stood looking at each other in silence.

"Do you wish things were different between us?" I asked after some time. She blinked a few times, likely thinking. I wasn't sure what I wanted to hear exactly.

"I don't know what that would look like. It's hard to imagine it, so I don't know. I've learned to make my peace with the way it is now. I just want our daughter to be happy."

"And what about *your* happiness?" I asked.

Rose shrugged, brushing her curls with her long fingers.

"Isn't that a part of motherhood? Sacrificing your own petty life stuff for the sake of your kid?"

"What would make you absolutely and completely happy, Rose?" I asked. She watched me again, trying to study me, like she was trying to dissect me open.

"Having the family I always dreamed of. Raising this child with someone I love," she said it in a whisper.

I could feel the adrenaline rushing through my veins. I wanted to pull her to myself, wrap my arms around her, and never let go. It wasn't just about the sex anymore. Yeah. I would always want to fuck her because she was fuckin' gorgeous—but it was about being with her too.

But there was something crucially important in what she'd just said. She wanted to be with someone *she* loved. It wasn't about me.

I nodded and thrust my hands into the pockets of my jacket.

"Well, I do hope you get what you want, Rose."

Her eyes had reddened a little and I thought she would cry. I didn't want her to cry. I wanted to give her whatever she wanted. Even if it was with another man. I just wanted her to be happy. I opened my mouth to speak. I was going to ask her who she was in love with, but Rose closed herself up. The moment had passed.

She had no interest in speaking to me anymore.

"I'm going to go," she said hurriedly. Before I could say anything, she rushed away. I had to let her go because it was the right thing to do. It wasn't me who could comfort her now. It was Diane and Monica she needed. She had people there to support her and I wasn't going to stand in her way.

I waited a few beats, watching her leave. I needed to calm myself before I could face the outside world again, to land myself back in reality. While I waited, I saw *him* walk in.

Will. Rose's ex. He had a bunch of flowers in his hand and he was looking around—undoubtedly for Rose. I felt a wave of rage when I saw him. My first instinct was to go up to him and drag him out of this place. Then his eyes fell on me and we were glaring at each other like some blood would soon be shed.

∼

It didn't look like this guy had the balls to approach me, so I walked up to him. There was a look in his eyes for a second like he was considering bolting out of there.

"If you're looking for Rose, you just missed her. She left with her friends to go celebrate."

Will tightened his jaw and stuffed the flowers under his armpit.

"Okay, well, I guess I'll catch up with her later."

He was about to walk away but I stopped him.

"It's a girl," I said. He turned to me again and his eyes grew wide.

"It's a girl?"

I nodded.

There was a smile on his face and I gulped. Maybe I was wrong about him all along. Maybe this was the guy Rose was supposed to be with. Was this what she meant when she said she'd be happy if she could be with the man she loved? Was Will the man she was in love with?

"Congratulations," he said and I smiled weakly. I couldn't get the thought out of my head now. Was I in their way? That wasn't what I wanted for Rose, no matter how I actually felt about her. I genuinely wanted her to be happy.

A happy mother would mean a happy home for my kid to be raised in too.

"Yes, it's a big day for all of us," I said.

Will just stood there with the flowers limp under his arm. He seemed to sigh over and over again. I wasn't sure if he had something on his mind or not, but I decided I would be the bigger man and say something.

"Hey, man, look, I'm sorry about the way I acted the last time."

He blinked like he was shocked, not expecting me to apologize.

"Yeah...well...yeah, I get it. You didn't know who I was and you saw red."

So maybe this guy wasn't so unreasonable after all. I nodded.

"Yeah, something like that. Rose explained the situation to me. She told me about your history."

"All of it?"

"Yes. As far as I know, and that made me despise you even more," I said.

Will looked away, sighing again and shaking his head.

"You have no idea, man. I've never been able to forgive myself for letting her slip out of my hands."

"You didn't. You *forced* her out of your hands because you behaved like a complete dick. You fuckin' cheated on her." I could feel the rage rising in me again and I knew I would have to calm down.

Will had that panicked expression on his face again, like he was worried I'd try to hit him. I held my hands up.

"Anyway, it's between the two of you. If Rose has decided to forgive you, then it's her choice."

"Is that what she said to you? That she's forgiven me?" He was excited again.

It made my stomach ache. I hated him having hope. It meant I couldn't have any.

"Those weren't her exact words, but yeah, I guess she's considering it."

I wasn't about to tell him what she'd just told me. I wasn't going to drop the L-word on him. Will was beaming already.

Yeah, he loved her too. I could see that. Maybe they were soulmates. They were meant to be together. To have a happy family—the one Rose always dreamed of like she claimed.

"Thanks for this, man," he said and I nodded.

"I want what's best for Rose and for our baby, even if it means the two of you working your shit out."

Will reached out and thumped my arm. I stiffened because I hated him touching me. This guy who'd once hurt Rose.

"Yes, that would be best for all of us," he said. "Anyway,

you know where she's headed? I'd love to catch up with her and give her these." He was talking about the flowers.

I shrugged. "They didn't specify a place. You could text her."

Will rubbed the back of his head with a hand.

"Yeah, she's not exactly been replying to my texts or answering my calls. She'd told me about this appointment earlier so I decided to surprise her. I haven't actually seen her in two months."

My eyes narrowed on him.

If she was in love with him, why hadn't she seen him in two months? If she wanted a future with this guy, why was she avoiding him?

"You think you could help me out? Find out where she's gone so I could surprise her?" Will continued.

I thought for a moment but then shrugged.

"Nope. I'm not. You can do it yourself. I'm sure she'll be easy to find if that's what she wants," I said.

When I was walking away from him now, I had a smile on my face.

35

ROSE

A few days later, I had lunch with my family. It had become our weekly ritual since the pregnancy announcement and this time I had a new piece of good news to give them. They were going to become grandparents to a precious little girl.

My siblings were just as excited. Lizzie was already setting some of her toys aside for her baby niece. Flora and Oz had a million questions about what pregnancy felt like and they couldn't stop doting on the growing baby bump.

My parents watched proudly as the family happily shared a meal. Once lunch was over and dessert was neatly tucked in, I was about to help Oz and Flora put the dishes away, but Mom said she would help them instead. They were all fussing over me—insisting that I needed the rest.

Lizzie went up for a nap and it was just Daddy and me in the living room. We sat on the couch, huddled together while the TV played some sitcom with loud canned laughter. It was just like old times. An exact replication of what my childhood Sundays used to look like.

There was something so comforting about this and I couldn't wait for my baby to experience it too.

Daddy had his arm around me as I sat there, staring and smiling at the screen.

"So, how is Duke?" he asked all of a sudden. Just for the sake of my family, I'd put on the rings again before I came here. I was glad Duke hadn't actually taken the rings back from me.

Although I knew this conversation with my parents about my marriage would have to happen soon.

"He's good, you know? Busy, but very excited about the baby."

Daddy was silent for a while and even though I was staring at the screen, I could sense him thinking. I didn't want him to continue with this topic. I wasn't prepared for this conversation.

"It's just that we haven't seen you guys together since that first time he came over."

I shifted in his arms and looked up at him. I was afraid he'd be able to see it in my eyes—the truth—that I was in love with a man who didn't love me back.

"You know what his work is like, Daddy. He's a busy man. He does important work and I don't want to trouble him with silly family meals."

"I didn't realize you thought our family meals were silly."

"That isn't what I meant, Daddy."

He nodded and patted my hand. He was still watching me and I tried to watch TV again, but it wasn't working. It felt like he'd caught me out. Like he knew.

"Is everything okay with you two?" he asked.

I waited a few beats, just to compose myself and then I shifted again, drawing away from him.

"I don't want the others to know, especially Mom because she'd worry."

"What is it?"

"Duke and I are separated."

Daddy went quiet again. I glared at him, hoping he would say something. Even if it was *I told you so*.

"I'm sorry, honey," was what he said instead and it absolutely broke my heart. I could see the disappointment in his eyes. As much as Daddy had been opposed to the idea at the start, I knew for a fact that he always liked and respected Duke. He had quickly warmed to the idea of our supposed marriage. And now it was over.

"Aren't you going to ask why? Aren't you going to reprimand me for making such a rash decision?"

Daddy reached for my hand again and patted it.

"What good will that do? As for asking why, it's not my business. I'm sure whatever reason you have for separating, it's a good one. You're making a choice for yourself and the baby."

I stared at him in confusion, my heart was beating fast. Every day, I was surprised by the people around me. By the people who loved and cared for me. Maybe it wouldn't be so hard to live my life without Duke, after all.

"I wish it wasn't like this, Daddy. I wish we could be together."

"You still love him?" he asked.

"I love him. I always have." It was the first time I was admitting it aloud and it felt good to actually do it.

He pulled me in for a hug this time.

"Just give me the word and I'll make sure he's kicked off the board. If it's the last thing I do before I leave that place!"

I leaned my head on my father's shoulder, surrounded by his love and his warmth.

"No, Daddy, I don't want you to do that. He's always wanted this. I want him to have it. Like a wedding present," I said.

When we parted, I had tears in my eyes. I was glad I could be somewhat honest with him. It was good to get it off my chest.

"We will have to tell your mother. It will eventually have to come out," he said and I nodded.

"I just feel like a failure, that I can't make him love me the way I love him."

Daddy hooked a finger under my chin, forcing me to face him.

"I'm sure he will see it one day, when you've moved on and living the best life you can. He'll know what he lost."

I smiled weakly at him but I didn't believe it. I was sure Duke would never know what I felt for him. I would always be the girl he accidentally knocked up.

Flora, Oz, and Mom came into the room just then and our conversation was cut short. The look Daddy gave me then meant that he wouldn't be disclosing it to the rest of the family yet. For that, I was grateful.

I could only handle one heartbreak at a time today. Instead, I placed a hand on my belly just as the baby kicked to remind me of her presence. At least I would always have her. A piece of Duke to carry with me everywhere.

∼

Will was the last person I expected to see when I took the elevator up to Monica's apartment. He was standing at the door like that time he'd stood outside my apartment a few months ago.

"Hey, I'm glad I found you. It wasn't easy," he said.

"How did you do it? I never gave you this address."

"I went to your office, asking to speak to you. Eventually, this girl named Monica came to speak to me when I demanded to see you. They were afraid I'd make a scene."

My cheeks burned up. I couldn't believe it. Why was he making a fool of me?

"Why are you doing this?"

"She said I could talk to you outside her apartment, but that was as far as I could go. It's your choice to let me in or not. But look, your friend realizes we need to speak to each other."

"Monica is just trying to be helpful. You have no right to be here when I've been ignoring you for two months."

"You said you needed time to think. I've given you enough time to think. I'm moving into the new apartment now, Rose, and you can move in with me. You don't have to live here anymore, share a small place with a co-worker."

"Monica is more than that. She's a good friend."

Will came toward me and I backed up to the door.

"What I mean is there is obviously a reason why you moved out of that guy's place, right? You don't want to live with him. And rightly so. Now is the perfect opportunity to move in with me and raise this baby girl together."

I stared at him for several moments, a little confused.

"Monica told you about the baby's gender too?" I asked. I was growing a little impatient with her now. She shouldn't have meddled or given Will this address.

"Not her, it was him. Duke Nolan. He told me you're having a girl."

I couldn't believe what I was hearing. None of this made sense.

"What? When?"

"At the clinic. I was there. I wanted to surprise you at your appointment but I was late. I got the time wrong and you'd left. He was still in the waiting room though and he told me."

I gulped. Suddenly, my throat felt dry. I hadn't seen Duke since that day at the clinic. I wanted to know how he was but I was too self-conscious to ask Diane.

"He didn't try to kill you?"

Will was smiling now. "No, he actually apologized to me!"

I leaned my back against the door. What was going on?

"He said what happens between us is our business and he doesn't want to come between us. In fact, he said he thinks you should forgive me for the past. That's exactly what it is. The past."

I leaned against the locked door while Will drew closer to me. I stared up at him, searching his eyes. What was Duke trying to tell me? That he wanted me to move on with my life and leave him alone? That I needed to be with Will so our kid could have a family life?

"If a crazy guy like him can see the logic behind that... what do *you* think, Rose?"

This time, he leaned in and kissed me gently on my forehead. Maybe I should have felt something, at least a spark, but instead, I felt clammy and cold. I fumbled in my purse for the keys to the house and whipped around from him.

"I think I need some space," I said.

"Rose!" Will's voice was harsher this time and he pulled the door handle so it remained shut. He'd never been physically aggressive like this before. I looked up at him and his eyes were narrowed at me.

"Do you hear what I'm saying to you? I need you back in my life. I've made a lot of changes to my life for you."

"I didn't ask for any of them. You made your own decisions."

"It doesn't matter. It's all done now. We can be together. A family with a beautiful baby girl."

I tried pushing the door again but it wouldn't budge. He was still clutching the door handle tightly. With his other hand, he fiddled with some of my curls, tucking them in behind my ear.

"You need to leave. Now. You're scaring me."

"I'm not trying to scare you, Rose. I'm trying to get you to see reason. I need you to come back to me. We can go back to having the life we always did."

This time when he clutched me and whipped me around, I kneed him in the groin. I was prepared for it. He howled in pain and I ran from him, darting for the stairs.

"Rose!" he cried after me. I could hear him making his way behind me and I ran blindly down a few steps until someone caught me.

Duke. He had his arms around me. He had me pinned to his chest.

"Rose? You all right? What the fuck do you think you're doing?" Duke barked at Will.

Will stopped in his tracks when he saw Duke. He still had one hand on his crotch, cupping it through his jeans like it was still painful for him.

"I'm just trying to have a conversation with her."

"She's running away from you. What does that say?" Duke growled.

Will eyed me and I looked away. My lips quivered a little and I leaned my head on Duke's chest.

"Get the fuck out. Get out before I call the cops and if I

ever see you near her again, I will break your jaw this time. I'm not going to warn you again."

I watched Will slink away by us down the stairs. Duke kept a hand sturdily on my waist.

"Are you okay?" he asked and I nodded.

"I'm fine now."

36

DUKE

I lifted Rose up in my arms and she didn't protest. I could sense she was trying to be brave, but her encounter with Will had zapped all her energy. She felt weak when I carried her into the apartment.

"Monica called me to say Will was waiting for you here. She said she just wanted me to know, but I felt like you could do with an extra hand."

Rose had her arms wound around my neck as I made my way to the small living room. There was a bright yellow couch there, just big enough for the two of us.

"Thank you for coming. Monica did well to tell you. I guess she sensed things weren't right with Will."

"He's losing it. He needs help," I said and gently placed her down on the couch. Rose laid her head back on the armrest.

"What can I get you?" I asked.

"I don't want you spending any more time than necessary in the kitchen. No fancy pea soup this time," she said in a steady voice. I smiled at her and dashed to the kitchen, returning with one tall glass of cold fizzy water.

"You read my mind," she said and drank thirstily from the glass.

"Are you sure you're okay? Did he hurt you? Do you want to go to the doctor's?"

"I kneed him in the balls," Rose replied. At first, she had a serious expression on her face and then she broke into a smile. I was grinning too.

"Guess I didn't have anything to worry about. You can definitely take care of yourself."

She wiped her mouth with the back of her hand. That mouth. Those beautiful glossy lips.

"He said some things to me, I don't know how true they are."

"Are you going to believe anything he tells you?" I asked.

Rose stared down at her feet, avoiding my eyes.

"He said you think I should forget about the past and just move in with him."

"He wishes I said that. All I told him was if that's what you wanted, I wanted you to be happy. But that was before he disclosed you hadn't answered his calls in two months."

Rose sighed.

"It just never felt right with Will again. There's something different about him. He's not the guy I thought I fell for. Or maybe I was too young and naïve to see the real him."

"He's kicking himself for losing you. For being a cheating bastard."

She put down the glass and sat on the edge of the couch, straightening up.

"Maybe he just wanted me back so I could clean for him and fold his clothes and entertain his dopey friends. I mean, that's all I was ever good for him. He probably just misses that."

I wanted to pull her into my arms and tell her I would never treat her that way.

I bit my tongue, but this time said the words.

"Rose, I would never treat you that way."

She blinked wide-eyed as she stared at me. It was like there were words on the tip of her tongue but she couldn't get them out.

I went to her, knelt down in front of her, and caught her gaze firmly.

"Do you hear what I'm saying to you, Rose? I would never treat you the way Will did. I am not that guy."

She opened her mouth but no sound came out.

"You are more than just the mother of my child. You're the girl who is bringing me to my knees. Life hasn't been the same since you spilt that coffee on me. Everything is upside down and only you can fix it."

She licked her lips and I hoped she had something to say. Anything. Even if she was going to reject me, I hoped she did it now. When I was on my knees and being honest with her.

"What does all this mean, Duke?" she asked.

We looked into each other's eyes. I could see her mind racing. She was trying to make sense of this just like I was.

"It means that I'm in love with you and I want you to be with me. Is that crazy?"

Once again, she dove into silence. Her hands were on her knees and slowly, I took them into mine.

"Tell me I'm crazy, that we don't belong together, and I'll stop now. Nothing has to change if you tell me to leave. Everything can go back to normal. I just had to tell you the truth before we moved on from this."

She had already started shaking her head.

"I don't want things to go back to normal. That isn't what I want. I want *you*. I always have."

I pulled her into my arms, tumbling back on the rug on the floor. For a pregnant woman, Rose seemed immensely light as she settled on me. We wrapped our arms around each other as our mouths went together. Our fingers weaved together, our bodies pressed to each other's. The kiss was deep and strong. I wanted her to know I wasn't going anywhere. This was just the beginning of something amazing.

She was breathless when I pulled away, smiling and bright-eyed.

"You have no idea how much I've wanted this. Talk about pregnancy cravings. You're mine!" She giggled at that. I grabbed her jaw and pulled her face to mine again, kissing her lips delicately this time.

"And you have no idea how crazy beautiful you look. Pregnancy suits you. Especially when it's my baby growing inside you."

She bit down on her lip and smiled hard. It was the kind of smile I always wanted to see on her face.

"Do it again, Duke. Kiss me again. Kiss me all the time," she said. But the door to the apartment opened. Monica and Diane burst in, shouting Rose's name.

37

ROSE

I was in a daze. None of this seemed real to me. Duke had just kissed me. He said he wanted to be with me. I wanted him to keep holding me, tell me over and over again the words he'd just said—because I just couldn't believe them. Was I hallucinating? Was this a dream?

Now Monica and Diane came rushing to me and Duke stepped away.

"Hey, you okay? Monica called me. She said Will was on his way to see you. She said he caused a scene at the office and was acting crazy." Diane was looking me over, checking me for bruises.

"I'm fine, really, I'm all right." I smiled at her and glanced at Duke. Diane caught that and she swung around to her brother.

"What are you doing here?" she snapped.

"Diane..." I tried to protest but Duke faced off with his sister.

"I came here because Monica called."

"We'll be fine here. You can leave now," Diane said.

"Diane, no!" I interjected.

"Sis, I know you're being protective of her, but we were actually in the middle of..." Duke tried to explain, but Diane was barely listening.

"Do you realize she's five months pregnant? The last thing Rose needs right now is for you to start an argument. She needs to rest."

"Diane, I'm not an invalid!" I screeched. Monica had come closer to me now and she gave me a smile of sympathy.

"We were not arguing," Duke said and his sister rolled her eyes. "In fact, we were doing just the opposite, but you don't have to believe me if you don't want to. Ask Rose."

Diane glared at him and then she finally spun around to face me.

"Rose, what's going on?" she asked.

I could feel the color rising in my cheeks. My heart was beating fast. So, this wasn't a dream after all. This was real. Duke was real. Those kisses had actually happened.

"We were...were..." I couldn't find the right words to describe it. Especially not under the steady gaze of three people who were waiting patiently for me to explain.

Duke decided to put me out of my misery and he came up to me and gently took my hand.

"We were in the middle of working out the finer details of our relationship," he said.

Diane's eyes grew wide. She looked up at Monica, whose mouth was now in a surprised "O" shape. Duke beamed at me and I broke into the broadest smile ever. I couldn't contain the excitement. And neither could the girls.

Diane screeched with delight.

"You two made up?" She pounced on her brother to hug

him, while Monica gave me a hug too. I could feel the happy spirit of celebration in the apartment. It was everywhere.

"I knew you'd finally get some sense in through your thick skull!" Diane exclaimed and Duke came to me again.

"Yeah, I'm an idiot. Blah, blah, blah."

"It's not all his fault. I've been stubborn too," I said.

"Okay, why don't we give these two some time to themselves? Diane, do you want to go get something to eat? Celebrate the good news?" Monica asked.

"Yes! I'm starving right now. This is amazing!" Diane couldn't stop gushing and eventually, Monica had to drag her out of the apartment. Even then, I knew she wouldn't be able to keep her out for very long.

Once the front door shut, Duke took me in his arms again.

"Is it a little mad that I can't stop holding you?" he asked.

I shook my head.

"If it is, then I'm mad too. I don't want you to stop."

We kissed and this time it was soft and slow, like we had all the time in the world.

"Why have we spent so much time apart?" he asked, brushing his fingers over the hair that had fallen on my face.

"Because things seemed too complicated, and we kept fighting and I was thinking about this baby."

"And neither of us wanted to admit it. Besides, I thought you were in love with Will."

I couldn't help but laugh at that.

"I don't think I was *ever* in love with him. You're the one who asked me to move in with you and fake-marry you so we could fool my dad. I didn't think you would ever want to be with me, for real."

Duke smiled and I leaned closer to him. It felt strange

how comfortable we were with each other already. Like I'd known him a lifetime.

"I didn't realize it at first either. The only thing I wanted was to possess you and your beautiful body," he said and kissed me softly on my neck. "And then slowly, I started to see what that really meant. It wasn't just your body I wanted to possess. I wanted *you* in my life. Permanently, but it felt too late for that." His mouth traveled down my neck and shoulders until he was cupping my left breast with his large hand.

I sighed and tipped my head back, pressing my eyes closed in surrender to him. I didn't want to miss a single second of this.

And just then, the baby kicked.

"Oh, my God! Did you feel that?" I squealed, pulling his hand over to my belly. She kicked again and this time Duke's face glowed with excitement.

"Is she trying to tell us something?"

Another kick, and Duke and I were laughing.

"Hey there, baby girl, it's Daddy. How are you doing?" He lowered himself as he spoke, so he was now at level with my bump. The kicking stopped by now but there was the baby's presence between us, like she was listening intently to us. She'd successfully managed to take his attention away from me. It made me smile.

"This little growing lady definitely knows how to get what she wants."

"We almost forgot about her there," he said, lifting my hand up to kiss it. "But before we talk about anything else, Rose, I want you to move back in with me. Today. Right now. I don't want to miss another minute with you and the baby. Can you do that for me?"

Duke peered into my eyes and I knew the answer was

yes. I wanted to live with him. That was what I wanted from the first time he touched me—I wanted to share my life with him.

∼

"Diane isn't going to be too happy when they return to the apartment and see we've cleared out." Duke was stepping into his penthouse...*our* penthouse...with my bags. He turned to give me a look which made me smile.

"Well, Diane's had her fun and she better get used to sharing you with me from now."

I followed him as he carried my bags to his bedroom. I stopped at the door, feeling a little weird. I'd never spent a night in this room before and now I was moving into it. He put the bags down and turned to me fully.

"You okay?" he asked.

I nodded, feeling a little teary-eyed.

"Sorry, it's just the hormones. I'm not actually crying. I'm happy."

He came up to take me in his arms again.

"That's okay, you can get it all out. But if there's something on your mind, you can tell me that too," he said.

He kissed my cheek and I laid my head on his chest.

"I just don't feel settled, I don't know how to describe it. I'm happy, I'm so happy to be here with you and start something new. Maybe it's because I've been moving around so much in these past few months, and the baby...and I'm just lacking stability." I was talking too fast. I wondered if my words were just coming out in a jumble. But Duke knocked his forehead against mine and smiled.

"You're right, we need to do something about it."

"No, nothing needs to be done about it. I'll be fine. I just need a few days to settle in and it'll be okay."

He took my hands and squeezed them tightly.

"Rose, you don't have to make excuses for yourself to me. That is the first thing you need to know about our relationship. You've pointed out a problem you're facing and we'll just have to look for a solution. We'll figure it out together, how to make you feel a little more settled."

He wrapped one strong arm around me and together, we walked into his bedroom. It looked exactly the same as it did that morning when he stormed out of it after kissing me.

"By the way, in the spirit of full disclosure—you should know that I told Daddy."

"Told him what?" Duke asked, spinning around to me.

"That we separated."

He let out a loud gasp of air.

"Well, we'll just have to fix that too," he said.

38

DUKE

First things first, I needed to make Rose feel comfortable and like herself again. I knew exactly why she was feeling so overwhelmed and tapped out, even though we were together now and our relationship was blossoming.

Too much had happened in the past few months. We met, we had sex, we had a whirlwind dramatic relationship, she ended up pregnant, and we spent a few months lying to the world about what our relationship really was. All the while, we continued to lie to ourselves about our true feelings too.

It was too much for me to handle and *she* was pregnant.

Luckily, I knew just the solution.

When we got on the private jet that was going to take us to our destination, Rose had no idea where we were going. I wouldn't even have told her we were going away for a vacation, but I wanted her to go for a checkup and get the all-clear from her doctor first.

"Are you seriously not going to tell me where we're headed?" she asked as we soared calmly through the air. I'd given up alcohol in the last few days, in solidarity with the pregnancy. So we were both sipping sparkling grape juice and holding hands.

"You'll see it yourself in time," I told her.

Several hours later, after Rose had spent most of that time napping on my shoulder, we landed at Kerry Airport in Ireland.

"Ireland? You brought me to Ireland?" she squealed with delight. "Oh, Duke, this is amazing!" She remained in my arms all the way to the car that was waiting to chauffeur us to Skibbereen.

"You're going to love this place," I said while we drove there. I watched her as she stared out at the lush green country through her window. This was exactly what she needed. What we both needed. A chance for us to get to know each other in private before the baby came.

We'd fallen in love very quickly, and we'd spent most of the time since then running away from each other. This was going to be our time to spend together in peace.

"Are we staying in a hotel?" Rose asked as we drove into the small town. I caught sight of the familiar places and I instantly felt at home.

"No. We're living in a house. Our house. I bought it last week," I said. She was surprised but then she was smiling.

"This is perfect, Duke, this is exactly what I needed. It's so beautiful here." Rose kissed me and I held her close to me. I wasn't thinking about work or the drug or the new project. I'd spent the past twenty years working my ass off. There were other competent people who could handle it now. Instead, it was time for me now to take care of the woman who was building my life.

∼

We spent the next two months in Skibbereen, disconnecting ourselves from pretty much the rest of the world. People back home in Chicago knew where we were and that we were doing fine, but they didn't know how to get in touch with us. It was only Laura who was privy to the information, and she was going to guard the secret with her life.

In those two months; Rose and I proceeded to build a home for ourselves in Ireland and get to know each other in a way that I had never known anybody else.

We spent our days shopping or building or painting around our new house. We even took up gardening. Rose did a little bit of farming too, inspired by the local zeal. By the end of the two months, we had a fully flourishing little veggie-kitchen-garden that she was immensely proud of.

In the evenings, we strolled by the river hand in hand and ate at the local café. In the little magical town of Skibbereen, everybody knew us now as the rich Americans who were living here and embracing the Irish country life.

Just like they did to me, they welcomed Rose in with their arms open and she thrived there. Everyone could tell she was pregnant and they fussed over her. She basked in the attention and adoration, and I fell even more in love with her. I could see a different side of her now.

I'd fallen in love with a beautiful and fiercely independent young girl...and she was now growing into a strong and social young mother. Even though the pregnancy was an accident, I couldn't have picked a better mother for my child. Every morning that I woke up beside her, I was grateful we'd found our way to each other eventually.

Two months went by and Rose looked even bigger now. More voluptuous. Even more beautiful, if that was possible.

One afternoon, she returned from working on the

garden while I was lounging in our sunroom, reading a book.

"Have you seen the sunflowers? They're enormous now!" she exclaimed, taking off her muddy gloves.

"Rose, honey, we have to go home," I told her, putting down the book. I'd been trying to broach the subject for a few days but I didn't want to see the look of disappointment on her face. The one I saw now.

"We don't have to, Duke, we can be here...hide away... have the baby here." She rushed toward me. I stood up and took her in my arms.

"We'll be back here, soon, in a few months. But we can't have the baby here. We need to be close to your parents, close to Diane and your friends. You'll regret it later if we hide away here."

Rose gulped and then she licked her lips. I was armed with another speech but she was nodding already.

"You're right. We have to go back. It doesn't mean the story is over."

"Far from it."

She kissed me abruptly. "This is why I love you, Duke Nolan, you always make me feel crazy and sane at the same time."

39

ROSE

When we returned to Chicago from Ireland, it felt like a whole different world now. I'd gotten used to the calm and quiet, to the unhurried-ness of Ireland. But Duke was right about the fact that we needed to return to Chicago for the sake of the baby.

Since we'd gotten together, we hadn't even had a chance to smooth things over with my family. As nervous as I was about it, Duke insisted we invite them over to the apartment. Along with Diane, Monica, Karen, and her family. We were going to host our first party as a couple, and I had no idea where to even start.

But it was Duke who took care of everything. He worked with the housekeeper to get the apartment looking ready for a celebration, and he arranged for caterers and servers for the night too. It was only going to be a small intimate gathering but he wanted to ensure that I didn't have an excuse to raise a finger.

Of course, Daddy was shocked by the invitation when I called them.

"We haven't heard from you in weeks. Do you have any

idea how worried we've been? Rose, what is going on? Are you two back together?"

"Everything is fine, Daddy, you don't have to worry about it. Just bring everyone for dinner on Friday and you'll see."

Friday arrived too quickly and I didn't feel prepared. I was nearly eight months pregnant now, just a few weeks away from our expected due date, and I felt like I was moving even slower. My feet were swollen, as were my fingers, and my hair had grown so thick that it seemed unmanageable now.

I'd spent hours the previous day shopping with Monica and Diane to find the perfect dress. It was long and flowy and a striking, electric blue to match my eyes. When Duke saw me in it, he stopped in his tracks at our bedroom door.

"Do you know what you're doing to me, woman?" he growled, coming to take me in his arms again. "At this rate, I'm going to have to tell everyone to leave so I can ravage you in our bed."

It was amazing how he always managed to make me laugh when I was feeling the most nervous.

But as it turned out, I had no reason to feel nervous at all. Everyone was happy to be there and to celebrate our love. Other than Daddy, the rest of my family didn't even suspect this was anything out of the ordinary. They'd just been worried when I went missing for a few weeks. But I was back now, more pregnant than before and as Mom said —glowing.

Karen, Monica, and Diane couldn't stop gushing about how happy they were for me too. Jasper and Duke seemed to hit it off instantly, so Karen and I exchanged looks of approval. Jessie was soon going to have a little baby to play with and we couldn't wait for the two of them to grow up together. It was going to be adorable.

Eventually, it happened—what I'd been dreading the whole night. Daddy took me aside when he found me alone, picking snacks for my plate because I was so hungry.

With a hand firmly on my elbow, he guided me out of the living room and led me to the quieter kitchen area.

"Rose, I need an explanation here. A few months ago, you told me you two were separated, and now you're playing happy families again? I hope this isn't all for show. I hope you're not doing this for our sake. Is this a lie?"

I could feel the tops of my ears burning up. I didn't know if I had it in me to lie to him again. I saw how hurt he was by all the drama in my life. I just wanted to tell him the truth.

"No, Barry, none of this is a lie." It was Duke. He must have seen Daddy take me aside, and now he joined us in the kitchen. I slinked into his outstretched arm. He must've had some idea how relieved I was to have him here.

Daddy stood back, studying us, but he wasn't saying anything.

"Look, Barry, I want to come clean here. You don't see any rings on our fingers at the moment because we're not actually married."

I tried to hide the gasp. Once again, we hadn't prepared for a conversation like this and Duke was taking a solo plunge. Something he was clearly good at.

Daddy's face turned even whiter now and I pressed my eyes closed, hoping for this to be over soon.

"What is that supposed to mean? I would love an explanation right about now."

"And I'd be glad to give it to you, Barry. I just need you to promise to listen to us with an open mind. To hear the whole story before you decide to react." While Duke spoke, he looked at me and smiled. "And you have to believe me when I tell you I'm crazy about your daughter. I have always loved her and nothing has made me happier than to find out she loves me too."

Daddy's shoulders seemed to relax now. He was prepared to listen to the story and Duke was ready to tell it. Once again, he had managed to make me feel like no burden was too heavy to bear. He was going to make it easy for us. At that moment, I realized I couldn't wait for the rest of our lives to unfold because I was lucky to spend it with him.

Now that I had him, I was never letting go.

EPILOGUE

ROSE

*A*va Elizabeth Nolan, a beautiful, green-eyed, blonde angel, was born four days before her due date.

My contractions started right in the middle of my baby shower which the girls had organized for me. Thankfully, all my friends were there to rush me to the hospital where Duke was waiting for me already.

It was a quick birth and it passed in a haze for me. All I could remember was Duke being there by my side the whole time, holding my hand, offering me sips of water and guiding me through the contractions.

Nothing was too painful, no mountain was too high to climb because he was by my side.

Once Ava was here, he wouldn't leave our side. I could see the look of worry on his face every time someone other than him or me was holding her. He watched her like a hawk. I knew instantly that this little girl was going to be the center of his world.

"You need to take a break, honey," I told him at the end of the day. The rest of our visitors had just gone home and I realized Duke hadn't slept or eaten in hours. Ava was asleep in my arms and I was comfortable and warm in the bed.

"I'm not going anywhere," he said and kissed me. "In fact, this was the moment I'd been waiting for all this while. For everyone to leave so I could ask you a very important question."

I blinked as I looked up at him.

"If you're worried about the germs, Duke, you don't have to. I made sure everyone sanitized..."

"No, Rose, this isn't about Ava. This is about you. About us. I didn't bring a ring because I already gave you one and this is beyond a ring or anything material we could ever possess."

My lips were sealed now as I watched him speak. My eyes filled up with tears of joy. Of all the days, Duke was choosing this day to ask me the most important question of my life. For real this time.

"Will you marry me, Rose Johnson? Will you be my wife? Sign a paper this time? I want to make sure it isn't as easy for you to escape me."

He was smiling and I smiled too.

"Yes, Duke. Yes!"

He kissed me while Ava slept between us. With his tongue in my mouth, his arms cradling me protectively, and my fingers wrapped around his strong muscular bicep—I felt like our little family was complete.

I was more complete now than I had ever been.

"I want to show Skibbereen to Ava, and my veggie garden," I said.

"So that's where we'll get married, as soon as you're ready," he replied, kissing my forehead again.

He held my hand and we stared into each other's eyes.

"Do you think all this would've happened if I hadn't

spilled coffee on your shirt that day?" I asked. He laughed at first and then a look of seriousness overtook his face.

"I would always have found my way to you, Rose. It was our destiny," he said.

∽

READ ALL THE NOVELS OF THE HOT BILLIONAIRE DADDIES SERIES HERE

HOT BOSS: A STAND-ALONE SINGLE DAD ROMANCE (BOOK 1)
HOT SURPRISE: A SURPRISE BABY ROMANCE (BOOK 2)

ABOUT SUZANNE HART

Thank you so much for reading my romances. I'm an avid reader who lives her dream of becoming an indie author. I enjoy writing about gorgeous billionaires that love to protect their sexy women.
I hope you love my books as much as I do!

Get FREEBIE!

https://dl.bookfunnel.com/4xfhgayq4p

facebook.com/SuzanneHartRomance
amazon.com/author/suzannehart
bookbub.com/profile/suzanne-hart

Made in the USA
Middletown, DE
15 May 2020